Praise for Charles ... in his Conor Bard mystery

HELL'S KITCHEN HOMICIDE

Books by Charles Kipps

Out of Focus

Cop Without a Badge

Hell's Kitchen Homicide

Crystal Death

CHARLES KIPPS

HELL'S KITCHEN HOMICIDE

A CONOR BARD MYSTERY

POCKET BOOKS
New York London Toronto Sydney

Pocket Books
A Division of Simon & Schuster, Inc.
1230 Avenue of the Americas
New York, NY 10020

This book is a work of fiction. Names, characters, places, and incidents either are products of the author's imagination or are used fictitiously. Any resemblance to actual events or locales or persons, living or dead, is entirely coincidental.

First Pocket Books paperback edition October 2010

POCKET and colophon are registered trademarks of Simon & Schuster, Inc.

For information about special discounts for bulk purchases, please contact Simon & Schuster Special Sales at 1-866-506-1949 or business@simonandschuster.com.

The Simon & Schuster Speakers Bureau can bring authors to your live event. For more information or to book an event, contact the Simon & Schuster Speakers Bureau at 1-866-248-3049 or visit our website at www.simonspeakers.com.

Manufactured in the United States of America

10   9   8   7   6   5   4   3   2   1

ISBN 978-1-4391-3994-3
ISBN 978-1-4391-4115-1 (ebook)

For Aida

HELL'S KITCHEN HOMICIDE

Chapter One

The Rhythm Bar was a brick barnacle clinging to the underbelly of Hell's Kitchen on Manhattan's West Side. You wouldn't want to be caught dead there, although a lot of people had been.

At least the Rhythm Bar had live music. And it wasn't like Conor Bard could afford to be picky. So here he was, onstage with a drummer, a bass player, and a guy with a beat-up electric piano. A white boy singing rhythm and blues.

"Papa was a rolling stone . . ."

Conor slid his hand along the neck of his Fender Stratocaster. His fingertips pinned the steel strings against the well-worn frets, coaxing a shriek from the vintage guitar.

"Wherever he laid his hat was his home . . ."

Conor looked up and found himself staring into a mirrored wall at his own image. He didn't like what he saw. The soft facial features molded from the clay of his Scotch-Irish heritage were more like craggy rock now. The brown hair falling just over his collar was more gray now. In fact, everything about him seemed more *something* now. Or was it *less* something? *When did this happen? Hell, I'm only forty-two.*

In one swift motion, Conor whipped the leather guitar strap off his shoulder, dropped the Stratocaster, crouched down, yanked a .38-caliber pistol from an ankle holster, and rose into a shooting stance.

"Police! Freeze!"

The man in Conor's sights was around fifty years old. White. A slight build. A tortured face. A hopeless expression.

Conor held his gun high, but even from the elevated stage he was having trouble getting a clear shot. If the man stood and ran, Conor would have to let him go.

After a collective moment of fear and confusion, patrons stampeded out the door. Conor now had a direct, unobstructed view of his target.

"On the floor!" Conor yelled. "Facedown!"

The man obeyed.

Conor jumped from the stage, rammed a knee in the guy's back, then clamped a pair of cuffs on his wrists.

The man twisted his neck around and looked up at Conor. "Not a bad voice," he said. "For a cop."

Conor led the cuffed man out of the club and handed him off to two uniformed cops.

"You coming?" one asked.

"Gotta get my guitar," Conor said. "I'll meet you there."

As Conor started back toward the bar, an unmarked vehicle, lights flashing and siren blaring, skidded to a stop a few feet away. An NYPD captain emerged from the car. He looked to be in his late forties, his military posture signaling he was as comfortable giving orders as taking them. He charged toward Conor.

"Are you Detective Bard? Conor Bard?" The captain's face was flushed and he was out of breath.

Conor was surprised to see a captain at a routine collar. "Hey, Cap. Yeah, I'm Conor Bard. But what are you doing here? I thought you guys only showed up when someone got killed."

"Well it's a goddam miracle no one *did* get killed."

Frank Reynolds wasn't happy. It was his turn to be the duty captain, a revolving assignment shared among all the captains in the department. Reynolds was covering the lower half of Manhattan, which meant he had to make an appearance at the scene if anyone was found dead south of Central Park. It could keep you running all night.

"According to what I just heard over the radio, you felt it necessary to draw your weapon in a crowd situation." Reynolds narrowed his eyes. "Is that correct? Or did I misunderstand the transmission?"

"I couldn't let him walk," Conor explained.

"Right. Better to risk the lives of innocent people."

"Trust me. They're not so innocent in there."

"So who the hell was this guy?" Reynolds demanded.

"You know how most people carry pictures of their kids in their wallet?" Conor began. "Well, my partner, Ralph Kurtz, carries old mug shots in *his* wallet. So every time we have a drink he pulls out these mug shots. And I always say, 'Ralph, can't we ever just have a drink without these scumbags?' And Ralph always says, 'Just look at the mug shots. Maybe one day you'll see somebody.' Tonight I saw somebody."

"That's touching," Reynolds managed. "Now, one more time, who *was* this guy?"

"Name is Robert Willis. Ten years ago, he was convicted of raping a sixteen-year-old girl, but then some hotshot lawyer got the conviction overturned. When Willis walked out of prison, the first thing he did was chop up his girlfriend. Seems she didn't wait for him like a good woman should."

"No excuse."

"I agree. He should've just dumped the bitch."

Conor and Reynolds squared off silently for a moment.

"Anyway," Conor continued, "after he butchered his girlfriend, Willis disappeared. Until tonight. Hadn't been for Kurtz and his mug shots . . ."

Reynolds was unimpressed. "I'm gonna have to write this up."

Conor shrugged. "Hey, do what you have to."

* * *

4

Conor drove to the One Eight, his precinct on West Fifty-fourth Street. He began the tedious process of filling out a DD5 form documenting the events that led to the apprehension of Robert Willis. As he filled in each line, Conor began to wish he had just finished his set at the Rhythm Bar and left Willis alone.

"Nice collar," Sergeant Amanda Pitts said as she sat on a chair next to Conor's desk.

Amanda Pitts was a fourth-generation cop. Thirty-seven years old. Not very pretty, but then again, she didn't try. She hardly wore makeup and when she wasn't in a uniform she dressed in loose-fitting, unflattering outfits. Amanda had been on the job twelve years and had distinguished herself as a detective. She took the sergeant's exam as soon as she was eligible, just as her former-cop father and former-cop grandfather had done.

Conor never opted for sergeant. Never intended to. Although it was a promotion in rank, only one out of five detectives apply for sergeant even with its higher base pay. The job was entirely different from detective: more administrative, less investigative. Conor liked the street. The precinct gave him cabin fever.

Amanda, on the other hand, relished her duties as sergeant so much that she didn't even care what shift she worked. Morning, noon, night; Saturday, Sunday, holiday—didn't matter to her. Put her on the schedule, she'd show up. Which created the illusion that Amanda was always at the precinct. Take tonight, for example. Sunday. Late. There she was.

"Pulling a gun in a packed bar?" Amanda said. "Wasn't the smartest thing you ever did."

"Wasn't the dumbest either."

"Captain Reynolds called me. Citing regulations."

Conor frowned. "Why is he so bent out of shape?"

"Maybe it's something personal," Amanda suggested.

"Can't be. I never met the guy before tonight."

"He's bucking for deputy inspector. Guess he wants to make it look like he plays everything by the book. Goes on record with me so if anything ever comes up he can say he reported the incident. That way he's clean."

"What about you?" Conor asked. "How are you going to handle this?"

"Me? I'll just write a letter for your file saying, 'Don't pull guns anymore in the middle of a set. It pisses off the paying customers.'"

Conor scribbled something on the form.

"Anyway," Amanda said, "Kurtz will be happy. Him and those damned mug shots."

Conor pushed the DD5 across the desk to Amanda.

"Schroeder in Cold Case was working on this guy," Amanda said. "I'll dump this piece of garbage on him if that's all right with you."

"Please," Conor said, happy to be off the hook.

A uniformed cop walked up to Amanda. "We've got a body over by the Hudson River."

"Where's Colaneri and Doherty?"

"On a job."

"What about Tomkins?"

"Out sick."

"Who's available?"

"Jenkins and Francelli."

Amanda made a face. "The rubber-gun squad? Forget it." She turned and looked at Conor. "How much you had to drink?"

"Look. Sarge. Please. I'm off today."

But Conor wasn't going home anytime soon.

It had gotten cold. Conor was shivering as he stood in the muddy, empty lot on the banks of the Hudson River. And it didn't warm him any to be looking down at a body. Male. Mid-fifties. Wearing a thousand-dollar suit.

Brian Cobb from the Crime Scene Unit walked up to Conor. Brian was forty-five years old. Six feet four at least. A graduate of the John Jay College of Criminal Justice, which was part of the City University of New York. Born and bred in Manhattan, no one would ever mistake him for a suburbanite.

"Shot six times," Brian said, delivering the information with no inflection. Brian's tone and expression never changed, regardless of the situation. He could tell you he'd won the lottery without any hint of excitement.

"White male. Age fifty-four," Brian added.

"How do you know how old he is?"

"Wallet, watch, cash, all still on his person."

Conor nodded. Either robbery wasn't the motive or the killer had been interrupted before he could take anything.

"Body temperature's ninety-six degrees," Brian continued. "I'd guess he bought it in the last hour, two hours at the most."

Conor checked his watch. It was almost midnight. *Shooting likely occurred sometime after ten.*

"Who found him?" Conor asked.

"Some guy walking his dog."

"Anybody take a statement?"

"Rossini." Brian pointed at various footprints in the mud that fanned out around the body. "Got a parade of shoe impressions. We're making casts."

Frank Reynolds appeared out of nowhere. "You again?"

"Yeah, I love the overtime."

"You smell like booze."

"What can I tell you? Some jerk in the bar spilled a drink on me."

Reynolds gave Conor a look of disdain then walked away.

"You two have some kind of problem?" Brian asked.

"Don't know what *his* problem is, but I've got no problem."

Conor turned his attention to the body again. Something about the face was familiar. "Is that who I think it is?"

"If you're thinking that's Walter Lawton," Brian said, "you're right."

Walter Lawton was one of New York's most successful criminal defense attorneys. You could kill somebody in Times Square on New Year's Eve in front of a million people and Lawton could still get you off.

Brian stared down at Lawton's body then turned toward Conor. "Looks like you caught yourself a big case, Detective."

Chapter Two

It wasn't long before reporters descended on the scene, asking questions, snapping photos, sniffing around for scraps of information. Conor wondered if these guys had a life beyond sitting in front of a police scanner. As he stared out at the encroaching army, he was reminded of a recent directive issued by the office of the police commissioner: The commissioner, and *only* the commissioner, was authorized to speak to the press. So Conor was obligated to avoid too much interaction with the assembled journalistic corps. He had already drawn fire from a captain. He didn't want to offend the commissioner.

It was no surprise that Walter Lawton's unceremonious end would bring out the media. His client list included a host of major mafiosi and billionaire businessmen with a penchant for white-collar crime.

Conor hated that distinction: white-collar crime. It made it sound more acceptable somehow. To

Conor, a crime was a crime. It didn't matter if the perpetrator was a CEO or a capo.

But the fact remained, since Lawton was the go-to guy for high-profile perps, that inquiring minds wanted to know how he'd met such an inglorious fate: sprawled in an empty lot by the Hudson River. Which was a long way from the hallowed halls of Harvard Law School, Lawton's alma mater.

Determined to offer as little information as possible, Conor told the reporters it was too early in the investigation to comment. But they persisted, firing questions without even pausing for an answer. No, Conor said, there were no witnesses. Yes, Conor said, it did appear to be a homicide. No, Conor said, there were no suspects. Since the reporters already knew the victim was Walter Lawton, Conor guessed that some cop must have slipped up and mentioned Lawton's name during a radio transmission. Which wasn't good if the next of kin had not been notified.

In this case, the next of kin was Lawton's wife, Holly. Conor was informed by officers on the scene that she was being given the grim news by the precinct chaplain, who had been dispatched twenty minutes ago. Conor would follow the padre shortly. He knew all too well that the first person you look at when one spouse winds up dead is the spouse who's still alive.

The place Walter Lawton called home was a testament to his billable time. A sprawling double-width townhouse on Park Avenue and Eighty-fifth Street. Conor guessed it was worth twenty million, give or take a mil. And as wives go, Holly Lawton probably cost more, assuming you could even put a price on her. Mid-thirties, tall and blond, Holly was one of those women who haunted Manhattan's Upper East Side like exquisite apparitions. If you tried to get near them they would simply float away. Unless, of course, you had Walter Lawton's money.

Conor stood facing Holly in the middle of the large foyer. "I'm sorry to bother you at a time like this," he said.

"It's all right," Holly replied. "You're just doing your job."

Conor found Holly's measured response rather odd, especially coming from a wife who had just found out her husband would no longer be gracing their spacious home with his presence. On the other hand, she had just become an extremely wealthy widow.

Conor was unnerved by everything about Holly. To begin with, her beauty was distracting. Perfectly coiffed hair, flawlessly applied makeup, a designer dress caressing her like a desperate lover. And this was one o'clock in the morning, for Christ's sake. What did she look like on her way out to a party?

As Holly took a step toward the living room, she wobbled. Conor touched her shoulder lightly, to steady her.

"I suppose I'm in shock," Holly said.

"That's understandable."

"Of course, if I weren't in shock, you might suspect me of killing my husband." Holly smiled. "Or maybe you already do."

Conor wasn't sure what to make of Holly's remark. While his experience as a cop told him that people say strange things in stressful situations, this was different. Instead of the unguarded ramblings of someone in distress, Holly's observation resonated more like a calculated statement, a preemptive strike from someone very much in control.

"Why don't we sit down, Mrs. Lawton."

Holly locked her arm into the crook of Conor's elbow. As he helped her navigate into the living room, crossing what seemed like an acre of plush oriental carpet, Conor looked around him. He wasn't much of an expert on art, but he was pretty sure the paintings hanging on the wall didn't come from Walmart.

They reached a large L-shaped couch. Holly eased onto the cushions. Conor sat in a nearby chair.

"Do we have to do this now?" Holly asked.

"If you can, Mrs. Lawton. Time is my enemy."

"Okay. But if Walter were here, he'd probably tell me not to talk to you."

"And why would he say that?"

"Why? He always told suspects not to speak with police."

Conor studied her for a moment. "You're not a suspect, Mrs. Lawton."

"Really?" Holly smiled patronizingly. "Walter always said the first person police look at is the wife."

"Would you like a lawyer present?"

"No," Holly said. "I have nothing to hide."

"Do you know where your husband was tonight?"

Holly stared off, tears finally forming in her eyes. "He was driving back from the Hamptons."

"Did you say he was driving?"

Holly nodded. "The car wasn't there?"

"No."

"Maybe he parked it. Maybe it's at the garage."

"Where's the garage?"

"Eighty-sixth and Lexington."

"What kind of car does your husband drive?"

"A Maybach."

Of course. A Maybach. Made by Mercedes but too expensive to be called a Mercedes. A limited-production vehicle like that would set you back half a million. The good news was that there weren't many Maybachs out there, even in Manhattan.

"What color?"

"Silver."

After a few more questions, Conor realized that the best he was going to get from her for the moment was the Maybach lead.

"Thank you for your help, Mrs. Lawton."

"Please find out who did this to my husband."

"I will. Don't worry."

Conor took out a business card and a pen. He wrote his cell phone number on the back of the card and handed it to Holly. "Here's how to reach me. Call me anytime. Twenty-four seven."

"Thank you." Holly looked past Conor. "Maritza. Will you please see this gentleman out?"

"Yes, Mrs. Lawton."

Maritza? Conor followed Holly's eyes to a Latina in her fifties who was standing in a doorway. Conor was startled. He hadn't noticed Maritza at all.

"Maritza's been here all night," Holly said. "With me."

Conor stood, looked at Maritza.

"You and Mrs. Lawton were here all evening?"

She hesitated, then answered, "Yes." She looked at the floor when she spoke.

Conor made a mental note: *The housekeeper seems nervous. Check out the wife's alibi later.*

Holly stared up at Conor. "Will I see you tomorrow?" she asked.

The question itself wasn't surprising. What was unusual about it was the pleading intonation and the way Holly glanced at Conor when she asked it. Conor had heard that tone, seen that expression before. It was what he recalled most vividly about the drunken nights he spent with some impromptu lover. They always asked him the same question: Will I see you tomorrow? And Conor always said yes.

This time he meant it.

Conor was so relieved when he left the apartment that he let out an audible sigh. The rich really were different, and it wasn't so pleasant to be reminded of that fact.

Finding the silver Maybach proved more difficult than Conor had thought. It was not parked at the garage, so Conor checked the DMV database and obtained the license plate number for the Model 57 S registered to Lawton. An APB was sent out, but still no hit after an hour. While Conor waited for word, Brian arrived.

"You still on the job?" Conor asked.

"Got to strike while the iron's hot." Brian proceeded with his report from the crime scene. "Six twenty-two-caliber shell casings recovered. Three slugs on the ground. Guess we'll find the other three when we dig into the body. But no murder weapon."

"So what do you think?" Conor asked.

"What do *I* think?"

"Give me a theory. Any theory."

"I think it's your basic carjacking. I mean, a Maybach? That's one hell of a score."

"You're probably right," Conor agreed. "Anyway, I hope that's what it is. Save me a lot of shoe leather."

Amanda walked up to Conor and Brian.

"Hey, Bard. They got your car."

"Where?"

"Flatbush Avenue in Brooklyn. Some black kid driving it. They're bringing him in now."

"What did I tell you?" Brian said. "Carjacking."

Chapter Three

Mike Boyd was sitting in an interrogation room, one hand cuffed to a chair. Conor, Amanda, and two uniformed cops stood in the observation area and stared at Mike through the glass.

"Just released from Riker's," Amanda offered.

"Let me guess. Grand theft auto?"

"You're psychic."

"So the guy likes cars," Conor said.

"Yeah. And maybe when he gets out of prison this time he'll actually buy one."

Conor studied Mike. He was young. And very scared.

"How old is he?"

"Twenty-four," Amanda said.

Conor started for the door.

"You want someone in there with you?" Amanda asked.

"Not yet."

Conor entered the interrogation room and took a seat across from Mike.

"Hey, Mike," Conor began. "Nice car you were driving."

"Look, man. You can't—"

"Whoa! Hold on. I haven't read you your rights."

"I know my rights."

"You want to waive your rights, talk to me?"

Mike didn't respond.

"Okay," Conor said. "Here we go. You have the right to remain silent. Anything you say can and will—"

"I *said*, I know my rights. And I want a lawyer."

"So you don't want to tell me where you got that Maybach?"

Mike didn't respond. Conor leaned in on him.

"All right," Conor began, "here's what I'm going to do. I'm going to lock you up in the Tombs. Then, fifteen minutes later, I'm going to have you transferred to Riker's Island. You remember Riker's. You just got out of there. And then I'm going to send you to Queens. Maybe Staten Island. Up to the Bronx. Over to Brooklyn. Then back to the Tombs. I'm going to keep you moving, give you a nice tour of the city's facilities. It'll take three days for a lawyer to locate you."

"Are you crazy? Even if I did lift that ride, what's the big deal? I'll do my bid."

"Go ahead," Conor said abruptly. "Call your lawyer." He stood, looked down at Mike. "And make sure you tell him you're being charged with murder."

Mike was freaked. "What are you talking about? I didn't kill nobody!"

"Glad to hear that." Conor hovered over him. "So I'll give you one more chance to waive your right to an attorney and tell me how you wound up driving the car of a dead guy."

"He's *dead*?" Mike began trembling slightly. "*Who's* dead?"

Amanda entered the room, but before she could intervene, Mike caved in.

"It was parked by the river. Engine running."

Amanda frowned at Conor. She wasn't entirely sure that whatever Mike said was going to hold up in court, but Conor didn't seem to care at this point.

"Parked by the river?" Conor repeated. "Engine running?"

"I swear," Mike whined. "I ain't killed nobody. I just took the car."

"Detective!" Amanda said. "Outside, please."

Conor looked at Mike.

"Stay here. I'll be right back."

Mike held up his cuffed hand. *Where am I going?*

Conor walked out of the room. Amanda followed him.

"You were treading on very thin ice in there," she said.

"Hey, he admitted to stealing the car," Conor countered. "Of course, we did catch him driving the thing."

"I don't care about the car. This is a homicide and I don't want some slick-ass attorney—"

"He didn't do it."

"Didn't do *what*?" Amanda was incredulous.

"He didn't kill Lawton."

"I know it's late, Bard, and you want to go home, but—"

"You see the way he reacted when I told him he was going to be charged with murder."

"How was he supposed to react?"

"Not with total surprise."

Conor looked down at his shoes, which were caked in mud from the crime scene, then pointed through the glass at Mike.

"Look at his feet."

The black boots Mike was wearing were clean. Not a speck of dirt.

"That field was a swamp," Conor said. "So how come there's no mud on his shoes?"

"Why don't we let the DA decide what to charge, okay?"

Amanda, more than a little annoyed, walked away. Conor stared at Mike through the glass. *No*, Conor told himself, *Mike's not the shooter. Too bad. This case could have been wrapped up by breakfast.*

It was five in the morning by the time Conor arrived home. His cramped one-bedroom apartment was in an old brownstone on Forty-eighth Street between

Eighth and Ninth Avenues. Banging pipes in the winter, electrical overloads in the summer. The furnishings were a mismatch of pieces from various stages of his life: a coffee table from his college days; a lamp with an NYPD insignia on the base, which he got when he was a rookie; a couch inherited when he and Heather split up.

Conor flopped on the couch and calculated its age. He and Heather bought it when she moved into his apartment. They lived together for a year and a half, and split up eight months ago. That made the couch a little over two years old, which wasn't ancient for a piece of furniture if it was well made. This one wasn't.

All Conor could remember about his time with Heather was the insanity of it. She was Ivy League–educated, came from a good New England family. An intellectual with a penchant for smoking joints who thought life was an adventure. And when life didn't measure up to her expectations, she created drama to fill the void. Upheaval made her feel alive. Conor, on the other hand, only wanted to end the day in a safe harbor. Heather created waves, violent storms. Conor could never relax around her. Heather made sure of that. Enduring a constant barrage of her unpredictable behavior, their relationship predictably unraveled.

Conor was never really in love with Heather. Although he depended on her in many ways, he often thought about ending the whole charade. Yet Conor was not the one to end it. Heather had pointed out that they were going nowhere. Conor was mildly surprised by hearing it said aloud even though he knew it was true. He had ignored the space between them until Heather had said it was there. Once the silence had been broken, they went from lovers to memories in an instant.

The last time Conor had spoken to Heather was a week ago. They had a brief conversation, catching up on each other's lives. Heather was vague, as if she had something to hide, but Conor didn't press for details. If she was concealing something, it couldn't be good. When he hung up the phone, he wondered what she was up to this time and a familiar feeling of impending doom overtook him. *Forget about her*, Conor told himself. But he couldn't.

He fell back on the couch. Exhaustion, both mental and physical, overtook him. In a dreamlike state of half slumber, he saw Heather smiling at him. And then she disappeared, leaving him alone somewhere. He felt empty. Afraid, even. Then a kiss on his cheek. A hand taking his. His nostrils filling with the scent of perfume. He spun around, pulled her against his chest. But it wasn't Heather in his arms.

It was Holly Lawton.

Conor jolted wide awake, sat upright. *Jesus*, Conor thought. *What was that?*

He inexplicably found himself hoping Holly Lawton was not a cold-blooded killer. But what if she *was* innocent? What then? No way he had a chance with her. Or did he?

Conor laughed at himself. After all, it was late, the hour when bizarre thoughts weren't afraid to climb out of the darkness. Time to get some sleep. Tomorrow was another day.

As Conor tossed and turned in his bed, he couldn't deny the fact that Holly Lawton, on some primal level, had entwined herself into his consciousness.

Chapter Four

Conor dragged himself out of bed, showered, and donned his "uniform"—dress pants, mock turtleneck, and a blue blazer. He hated wearing ties, and in fact owned only five of them, preferring comfort over fashion during the long hours he put in on the job.

Ralph Kurtz was sitting at his desk when Conor arrived at the precinct. Seven days shy of sixty-two, five feet eleven, a little overweight, he was wearing his usual cheap suit, garish tie, and a pair of size-13 triple-E shoes on his large, wide feet, which made the term *flatfoot*, slang for police officer, particularly appropriate.

Ralph had rejected retirement at every milestone—twenty years, thirty years, forty years—and was determined to remain on the force until they made him leave. That would be in exactly one week. But Ralph didn't plan to retire even then. The district attorney's office didn't have a mandatory retirement age, so he had already lined up a job as an investigator on the DA squad.

"You had a busy night, I see." Ralph held up a copy of the *New York Post* and waved it at Conor. The headline blared, *Mob Attorney Slain on West Side*. There was a huge photo of Walter Lawton.

"And there's a nice picture of you on page five," Ralph added, holding out the *Post* to Conor.

"Let me see that." Conor grabbed the paper and flipped to a photo of himself standing in the middle of the crime scene chaos.

"The commissioner's going to love reading your comments," Ralph said with a smile.

"Jackals." Conor tossed the *Post* onto his desk.

"You should've called me," Ralph said.

"It was late. I'm sure you were asleep. But you're right about it being a busy night. I got Robert Willis for you too. You see the DD5?"

"Yeah. That sick bastard is finally gonna pay."

"Walked right in the club like he didn't have a care in the world."

"Nice collar. So don't give me a hard time about my old mug shots anymore."

"I won't."

"Anyway," Ralph said. "This guy Lawton? A dead lawyer? What's the big deal? You know how I feel about lawyers."

"Yeah, I know. But we still have to investigate."

"Don't worry. I called Lawton's office. They're expecting us at nine thirty."

Ralph was like that. Always on top of any situation. He loved the work. Even the minutiae. Ralph would research a case to death then spend days poring over the evidence. He had a reason for his obsessive dedication—Ralph had once confided to Conor that the job was the only thing that kept him from going nuts after his wife, Laura, died two years ago.

"I spoke to forensics," Ralph said. "No gunshot residue on the suspect they brought in."

"Plus, there was no mud on his shoes," Conor said. "That kid's not the shooter."

"He could've had an accomplice," Ralph speculated.

"Possible," Conor allowed.

"What's the story on the wife?" Ralph asked.

"I don't know. She wasn't too torn up about the whole thing."

"She has an alibi, of course." Ralph didn't hide his skepticism.

"Yeah. The housekeeper."

"Who happens to be on the wife's payroll."

Ralph held up a piece of paper.

"I filed a request for phone records on the Lawton residence, Lawton's private line at his office, and both Lawton's and the wife's cell phones."

"Good," Conor said.

"And you want to hear something funny?"

"What?"

"I Googled Lawton. Came across this Web page where they tell you the origin and meaning of names."

Although Ralph had a variety of restricted law enforcement and legal databases at his fingertips, he also would use consumer search engines to surf the Internet, especially when a high-profile victim was involved. According to Ralph, the information he garnered on these forays into cyberspace gave him a broader view of the case.

"Guess what the name *Lawton* means?" Ralph asked.

"I don't know. What?"

"It's an old English word for 'burial mound.' Looks like Lawton's living up to his name. Or maybe dying down to it." Ralph chuckled at his own joke, then checked his watch. "Better head over to the law office."

Ralph was never late.

Walter Lawton's office was impressive even by New York standards. Conor and Ralph looked like toy action figures as they stood in the double-height lobby waiting for someone to lead them into the inner sanctum.

"This guy had a lot of powerful friends," Ralph said.

That was yet another Ralph Kurtz trait: stating the obvious.

"They're no good to him now," Conor said.

Ralph rubbed his chin. "Don't be so sure."

Actually, Ralph was right. A victim this connected could pull strings from the grave.

"Hello, Detectives." The voice sounded like it was coming from the mouth of a prepubescent girl.

Julie Hahn, a pretty young woman in her early twenties, approached them. Petite, with short brown hair, she was dressed in a tailored gray jacket with a matching skirt, obviously trying to project Manhattan business cool. It might have worked had it not been for the voice.

"You must be Miss Hahn," Ralph said. "I'm Detective Kurtz. We spoke on the phone."

"Yes," Julie acknowledged.

Ralph motioned toward Conor. "This is my partner, Detective Bard."

Julie straightened her posture, as if to signal her importance. "Pleasure to meet you."

As Conor looked at Julie, the first word that popped into his mind was *yuppie*. Of course, the term hadn't been relevant for over twenty years. Then again, Conor thought, neither had he.

"I'm a junior partner here," Julie explained. "I've been assigned to interface with you."

Conor and Ralph exchanged a glance. *Interface?*

Julie motioned across the lobby. "This way, please."

Conor and Ralph followed her down a seemingly endless hallway.

"Everyone in the office is extremely upset," Julie said, shaking her head back and forth.

"I'm sure they are," Ralph offered, trying not to sound too jaded.

"Do you have any idea who might have done this to Mr. Lawton?" Julie asked.

"Do *you*?" Ralph asked.

"I can't imagine. He was such a nice man."

They walked to a door and entered a small conference room.

"Please. Detectives. Have a seat."

Conor and Ralph sat across from each other. Julie sat at the head of the table. She looked at Ralph.

"When we spoke earlier I said the law firm would do everything it could to assist your investigation."

"Thank you," Ralph said. "We really appreciate that."

"You asked for our client list."

"Yes. That would be very helpful in the investigation."

"I'm sorry," Julie said. "I'm afraid I can't accommodate you without a warrant."

"I understand your concerns but—"

"The partners held an emergency session this morning and it was the consensus opinion that we must not do anything to violate attorney-client privilege."

Ralph started to say something.

Julie interrupted, "I'm not authorized to say any more than that." She stood. "I'll show you out now."

Conor and Ralph exited the office building and walked down the street.

"Is she even old enough to drink?" Conor wondered aloud.

"What?" Ralph teased. "You want to take her out?"

"Yeah. *Right*."

"I know what you mean. They get younger and younger. Or is it that we get older and older?"

Conor was annoyed. "Couldn't she have asked for a warrant on the phone? Instead of making us come all the way over here?"

"She's a lawyer. What do you expect?"

They stopped at the car. Ralph climbed behind the steering wheel. Conor hated to drive.

"So we get a warrant," Conor said.

Ralph frowned, thinking. "Or . . ."

"Or what?"

"I'm starting at the DA's office in two weeks. Right after NYPD kicks me to the curb."

"You're a senior citizen. What can I tell you?"

Ralph ignored Conor's gibe. "Maybe I can get somebody at the DA's office to run a list of cases where Lawton was the attorney of record. Faster than a warrant."

Chapter Five

The trip to the DA's office was worth it. Conor and Ralph returned to the precinct with a box full of case histories spanning the last five years. They had wanted to go back further in time but Ralph's contact at the DA's office said that five years was the best he could do without making a formal request, and that could take days.

"Five years should be enough," Ralph said as they sifted through the documents. "If any of *these* guys had a grudge against Lawton, they wouldn't wait too long to settle the score."

It seemed no client with a checkbook was too unsavory for Walter Lawton. Besides the mob bosses and the Wall Street bonus babies, there were an assortment of petty thieves, wife beaters, smugglers, rapists, and even child molesters.

"I bet if we laid all their rap sheets end to end," Ralph said, "they'd reach L.A."

He looked down at one of the files and tapped a page.

"Check this guy out."

Conor leaned over Ralph's shoulder. "Salvatore Zeffri."

"Murder for hire," Ralph observed. "And look. His *alleged* weapon of choice was a twenty-two-caliber handgun."

Ralph often used the word *alleged* mockingly. Most cops did.

Assassins generally preferred a .22. Small-caliber bullets tended to bounce around inside the body, ricocheting from bone to bone. This resulted in maximum internal damage with a minimum of mess. When Conor was standing over Walter Lawton's body and learned there were .22 shell casings at the scene, he had considered the possibility that the shooter wasn't an amateur.

Conor read more of the dossier on Salvatore Zeffri. "Lawton got the guy acquitted. It's not like you kill the person who kept you out of jail."

"Yeah," Ralph agreed. "But it's not like he has anything against blowing somebody away for money either."

"Which means?"

Ralph motioned to the file. "Unless you have a better idea, we start with Zeffri."

Salvatore Zeffri lived in a modest house on a nondescript block in Ozone Park, Queens. It was the kind of street that wiseguys loved. No ostentatious mansions here. Nothing to draw attention. Just a quiet, seemingly benign community providing perfect camouflage for violent residents.

Salvatore Zeffri was not home, so Conor and Ralph canvassed the neighbors. Most of them refused to talk.

"Sorry, I'm late for work," was all the man in a paint-splattered jumpsuit would say as he climbed into a pickup truck and drove off.

Others denied even knowing Salvatore Zeffri.

"Never heard of him," a middle-aged man said as he hurried down the street.

Finally, a woman walking her dog told them that Zeffri owned a kennel.

"I board my dog there when I go on vacation," the woman added before walking away.

Ralph frowned. "A kennel?"

"Guess he likes dogs," Conor observed.

"Right," Ralph said. "So did Hitler."

Canine Care Kennels was located in nearby Hillside. It consisted of two acres, a house, which served as the office, a one-story building where the actual kennels were located, and an outdoor dog run surrounded by chain-link fence.

Conor and Ralph found Zeffri walking along the fence. He was handsome, elegant, forty-five years old. The cocksure way he carried himself made it hard to picture him shearing a poodle.

Zeffri looked up and saw Conor and Ralph approaching. He made them immediately. "Good afternoon, Detectives."

"Salvatore Zeffri?" Ralph asked.

"That's me."

"I'm Detective Kurtz. And this is my partner, Detective Bard."

"Can I see some ID?"

Conor and Ralph complied.

"One can never be too careful," Zeffri said as he studied the badges and IDs for a moment. He feigned apprehension. "Should I call my lawyer?"

"He's dead," Ralph pointed out.

"Yes. Poor Walter. I heard about it on the news. A terrible tragedy."

"Not so terrible," Ralph said.

"He doesn't like lawyers," Conor explained.

"Who does?" Zeffri asked. "So what can I do for you? Would you like to board a dog? Our rates are extremely reasonable."

"Let's stop playing cat and mouse at the dog kennel," Ralph said, done with the game. "We were just wondering where you were last night."

"I'll have my attorney call you," Zeffri said.

"They have phones in Hell?" Ralph asked.

Zeffri smiled. "My *new* lawyer, Megan Hollister. She'll be in touch. Now, if you'll excuse me, I have to feed the boarders."

Zeffri walked away. Conor waited until Zeffri was out of earshot then turned toward Ralph.

"Cat and mouse at the dog kennel?" Conor laughed. "Forget the DA's office. You ought to try standup comedy."

"I'd lay you odds this place is a Mafia front. Money laundry."

Conor looked at Ralph with an expression of mock surprise. "What? You don't think Zeffri is an animal lover?"

But Ralph wasn't paying attention. He was scanning the property like a prospective buyer. "After we close the case," he said with conviction, "we should close this place."

"A comic *and* a poet?"

They started walking off the property.

"Take me to the wife," Ralph said. "I want to see if she's as gorgeous as you say she is."

Chapter Six

Holly was impeccably dressed, appearing fresh and well rested. Glowing, even. Apparently she hadn't had too much trouble sleeping after the bad news. Conor and Ralph sat with her in the "Florida Room," as she called it, a glass-enclosed patio full of plants and flooded with sunlight.

"I understand you arrested the man who killed Walter," Holly began, catching Conor and Ralph off guard.

"We apprehended someone who was driving your husband's car," Conor explained. "But he has denied killing your husband."

Holly rolled her eyes. "Well, of *course* he would deny it."

Ralph bristled over the fact that Holly was aware they had made an arrest. "How did you find out about this?"

"I'd rather not say. I don't want to get anyone in trouble, if you know what I mean."

Holly, by virtue of her marriage to Walter Lawton, obviously had contacts in the DA's office. Ralph vowed to himself that his first order of business when he arrived there would be to find whoever was using the office in order to gain favor with the social set. The more he thought about it, the more pissed off he became—and the less attractive Holly Lawton seemed to him.

"Until we're sure we have the right person," Conor said, "our investigation will be ongoing."

Holly waved her hand in a dismissive manner. "He *was* driving my husband's car, wasn't he?"

Conor ignored the question. "Did your husband have any enemies?"

"Enemies?" Holly repeated. "I suppose there were people who had a reason to dislike him."

"Anyone in particular?" Conor asked.

"Sure, a few clients were upset at Walter. But Walter couldn't help it if the jury didn't—"

"Anyone who stands out in your mind," Conor pressed.

Holly thought for a moment, then: "There was this *one* man. A Russian. Walter did everything he could for him but—"

"Do you remember his name?" Ralph cut in, losing his patience.

"No, I'm sorry. But I *do* remember that after he was convicted he threatened to kill Walter. And now he's suing the firm for incompetent counsel."

Ralph pulled a pen and notebook from his pocket.

He hated taking notes—usually he would just pretend to jot down something relevant—but he had discovered over the years that merely the act of holding a pen over a blank page caused suspects to make minor adjustments to their previous stories. Confronted with the reality that what they said was about to be written down, they often would attempt to be precise in their recollections, *too* precise, recalling exact times right down to the minute. Nobody remembers exact times. Unless you are making it all up.

"Last night." Ralph held up the pen like a baton. "You told Detective Bard that you were home all evening. With your maid, Maritza?"

"My *housekeeper*, Maritza." Holly said it as if to scold Ralph for not knowing that the upper crust shy away from the word *maid*.

"I assume your *housekeeper* will give us a statement to that effect." Ralph made no attempt to hide his disdain.

"Of course."

Ralph wrote something in the notebook. "Is she here now?"

"No. This is her day off. She'll be back tomorrow."

Ralph snapped the notebook shut. "Then we'll stop back by tomorrow and take a statement." His tone bordered on contempt.

"Do you know someone named Salvatore Zeffri?" Conor asked.

"Zeffri?" Holly said, shifting in her chair.

"Salvatore Zeffri," Conor repeated. "You know him?"

Holly cleared her throat. "No. I mean, I don't think so."

Ralph opened the notebook again. "You don't *think* so?"

Holly drew in a breath. "Wait. Wasn't he one of my husband's clients? Yes. That's where I heard the name."

"But you don't *know* him?" Ralph said.

Holly's face flushed and her hands curled into tight little fists. She glanced at Ralph's notebook. "*Know* him?"

Conor studied her. It was a simple question. Ralph held the pen over the notepad, apparently poised to write down whatever she said.

"No," Holly finally said. "I don't know him."

Conor looked at Holly—her facial expression, her body language, her blinking eyelids, all led to an undeniable conclusion: as adept as she might be in other areas of her stress-free life, Holly Lawton was not a very good liar.

Conor and Ralph, still holding his notepad, walked out of Holly's building and headed down the street.

"I hate women like that," Ralph fumed.

"Oh, *really*? I didn't notice."

"They think the world owes them."

"Looks like the world already paid up," Conor observed.

"She was lying," Ralph said, once again stating the obvious. "She knows Zeffri."

"Seems that way."

Ralph squinted, which he always did when he was on to something. "What if the wife wanted to dispense with her husband? She'd have no trouble paying for the job in more ways than one. So what would stop her from going to a guy like this?"

Conor didn't have to ponder the question very long. "Nothing would stop her."

A lying widow? That automatically put her high on the list. Maybe not the shooter but definitely a possible accessory. Yet whatever her involvement might or might not be, Conor knew one thing for sure. The way the investigation was going, the only thing that would be easy to pin on Holly Lawton was a very expensive piece of jewelry.

Conor glanced at Ralph's notepad. "You take any notes?"

"Yeah," Ralph replied. "Got to pick up some milk on the way home."

Back at the precinct, Conor and Ralph dug into the box of Lawton's cases again. They finally found a client with a Russian name who fit the bill: Anatoli Sidorov. The FBI had snared Sidorov under the provisions of the Racketeer Influenced and Corrupt Organizations Act. RICO was enacted in 1970, providing law enforcement with a way to prosecute individuals not just for single offenses but also for their role in ongoing criminal activity.

"The feds nailed him on a RICO," Ralph said. "Like Gotti."

Conor scanned the file. "Life without the possibility of parole. That'll tick you off."

A quick check of the legal database turned up the suit Sidorov had filed against Lawton. Ralph read from the computer screen. "Incompetent counsel. Just like the wife said."

Conor flipped through Sidorov's file. "He's being held at Otisville."

The Federal Correctional Institution in Otisville was in Orange County, New York. Ralph lived in Harriman, about half an hour from there.

Ralph stood. "Come on. That's my hood. I know all the shortcuts. I'll get us there in an hour twenty."

Conor ached for sleep. Every fiber in his body felt frayed. However, since the possibility did exist that Anatoli Sidorov had something to do with the murder of Walter Lawton, there was no choice.

"All right," Conor said as he pushed himself out of his chair. "Let's hit the road."

Chapter Seven

Ralph drove, not like a normal person but like a blind rat in a maze. He ate a sandwich, fiddled with the radio, and read the *Daily Racing Form*, which was draped over the steering wheel, all at the same time. Once in a while he looked at the road ahead.

Conor frowned as the car veered onto the shoulder.

"Jesus, Ralph. Watch where you're going."

"I know where I'm going."

Ralph, holding the sandwich between his teeth, yanked the steering wheel to the left with one hand and continued to twist the knob on the radio with the other.

"Gotta get the results," he explained, his voice muffled through the ham and cheese. "Got a C-note on Sassy Sue in the second."

That was another thing about Ralph. He loved

the ponies. When he wasn't working on a case, he was at the track.

Ralph finally tuned in to the station he wanted. A static-filled commercial blared over the speakers.

"The reception's terrible up here," he said as he pulled the sandwich from between his teeth. "Anyway, Sassy Sue's the only filly in the race. Sometimes you've got to bet on the ladies."

Conor smiled. Horses, maybe. But he'd bet on the real ladies a few times. So far not even one had made it across the finish line.

He checked his watch. "Are we there yet?"

"You sound like a kid."

The commercial faded to silence. A DJ's upbeat voice filled the void.

"And now here's Marv the Blade with the racing report from Belmont Park."

"In the first it was Broadway Blues by a nose, followed by Stonegate and then Harry's Tweed. In the second . . ."

Ralph reached over and turned up the volume.

". . . Roman Candle burned up the track . . ."

Ralph hit the steering wheel with his hand.

". . . running away from Star Mountain and . . ."

Ralph snapped off the radio. "Remind me. Never bet on fillies."

"I will."

They rode in silence for a mile or so as Ralph stewed.

"So we've got the wife," Conor said. "And we've

got a professional killer with a penchant for twenty-two-caliber firearms. And now we're going to see what the Russian has to say for himself. The field's getting pretty crowded."

Ralph popped the last bit of ham and cheese in his mouth. "The more the merrier. Makes for a more interesting race."

"Yeah," Conor teased. "But the problem is, you never pick a winner."

Ralph chewed. Conor waited for him to counter.

"That's all right," Ralph finally said. "We're not looking for a winner here, we're looking for a loser."

Conor and Ralph went through the security check at the prison and proceeded to an interview room. There were three folding chairs, nothing else.

"You want to start?" Ralph asked.

"Okay," Conor said. "You come in when you see an opening."

Their tag team approach to interrogation had served them well in the past. Two against one. The odds were in their favor.

The door opened. A guard led Anatoli Sidorov into the room. He was fifty-two, six feet tall, broad-shouldered. The Otisville-issue outfit he was wearing was too small and the close-cropped prison haircut accentuated his wide forehead. He didn't walk, he lumbered. And, surprisingly, he was uncuffed. A small measure of respect granted him by the guards, perhaps. The cumulative effect was that he didn't seem sinister at all, at least not in the way he had been portrayed by the feds, and he even possessed a certain Eastern European charm. Definitely not the character Conor and Ralph had expected.

"I'm Detective Bard," Conor said. "And this is my partner, Detective Kurtz."

Sidorov motioned to the chairs. "Please. Have a seat."

His demeanor was that of a host, not a prisoner, a cordial manner intended to create the illusion he was still in charge. Which was something Conor had noticed before when he'd dealt with fallen antiheroes. They never totally relinquished the aura of their once-unchallenged mantle of absolute clout.

"Sorry I can't offer you some fine Russian caviar," Sidorov said as they all took a seat.

"Mr. Sidorov," Conor began, opting to address him formally instead of using his first name. "We want to talk with you about the murder of Walter Lawton."

Sidorov's face brightened. "That was very good news."

"I'm sure it was," Conor said. "Lawton's inadequate defense got you convicted."

"And you think that gives me motive?" Sidorov asked.

"Maybe," Conor replied.

"Not *maybe*. *Definitely* that is very good motive." Sidorov leaned in on Conor. "People told me he was the best lawyer. That was not true. He did not care about my case. He had many other clients. He was a greedy man, Detective. A greedy man. And because of this, I am sitting here. *Me.* An honest immigrant who did nothing wrong."

"So you're saying you had no involvement in the murder of Walter Lawton?" Conor asked.

Sidorov appeared pained. "It hurts me that you would accuse me of something like that. I don't kill anyone." He smiled. "Even if they deserve to be killed."

Ralph jumped in. "According to his wife, you *threatened* to kill him."

"Yes. I did that," Sidorov said without apology. "I can only blame my Russian blood. But I did not mean a word of it. I wanted to hurt him much more by taking his money. That is why I sued him instead of . . ." His voice trailed off.

"Instead of what?" Ralph asked.

"Instead of spanking him."

But Conor knew full well how the sentence would have been completed had Sidorov finished it. *Instead of killing him.*

Conor made a play on Sidorov's ego. "But you still have the power to order a hit, even from in here."

"A hit? I don't know what you mean by that. A hit? Like what?" Sidorov mimicked a baseball player swinging at a pitch. "Like to hit a ball with a bat?"

"According to the transcript of your trial," Conor pressed, "you know very well what I mean by a hit."

"Lies. All federal lies. Ever since we were first in space with our little dog, your government has hated everyone who is Russian. That is why my new lawyer is Russian immigrant like me. I have filed an appeal and I will be out of here soon. And when I am out"—Sidorov slapped Conor's shoulder—"I take you to good Russian place in Brooklyn where the girls are hot and the vodka is cold."

He laughed a big belly laugh. Conor laughed too, even though the joke was on him.

Chapter Eight

Conor and Ralph exited Otisville and headed to the car.

"You see the way Sidorov handled himself?" Ralph said. "I almost liked the guy. A ruthless, likable guy. That's the kind of guy who inspires loyalty."

"Yeah," Conor agreed. "I know what you mean."

"But don't get me wrong. He's a bad guy. And I'd guess he still wields a lot of power on the outside. Just because he's locked up doesn't mean he isn't capable of ordering Lawton's murder from his cell. But, to tell you the truth, I think somebody else beat him to it." Ralph turned and looked back at the prison. "The thing that really bothers me is he might conceivably win on appeal."

"You think so?"

"Yeah. I do." Ralph was becoming agitated. "Some lawyer finds a bullshit technical loophole, Sidorov walks right out the doors we just walked out of. I mean, we bust our ass, risk our lives, then some mook with a law degree in his hand puts these scum back on the street. And you wonder why I can't stand lawyers."

"Thanks for filling me in," Conor teased. "Now I don't have to wonder anymore what you have against lawyers."

"Yeah? Well, you just watch. Sidorov is back in Brooklyn within a year."

"I hope so. The place with the hot girls and cold vodka sounded great."

They stopped at the car.

"Drop me off," Ralph said. "I'll take the train in tomorrow."

"No. *You* drop *me* off. The thought of driving back to the city right now . . ."

"All right." Ralph checked his watch. "Come on. There's a train out of Harriman in eighteen minutes."

"Can we make it?"

"If we use the flashers."

Ralph smiled. Even after all these years, he loved the lights and sirens.

The ride was not for the faint of heart. Ralph drove with the determination of a Nascar driver but not the skill. He hit the curb so hard during a sharp right turn, Conor was convinced they must have lost a wheel. But the objective was achieved. Conor arrived at the station with three minutes to spare.

He boarded the train and almost immediately dozed off in the seat.

After arriving at Grand Central Station, Conor took the shuttle to the Times Square subway station, then, to wake himself, walked the twelve blocks to the precinct. By the time he got to his desk and started writing the DD5 on the Sidorov interview, it was almost nine o'clock. *I'll do it in the morning*, Conor thought as he shoved himself away from his desk.

Conor left the precinct and headed down the street. He stopped at the corner and, realizing he hadn't eaten dinner, wondered whether to duck into Fu Ying and pick up some Chinese food. Then what? Eat it alone in his apartment? Conor thought about Ralph. Since his wife had died two years ago, Ralph went home every night to an empty house. *No wonder Ralph is so obsessed with the job.* Conor decided to grab some fried rice, then go back to the precinct and work on the DD5.

"Excuse me, do you know a restaurant called Thalia?"

Conor turned. The voice belonged to a young woman who appeared to be in her thirties. She was pretty, with olive Mediterranean skin, jet black hair, and a body most American women would try to shed in the gym. But her curves exuded a sensuality that skin and bones could barely approximate. She spoke with a slight foreign accent that only served to heighten her appeal.

Her question had been directed at another woman, who appeared to be in a hurry.

"I'm sorry," the other woman said as she kept walking. "I don't live in the neighborhood."

The woman crossed the avenue, leaving the young dark-haired woman standing there bewildered. Conor wondered what to do. Meeting women on the street was not the greatest idea. He'd done it before—always a disaster. Still, pointing her in the right direction couldn't hurt.

The woman started down the block. Conor followed her, caught up with her.

"Are you lost?" he asked.

The woman stopped, turned, and looked at Conor. She seemed a little startled.

"Well, you *look* lost," he said.

"No, I'm fine, thank you."

She started walking again. Conor matched her pace.

"Thalia's on Fiftieth," he said. "Come on. I'll take you there."

The woman hesitated. Conor pointed down the street. "That's my precinct back there."

He removed his gold shield from the breast pocket of his jacket and held it so she could see it.

"Honest," he said with a smile. "I'm a cop."

The woman looked at the badge, then at Conor. "If it's not out of your way . . ."

"Not at all," he said as he put the shield back in his pocket. "I live on Forty-eighth."

They crossed Eighth Avenue and walked south toward Fiftieth Street.

"I'm Detective Conor Bard."

"Monica Kodra," the woman said.

"Nice to meet you."

Conor tried to place the accent but couldn't. "Where are you from?"

"Albania."

"I don't know too much about Albania," Conor admitted.

"Don't feel bad. Most people don't."

"The other day I was doing a crossword puzzle and the clue said: 'Albanian coastal city.' I had no idea."

"Well, at least you know Albania has a coast. That's good."

"I take it you don't live in Hell's Kitchen," Conor said.

"Hell's Kitchen?"

"That's what this neighborhood is called."

"No. I'm meeting someone."

"Someone who lives around here?"

Monica laughed. "You ask a lot of questions."

"I'm a detective. I can't help myself."

They stopped in front of Thalia.

"What time are you meeting your friend?"

"Ten."

Conor looked at his watch. "It's not even nine."

"I didn't want to be late."

The way she said it, so sincerely, made Conor

smile. Heather had never cared if she kept someone waiting an hour or even more.

"Can I buy you a drink?" he asked rather clumsily.

Monica waited an appropriate amount of time before answering. "Sure," she finally said. "Why not?"

Chapter Nine

Conor and Monica took a seat at the bar. The bartender was a tall redhead named Kristen. Conor was surprised she was still there. Although Thalia once had a lively late-night bar scene, the owner had developed the place into more restaurant than watering hole. As a result, the bevy of cocktail waitresses Conor had known and loved had moved on to other spots. And so had he.

"Hey, Conor. Where you been hiding?" Kristen asked.

"Been busy fighting crime," Conor said.

"Not going too well, is it?" Kristen laughed. "So, what can I get you?"

Conor turned toward Monica. "What would you like to drink?"

"A red wine, please."

"Cabernet? Merlot? Pinot Noir?"

"Whatever you think." Monica's vaguely embarrassed expression told Conor she wasn't much of a wine aficionado. He found that endearing. Heather would have asked for the wine list, decided that nothing by the glass was worthy of her palate, *then* ordered a bottle of the most expensive wine on the list. And *then*, after sipping less than half a glass, would've decided she'd rather have a cosmopolitan.

"We just got a nice Australian Shiraz in," Kristen said.

"You like Shiraz?" Conor asked Monica.

"I've never had one."

"I think you'll like it," Kristen said. "If you don't, I'll give you something else."

"Okay."

Kristen looked at Conor. "The usual?"

For Conor, the usual was a Ketel One martini. Straight up. Twist. No vermouth. All the bartenders in Hell's Kitchen knew that well. On some nights, too well.

"Yeah. Thanks, Kristen."

Kristen drifted away to fill the order. Conor rotated on his bar stool and faced Monica. "How long have you been in New York?"

"Five and a half months."

"Do you like it?"

"I love it. But unfortunately I have to go back to Albania next week."

"When next week?"

"Tuesday."

"Why? Your visa expiring?"

"Yes."

"Tourist visa?"

"No, actually a work visa. I'm in the business development department at the Albanian American Bank. They sent me over to meet with some of their expatriate clients living in New York."

"Where are you staying?"

Monica smiled. "You *do* ask a lot of questions, don't you?"

Conor threw his hands in the air. "A man can't win. If he doesn't ask questions, a woman thinks he isn't interested in her. But if he *does* ask questions . . ."

Monica laughed.

"You really think I ask too many questions? Oh. Sorry. That's a question too, isn't it? Sorry, that was *another* question."

Monica laughed again. As far as Conor could tell, he had charmed her somewhat. At least he hoped so. A sexy young woman leaving the country in a week? If they did wind up in bed, the goodbye was already built in. *It doesn't get any better than that*, Conor thought.

"I'm staying in one of the bank's corporate apartments on the East Side," Monica said as her laughter faded.

"So, tell me about Albania. And may I point out I did *not* phrase that in the form of a question."

As Monica talked about her country, Conor found himself increasingly curious about the small Balkan nation. She recounted that, historically, Albania was constantly the target of occupation by foreign powers. Monica herself had endured years living under Communist rule, which led to a collapsed economy and spirit-killing poverty. As he listened, Conor was reminded that outside the United States life often wasn't easy—something Americans would rather not think about.

"It's much better these days," Monica said. "Now that the Democrats are in power."

Although Monica called Tirana home, she had grown up in northern Albania.

"They still practice the Kanun in the north." Monica explained that the Kanun was a fifteenth-century code of law in which women had few rights.

"What's wrong with that?" Conor asked.

Monica smiled. "If you want to practice the Kanun, you'll have to move to north Albania. And I don't think you'd like it very much."

The hour had passed like minutes. Conor drained the last of his martini. Monica still had half a glass of Shiraz.

"Is the wine okay?" Conor asked.

"It's very good. Thank you. It's just that I'm not much of a drinker." Monica seemed suddenly nervous. She looked up at a clock hanging on the wall behind the bar.

Conor realized that for whatever reason, Monica would prefer that he not be sitting there when her friend, male or female, arrived.

"I better get going," Conor said. He turned toward the bar. "Hey, Kristen. What's the damage?"

"It's on me, Conor. Just show your face around here a little more often."

"Will do."

Conor left a tip, then looked at Monica.

"I'd love to see you again," Conor said.

"That would be nice," Monica replied.

Happy to have Monica's cell phone number tucked safely away in his pocket, Conor didn't relish facing his empty apartment just yet, so he decided to swing back by the precinct. On the way, he stopped at Fu Ying and picked up an order of chicken with cashews.

Conor sat at his desk and ate the Chinese concoction right from the carton. In between bites, he called the Rhythm Bar and told the owner he couldn't be there the following night. As much as he wanted to lose himself onstage, singing songs in the middle of a homicide investigation would not create the best impression.

The owner wasn't happy, but then again, what could he say? Conor had protected the Rhythm Bar over the years, calling off the city health inspectors on more than one occasion and making minor offenses disappear as if they had never happened.

"The band can handle it without me," Conor said.

Canceling gigs was something Conor was often forced to do because of his caseload, which was ironic because he never really thought of himself as a cop.

That was his day job. He was a musician. A performer. A songwriter. Most nights off he spent singing in the Rhythm Bar or some other joint. Not exactly the fast track to stardom. Still, Conor was a dreamer, always had been. Someday he'd make a CD. It would be a hit. He'd retire from the force.

Amanda walked up to Conor. *Jesus*, he thought. *Does she ever go home?*

"Conor," Amanda said, her voice somber. "Reynolds called. He's pressing for a disciplinary hearing."

"You're kidding."

"Don't worry. I'm sure you'll just get a slap on the wrist."

Amanda was probably right. He drew his weapon in a crowded bar? So what? He got a killer off the street. The incident warranted a minor reprimand at worst. Even so, it was one more frustration in Conor's increasingly frustrated life.

As Conor stood to leave, he noticed something in Ralph's in-box. He picked it up and discovered several pages of phone numbers. On top was a list of calls made in the past two weeks from Lawton's private office line. Under that were his cell phone and home phone records. On the bottom of the stack, Conor found Holly Lawton's cell phone activity. He sat back down and went through the numbers. One on Holly's list stood out because of the sheer volume of calls both incoming and outgoing.

Conor reached for the phone and dialed the number. It rang three times and went to voice mail.

"Hello. This is Sal Zeffri. I'm not available right now. Please leave a message."

Conor hung up the phone and leaned back in his chair. Holly Lawton and Salvatore Zeffri burning all their mobile minutes chatting each other up?

Why?

Because Holly and Salvatore conspired to kill her husband, of course. What other explanation could there be?

Chapter Ten

Despite learning that Holly Lawton and Salvatore Zeffri obviously were well acquainted, Conor wasn't basking in some eureka moment. He was troubled by it all. This was too easy. Zeffri was a wiseguy, so he knew all about phone records. Could he have been so careless? Sure, a woman as seductive as Holly could render a man stupid in a heartbeat—Conor knew that firsthand—but an iceman like Salvatore Zeffri? Conor guessed that even Holly couldn't melt him. And what about Holly? How many times must she have seen one of her husband's clients tripped up by something as easily attainable as phone records? Yet she was so cavalier in her communication with Zeffri.

How to handle the situation? Should he be direct, question her about it? Should he use the information to catch her in another lie? Should he set a trap for Zeffri?

Conor felt confused. He realized that without

much sleep, his productivity was plummeting. The best thing to do was to go home and let his brain process the overload of information while he slept. He glanced at his watch. It was ten thirty. *Why is that important?* Then he remembered.

After a short ride, the cab deposited Conor on Forty-third Street and the West Side Highway. He crossed the highway and made his way to the vacant lot where Lawton was killed. The way Conor saw it, most people were creatures of habit, especially dog walkers, and this wide-open expanse of real estate was a great place to unleash a pent-up pet. After all, Lawton's body had been discovered by a dog walker. If he had been shot after ten o'clock, as Brian Cobb had speculated, maybe someone else was out with their dog and saw something.

A couple walking their golden retriever told Conor they didn't usually come to the lot this late except when they went out to dinner. The night Lawton was killed they had walked their dog at nine, so all they knew about the murder was what they'd read in the newspaper.

A few minutes later, a short, middle-aged woman appeared and removed the leash from a terrier. The dog made a frenzied beeline toward Conor. As the crazed little animal yelped at him, Conor was glad it wasn't a German shepherd.

"Rusty!" the woman yelled. "Come back here."

"Excuse me," Conor said as he appeared out of the darkness and held up his shield. "Detective Bard. NYPD."

Despite the shield, the woman seemed terrified, leaning away from Conor, cowering slightly.

"If you don't mind," he continued, "I'd like to ask you a few questions."

The woman took a step away from Conor. "About what?"

"There was a man shot here last night."

The woman covered her mouth with her hand. "Shot? Here?" She frowned. "Oh, my God! Was it that lawyer? I saw the front page of the *Post* but I didn't have a chance to read the article. He was shot *here*?"

"Did you walk Rusty last night?"

Hearing his name, Rusty cocked his head, frowned quizzically at Conor, and stopped barking. *Maybe Rusty saw something*, Conor mused.

The woman identified herself as Jennifer Grant. She recalled seeing the Maybach. "I thought it was strange, the engine running and all. And then this guy jumped in the car and drove off."

"Can you tell me what he looked like?"

"Not really. It happened so fast. But I *could* see it was a black man."

Conor nodded. That, of course, was Mike Boyd.

Jennifer wrinkled her nose. "Now it makes sense."

"What makes sense?"

"When I was leaving the house to walk Rusty, I

heard these noises. Like, *pop, pop, pop, pop!* I thought it was a car backfiring. Or firecrackers. I never thought—"

"What time was this?"

"Ten forty-five."

"Are you sure it was ten forty-five?"

"I always walk Rusty at ten forty-five. Dogs need a regular routine, you know. Otherwise they lose their sense of time."

Conor felt informed. He had no idea dogs even cared about the time. Jennifer pointed toward the river.

"And I saw somebody over there. That's why I didn't let Rusty off the leash. As soon as he did his business we went home."

"Can you give me a description of the person you saw by the river?"

"No. I'm sorry. It was too dark." Jennifer waved her hand. "The city ought to put lights up here. It's just not safe. And now where am I supposed to walk Rusty? It's dangerous without lights. Can't you do something? Talk to somebody with the city?"

"I'll file a report," Conor assured her. "Anything else you remember?"

Jennifer thought for a moment. "Oh, yes. He threw something in the water."

"In the water? Are you sure?"

"Yes. I heard a splash."

What might the NYPD scuba team find if they were called in? The murder weapon?

Conor extracted as much information as he could from Jennifer and took down her contact information. Then he made his way back across the highway. His cell phone rang. He slipped it out of his pocket and checked the caller ID. It was a number he had just seen on the printout at the precinct. Conor frowned. Holly Lawton was the last person he expected would be calling him.

He answered the phone. "Bard."

"Detective. It's Holly Lawton."

"Hello, Mrs. Lawton."

Holly started to cry.

"Mrs. Lawton. Are you all right?"

"No."

"What's wrong?"

"I'm scared," Holly said, her voice trembling.

"Are you in danger? Is somebody there?"

Holly didn't answer.

"Mrs. Lawton?"

More silence. And then: "It's my fault Walter is dead," Holly sobbed. "It's all my fault."

Chapter Eleven

When Conor arrived in front of Holly Lawton's townhouse, he stopped to collect himself. What was he about to hear? A confession?

He rang the buzzer. After a moment, the door opened, revealing Holly in a long silk robe. There was a slight puffiness around her faintly red eyes. Other than that, she looked as if she were ready for a photo shoot.

"Oh, thank you, Detective. Thank you for coming."

Conor looked past Holly into the dimly lit foyer.

"Are you alone, Mrs. Lawton?" His hand moved slowly in the direction of his gun.

"Yes," Holly said. "I'm alone."

She took Conor's hand and led him through the apartment to the living room. It seemed to Conor a peculiar thing for her to do, taking his hand, considering the circumstances. Her hand felt like dead weight in his and he wanted to disengage their entangled fingers, but her grip was so tight he would have had to literally rip himself away.

Holly sat on the couch and pulled Conor down beside her. She stared at him for a long time. Finally, she released his hand and said, "I know I shouldn't have done it. I knew it was wrong. But . . ."

While Holly searched for words, Conor wondered what to do. Should he just let her talk? Or should he advise her of her rights?

Conor was reasonably certain that a Miranda warning wasn't required in this case. Holly was not in a custodial situation, as in an interrogation room where a suspect's freedom is limited even though they are not technically under arrest. Still, she had been married to a lawyer. She knew all about Miranda warnings. If Conor allowed her to continue, she could later hire an attorney who might argue that her movements were constrained in some way, that she actually had been in some degree of custody.

So was this a way to confess to her husband's murder only to have his procedural screwup make it inadmissible in court? After the incident at the Rhythm Bar, Conor didn't want to take the chance.

"Mrs. Lawton. At this point, I must advise you that you have the right to remain silent."

Holly tilted her head to one side and stared at Conor. "What do you think I'm going to say?"

"I'd rather not venture a guess."

"I did not kill my husband."

"But you told me on the phone it was your fault."

"It was."

Tears formed in Holly's eyes. Conor wondered where this was going.

"In what way was it your fault?"

Holly wiped her eyes with a finger, took a breath. "I suppose by now you've gotten my phone records."

Even though Conor realized that Holly was well aware he would have already requested her phone records, he decided not to confirm to her that he did, in fact, have them in his possession. Yet whether he actually had them or not didn't matter. It was an eventuality that she had anticipated early on and was prepared to confront.

Holly stood and paced in front of the couch. She caught a reflection of herself in a wall mirror, paused to admire the image, then spun around and looked at Conor.

"I had an affair with Sal Zeffri," she blurted out. "If you must know."

In some strange way, Conor was profoundly disappointed in her. Apparently, he couldn't hide it. Holly looked at him hard.

"Don't judge me," she said sharply.

"I'm not judging you, Mrs. Lawton."

"My marriage to Walter was over long ago. We've been nothing more than roommates for years. When I met Sal . . ."

Holly's voice trailed off. The reality of what she had done struck Conor hard. If she was so hot and bothered at least she could have chosen someone outside her husband's professional circle.

Holly flicked her hair with her hand. "I'm not proud of what I've done. Really, I'm ashamed of myself. But you must believe me when I tell you I had nothing to do with Walter's death."

"I believe you," Conor said. He wasn't sure what to believe at this point. All he knew was that he wanted her to keep talking.

Holly searched Conor's eyes. "Are you sure?"

"I'm a detective," he said. "I can tell when someone's lying. And I can see you're telling the truth."

Holly smiled, certain she had taken Conor in. He smiled back at her. The psychology of it was simple. No one would ever commit a crime unless they thought they were smarter than the cops who would eventually be on their trail. And that's what Conor wanted her to think, that she was smarter than he was.

"I'm sure you're sorry about what happened," he said. He knew better than to say "What you *did*."

"I *am* sorry about what happened," Holly said.

She returned to the couch, sat too close to Conor. Now feeling as though she had an ally, she began to open up. "Sal and I started seeing each other three months ago. It was wonderful at first. But then Sal became possessive. Accused me of seeing other men."

"But you weren't seeing other men, were you?"

"No. I was *not*." Holly's tone was defiant. "So last week, I told Sal I couldn't do it anymore. He went nuts. Started calling me twenty, thirty times a day."

She took Conor's hand again. "Sal is a very violent man. I think he may have killed Walter."

Conor almost laughed out loud. What a scenario Holly may have set in motion. Hook up with a contract-killer lover. Mess with his head. Drive him insane enough to murder his rival. *Then* finger the jealous lover and walk away with millions of dollars. *Beautiful*, Conor thought. But even in his sleep-deprived state he was able to focus on the real questions in the investigation. Where was Maritza, the housekeeper? Wasn't she supposed to verify that Holly was home last night at the time of Lawton's murder?

Conor slowly pulled his hand away from Holly's.

"You told me you were home last night with your housekeeper. I'd like to stop by and confirm that with her if you don't mind."

"I lied."

Of course you did, Conor thought.

"Maritza won't be here tomorrow. I sent her back to Chile for a while."

Chile? What if he wanted to bring Maritza back from Chile or at least contact her to take a statement? Could a subpoena reach across borders? What were the international implications? He'd have to consult the DA on that one. But even if he did transport Maritza back to New York, how reliable a witness would she be? Holly probably sent Maritza south with a first-class ticket and a pocketbook full of cash. Maritza would likely say anything Holly wanted her to say.

"So were you home last night or not?" Conor asked carefully.

"Not until ten."

Lawton was presumably killed at ten forty-five. Conor rubbed the back of his head. Was she lying about when she got home? Or was she about to sell Sal down the river? Maritza, of course, could pinpoint the time, something Holly obviously didn't want to happen. He decided to coax as much specific information from Holly as possible. Even if she was not being truthful, he needed to get her on the record with something. He could always trip her up using her own words later.

"Mrs. Lawton. Were you with Sal Zeffri last night?"

"Yes. He insisted on seeing me. Said if I didn't meet him he would tell Walter about our affair."

"Go on."

"Sal picked me up on the corner and we drove around the city. At some point he started screaming at me. So I jumped out of the car when he stopped for a light on Second Avenue."

"What time?"

"I don't know. I walked home. And when I got here, it was ten."

"Where on Second Avenue?"

"I think it was Sixty-second, Sixty-third, something like that."

Conor calculated the distance. A little over twenty blocks. Depending on how fast she walked, she could have gotten out of the car around nine fifteen, nine thirty. Assuming, of course, that anything this woman said was true.

"I'm afraid, Detective. Sal is capable of anything."

As Holly leaned closer to Conor, her robe fell open. She wasn't wearing anything underneath.

"Please don't leave me alone," Holly whispered.

Chapter Twelve

Conor fled the townhouse like someone who had just seen the Devil. *Same thing*, he thought. A beautiful, sociopathic, nude nymphomaniac sitting next to him. Even Satan himself would be hard-pressed to conjure up a scene so tempting to a red-blooded heterosexual male. In fact, there was a moment, a purely irrational moment, when Conor actually contemplated staying there—but he wasn't quite ready to sell his soul.

Conor walked for blocks, not really caring which direction. He couldn't stop thinking about the delectable but morally bereft Holly. At least there was one good thing about the widow Lawton: she made Heather look like an amateur.

Conor somehow wound up in front of his apartment, pulled the mail out of the mailbox, and made his way inside.

One item in the bundle was a small manila envelope. Conor tore it open and took out a CD and a letter, which was from Sony Records. He had met an executive from Sony while working security at a launch party for one of their artists. The executive had promised to listen to Conor's music. This was the reply:

> *Dear Conor, Sorry it took so long to get back to you but I wanted our A&R staff to hear your material. Unfortunately, I was unable to gain the kind of support that would be necessary to sign you to our roster.*

Conor tossed the CD across the room like a frisbee, then crumpled up the letter and let it drop to the floor. He walked to the refrigerator, pulled a bottle out of the freezer, and half filled a water glass with vodka. One vodka led to a second. And a third. But the sting of yet another rejection proved impervious to intoxication.

A ringing cell phone jolted Conor awake. He had fallen asleep, fully clothed, on the dilapidated couch. He glanced at his watch. It was ten thirty. He fumbled for the phone, found it on the floor under the coffee table, checked the caller ID.

"Hey, Ralph," Conor rasped into the phone. "What's up?"

"Obviously not you."

Conor stood and realized he was still drunk.

"I'm on my way."

Conor arrived at the precinct and found Ralph in midconversation with Brian, who had documented all the footprints in the mud and had brought photos of each distinct set.

"There are seventeen individually distinguishable shoe patterns," Brian noted. "Now, I can't tell you for sure that they were all made Sunday night, but I'd guess they were because it rained the whole afternoon. Prior to Sunday night, the ground would've been too hard to create such detailed impressions. I've matched most of the sole patterns with known samples, and I'm in the process of contacting manufacturers to classify the others."

Brian finished his analysis of the footprints and left the room. Ralph looked at Conor.

"Nice of you to stop by," Ralph said. He leaned back in his chair, crossed his arms. "Looks like you had an interesting night. Want to tell me about it?"

"Yeah. As soon as we call the Harbor Unit."

"Why are we calling the Harbor Unit?"

"Because I think I have a fix on the murder weapon."

Ralph frowned. "Why didn't you tell me?"

"I just did."

* * *

Conor and Ralph stood on the bank of the Hudson River and watched as Harbor Unit scuba divers plunged into the frigid, murky waters. It had been two hours since Conor had recounted the events of the previous evening, and Ralph still couldn't believe it.

"You mean like nothing on? Nothing at all under the robe?"

"Ralph. How many times I've got to tell you? Nothing. Completely naked."

"Unbelievable." Ralph frowned. "You sure you went home?"

Conor was tired of Ralph's questions. "Okay. You want the truth? I stayed there all night. It was incredible."

Ralph did a double take then realized Conor was putting him on. "You bastard," he said.

They stared at the river, hoping the diver would break the surface soon.

"So Zeffri and the wife are calling each other every day," Ralph said. "We know the wife's take on it. Now we need to hear Zeffri's explanation."

"You want to head over there? Rattle Zeffri's cage? We could check back with Harbor later."

"Yeah," Ralph said. "Let's go."

They headed toward their car.

"Hey, guys!"

Conor and Ralph turned. A scuba diver was bobbing in the water.

"I've got a gun," the diver shouted.

* * *

Conor and Ralph sat at their desks waiting for ballistics on the weapon pulled from the river. It was a Beretta 21, a semiautomatic, subcompact .22-caliber handgun known as the Bobcat. A diminutive little piece of steel and aluminum but it gets the job done.

"It's a twenty-two," Ralph said. "That's good. I mean, what are the odds that a twenty-two, *not* the murder weapon, would wind up a hundred feet from the place where Lawton was killed *with* a twenty-two."

"Well, I hope this gun leads somewhere," Conor said. "Because right now we've got no real leads, no evidence other than circumstantial, no clear suspects."

"Unless you count the wife and the contract killer," Ralph offered.

They both laughed. They couldn't help it.

"Speaking of contract killers . . . ," Ralph said.

This time, Conor and Ralph found Zeffri at home in Ozone Park. He was wearing a jogging suit, doing stretches in the front yard.

"Detectives," Zeffri said. "I was just about to go for a run."

"We wanted to ask you a couple of questions," Conor said.

"I told you. My attorney will contact you."

"Come on," Conor said. "These are simple questions."

Zeffri was curious. "Like what?"

"Like, do you know Holly Lawton?"

The mention of Holly's name got an immediate reaction. Blood rushed to Zeffri's face. He exploded into a sudden rage. "You have no right to harass me like this! Get off my property! This is trespassing."

Holly was right about one thing, Conor thought. *The guy's got a short fuse*.

"We were just wondering," Ralph said. "Did you kill Walter Lawton so you could have Holly to yourself?"

Zeffri took a deep breath, clenched his fists. He seemed to realize that losing his cool was a mistake.

"Before you accuse me of anything, Detectives, don't you think you should have proof?" Zeffri's voice was even, his demeanor eerily relaxed.

That was a freaky transition, Conor thought. Calm, irate, then under control again. All in the space of a few seconds. *This guy's a real psycho*.

"All right," Ralph allowed. "We can't prove you screwed her. But we *can* prove you've been calling her twenty times a day."

Zeffri waved his hand dismissively. "So what?"

"So that's a little obsessive," Conor said. "Don't you think?"

Zeffri smiled. "Why don't I stop by this afternoon? With counsel."

"When?" Ralph asked.

Zeffri checked his watch. "How's three o'clock?"

"Three o'clock," Ralph repeated.

"See you then," Zeffri said, then started to jog down the street.

"Just one more thing," Ralph called out.

Zeffri stopped, turned, and looked at Conor. "Who is he? Columbo?"

"You ever own a twenty-two-caliber handgun?" Ralph asked.

Zeffri gave Ralph a look that could kill without a gun, then sprinted down the street.

"He's not such a bad guy when you get to know him," Ralph said as he watched Zeffri round a corner and disappear from view.

"You know, Ralph, I think I'm going to miss you."

"No, you won't."

"Really. I will."

Ralph looked at Conor. "Yeah? Well the sarge told me a detective is transferring in when I retire. Going to be your new partner."

"It won't be the same," Conor insisted.

"Well, you're right about that. She's nothing like me at all."

Conor was surprised. "*She?* They're giving me a *woman*?"

"You got something against women?"

"I *love* women," Conor insisted. "Too much. All I'm saying is—"

"I met her," Ralph cut in. "Blond. Huge gazongas. Gorgeous girl."

"I can work with a woman. No problem."

"I'm kidding. You're not going to be *that* lucky. They'll probably stick you with Jenkins or Francelli."

Conor frowned. "The rubber-gun squad?"

Ralph chuckled. "Yeah. You're going to miss me all right."

Conor and Ralph drove back to the precinct. Brian was waiting for them.

"I've got good news and bad news," Brain said. "Which do you want first?"

"The good news," Conor said.

"The good news is that the twenty-two pulled out of the river is definitely your murder weapon. We test-fired it and the ballistics match the slugs found at the scene."

"What's the bad news?" Ralph asked.

"The bad news is that the gun was clean. I mean *completely* clean. Usually they forget the trigger guard. You know, when they wipe it down they have to hold it somewhere. But not this piece. And another thing. The shell casings? Nine out of ten times we get a thumbprint off the casing. Not this time. And the clincher? The serial number's been filed off."

Twenty-two-caliber weapon, no prints. No prints on the shell casings either. Serial number obliter-ated. A professional job for sure. But with no forensic evidence to link the gun to a suspect, the killer would likely never be caught. And considering all the murderers for whom Walter Lawton had gained an acquittal, it seemed somehow fitting to Conor that Lawton's own killer might never be brought to justice.

Chapter Thirteen

"**W**ell, at least we have the weapon," Conor said. "We'll just have to start trying to match it to other crimes."

"It's a long shot," Ralph noted.

"Yeah. But right now it's our only shot."

Amanda walked up to them.

"The DA's taking Mike Boyd before the grand jury next week. Seeking an indictment for murder one."

"Oh, come on," Conor said. "We all know that kid didn't do it."

"I don't know if he did or didn't," Amanda said. "But, hey, Bard, it's good to know you haven't given up on your psychic abilities."

"I have a witness who saw a black suspect steal the Maybach," Conor said. "The witness corroborates Boyd's version of the story."

Amanda gave Conor a look. "We *know* he stole the car."

"Yes," Conor replied, "but the witness also saw

someone else by the river at the time the Maybach was being stolen, potentially the shooter. And the gun Harbor fished out of the river? Definitely the murder weapon. So my witness puts Boyd in the car while someone *else* was throwing the gun in the river."

"You watch *Law and Order*, don't you, Bard?" Amanda smiled with a hint of sarcasm. "We're the order part. If the law part wants to charge him with murder, that's their business."

"I know," Conor replied. "But what's the rush?"

"District attorney wants to make sure Boyd stays on ice until there's someone else to go after. If and when there is, DA can always knock the charges down to grand theft auto. Besides, word is that one of Lawton's political pals is leaning on the DA."

Ralph crossed his arms. "So it doesn't matter who he charges as long as he charges somebody?"

"Why are you asking me?" Amanda said impatiently. "You're headed to the DA's office. Ask him."

Amanda started walking away. She stopped and looked at Conor. "Get me a DD5 on your witness. I'll pass it along to the assistant DA assigned to Boyd's case." She continued out of the room.

"Yeah," Ralph said. "I'll talk to the DA. You bet I will. A lot of things have to be fixed in that office."

Conor and Ralph looked at each other. They both knew that in a few days, the case would look like an ice cube.

"If this kid Boyd is innocent," Ralph said in a way that was more a statement of fact than an open argument, "then we better get somewhere on this thing fast."

"Good afternoon, gentlemen."

Conor and Ralph turned to see Megan Hollister approaching. She was in her mid-forties with dark brown hair, attractive but certainly not beautiful, six feet tall in bare feet. Today she wore high heels, elevating her to an imposing height of six-three, and sported a rather revealing dress that strained to confine her cosmetically enhanced breasts. Flanking her was Salvatore Zeffri.

"I understand you've been harassing my client," Megan growled as she stopped and loomed over Ralph's desk.

"I'm sorry, Counselor," Ralph said, feigning contrition. "We didn't mean to upset Mr. Zeffri."

"All right," Megan said. "Let's get this over with."

The four of them reconvened in a conference room. Megan got right to the issue at hand.

"I assume you have nothing that ties my client to the murder of Walter Lawton."

Conor and Ralph didn't respond. They found themselves staring at Megan's breasts.

"I didn't think so," Megan said. "Which means that Mr. Zeffri is under no obligation to tell you anything at all."

"Yes," Ralph said. "But if he didn't have anything to do with the murder of Walter Lawton . . ."

"That's beside the point, Detective, and you know it."

Megan stood and paced alongside the conference table. It was one of her favorite tactics.

"However," she went on, "we *are* prepared to answer a few questions in the interest of putting an end to your unwarranted trespassing on Mr. Zeffri's property."

Ralph didn't waste time. "Did you kill Walter Lawton?"

"No."

"Where were you Sunday night?" Conor asked.

"Which Sunday we talking about?"

"You know which Sunday," Ralph said.

Zeffri looked at Megan.

"For the record," she began, "my client had an affair with Holly Lawton, which may be morally offensive in the Bible Belt but in New York, as far as I know, is not a crime."

Megan was being smart. Even if she didn't know the salacious cat was already out of the bag, she knew the tryst would become public at some point. Better to get it on the table now.

Megan looked at Zeffri. "You may answer the question."

"I was with Holly Lawton," Zeffri said, a smirk on his face. He taunted Conor with his eyes. *In your dreams, Detective.*

"Until when?" Conor asked.

"Eleven."

"That's not what Holly Lawton told me," Conor said.

"Holly Lawton is a compulsive liar," Megan inter-jected.

Megan walked to the head of the table. She reached down, grabbed the plunging neckline of her dress between her thumb and forefinger, and hoisted it higher. The meeting was coming to an end. Time to holster the weapon.

"If you feel you have the need to ask my client any further questions, you must contact me first." Megan tapped Zeffri on the shoulder. "Salvatore. Let's go."

Zeffri stood. He and Megan walked out of the room.

"Zeffri said he was with her until eleven," Conor noted. "If he killed Lawton at ten forty-five, he's looking for the wife to provide an alibi. But she makes the time more like nine thirty, leaving poor Salvatore hanging out to dry."

"The stakes are high," Ralph began. "The wife knows that. We know it. The problem is, she's shuffling the deck and we've been dealt a hand with no aces."

Ralph could sum up any situation with a gambling analogy. For some reason, that always prompted Conor to answer with an analogy of his own.

"This case isn't just turning cold," Conor observed, "it's beginning to look like Antarctica."

"So we dress warm and hope for a royal flush," Ralph said, punctuating their odd but effective form of verbal shorthand.

* * *

Conor walked home from the precinct. Somewhere during the day he had gone from slightly inebriated to hungover, and a mean-spirited headache was making itself known. Still, he had wanted to work the case a little more, but how? Interrogate whom? Examine what evidence?

Stepping into his apartment at seven o'clock during a homicide investigation made Conor feel like he had been sent home early from school. He dropped onto the rickety couch and decided to order in some food, watch a little TV, then get to bed early. When he picked up the phone he heard the stutter dial tone indicating he had voice mail. He pushed the speakerphone button, speed-dialed his access number and password, then waited for the electronic voice.

"You have two new messages and no saved messages."

He hit the 1 key. "First new message."

"Hey, Conor, it's Veronica. Where have you been? Love to see you sometime. Call me."

Conor grimaced. Veronica was a mistake he made right after he and Heather split up. Hell, Veronica was a mistake half the precinct had made at one time or another. He pressed the 3 key.

"Message deleted. . . . Next message."

"Yes, I'm calling Conor Bard." A man's voice resonated from the small speaker. "This is Tony Landis from East Coast Records."

Conor sat upright, leaned over the phone.

"I believe you sent a CD to Ron Moseley some

time ago. He left the company. But I happened to come across your CD and gave it a listen. I'd like to talk to you about it. Please call me at 212-555-7739. Thank you."

Conor played the message again just to be sure he wasn't dreaming, saved it for posterity, then hung up and fell back on the couch. *The hell with the Lawton case*, Conor thought. He was about to be discovered. But it was just a phone call. Would it really turn into a recording contract? Maybe, maybe not. Yet it *was* a possibility and he wanted to share his excitement with someone. That used to be Heather. Well, not really. Whenever Conor wanted to commemorate one of his small victories, Heather would always find a way to make the celebration all about her.

Conor looked down at the coffee table, saw a folded piece of paper, and smiled.

It was Monica's cell phone number.

Chapter Fourteen

Monica was free for dinner. They decided to meet at nine o'clock at Maria Pia, a cozy Italian restaurant near the precinct, on the first floor of a brownstone on Fifty-first Street, just off Eighth Avenue. Conor liked it there, knew the owners and the staff. In many ways, it felt more like home to him than home.

Conor took a quick shower, dressed carefully, and made his way up Eighth Avenue. He slowed down in front of Thalia, then, almost involuntarily, turned and walked inside.

Kristen look up at him. "Two nights in a row. I feel like I hit the lottery."

"Hey, Kristen."

"The usual?"

"Not tonight. I've got to be somewhere."

"So what can I do for you?"

"The woman I was here with last night?"

"Yeah?"

"After I left . . . I'm curious."

Kristen gasped in mock outrage. "You want me to betray the Secret Society of the Sisterhood?"

"I'd just like to know who met her here, that's all."

"You *really* want to know?"

Conor nodded. Kristen stared off as if she were imagining the scene.

"Okay. This tall, dark, and extremely handsome man came in. They made out at the bar for a while then he swept her off her feet and carried her away to what I can only assume was a night of unbridled passion."

"Kristen."

"Boy, Conor, you're really getting paranoid about women."

"Hey, *you* met Heather."

"You've got a point."

"So who was it?"

"Well, this man came in."

Kristen let Conor hang there for a moment before continuing.

"And he had a little girl with him. I don't know. About seven or eight, maybe. They sat at the bar with your friend. The guy had an espresso. The little girl had a cranberry juice. And then they left."

"When they were at the bar, what did they say?"

"I don't know. They were speaking some foreign language."

"Albanian," Conor said.

"How exotic."

"Thanks, Kristen."

Conor started for the door.

"Hey, Conor," Kristen called out. "Where *is* Albania anyway?"

Conor felt a little guilty, but he hadn't done anything so terrible, had he? Besides, he told himself, the cop in him made him do it. He walked up Eighth Avenue wondering, *Who was the man? And who was the little girl?*

Monica was sitting at the bar when Conor walked into Maria Pia.

"I hope I didn't keep you waiting too long," Conor said as he glanced at his watch. It was five minutes before eight.

"She got here at seven thirty," Luca said as he stepped up next to Conor.

Luca was the manager. Mid-twenties, born in Italy, he had come from a family of restaurateurs.

"I offered her a Rosso di Montalcino," Luca told Conor. "In Italy, we call it Baby Brunello."

"It's really nice," Monica said.

"How about you, Conor? The usual?"

"What else?"

Conor led Monica to "his" table, against the wall near the front of the room. He pulled out her chair then took a seat across from her.

"Thanks for coming to dinner on such short notice," Conor began. "I just got some good news and I wanted to celebrate."

"Good news?"

"A record company wants to talk to me about a CD I sent them."

Monica was confused. "A CD? You mean, a *music* CD?"

"I play guitar," Conor explained. "And I sing. Sometimes I work with a band at a place called the Rhythm Bar. Anyway, I'm hoping the phone call leads to a recording contract."

"Can I see you perform sometime before I leave?" Monica asked.

"I wish you could. But I had to cancel all my gigs this week."

"Why?"

"I'm in the middle of a homicide investigation."

"A murder?"

"Maybe you read about it. Big-time lawyer shot and killed. Name was Walter Lawton."

Monica shook her head no.

Conor was surprised. "It's been all over the news."

"I'm afraid I've been putting in long hours at the bank," Monica explained. "I haven't read a newspaper or turned on a television for a week."

"Anyway, I caught the case."

"You know who did it?"

"I've got my theories."

Fragments of the investigation began to avalanche into Conor's head. He shrugged it off. He wasn't here to discuss a homicide investigation.

"I can't really talk about it," he said.

"Well, congratulations on your record deal."

"It's not a deal yet. Just some interest."

A waiter arrived with menus. Monica scanned the page for a moment.

"*Zuppa di porri*," Monica said. "Leek soup."

"You like leeks?" Conor wanted to know.

"I like to *eat* them," she replied. "But I didn't like them so much when my mother baked them and then squeezed the liquid into my ear."

Conor frowned. "Your *ear*?"

"That was the treatment for an earache in Albania. Squeezed leeks."

"Did it work?" he asked.

"Yes."

"Great. I'll keep that in mind if I ever have an earache and can't find a drugstore."

Monica laughed. Conor was beginning to like the sound.

After they ordered, Conor was tempted to babble on about his music but he'd learned long ago that the best way *not* to charm a woman was to talk about yourself.

"Tell me about your family back in Albania."

"My mother and father still live in Shkodër. In the north."

"Your father practice the *Kaboon*?"

Monica laughed. "The *Kanun*. With an *n*."

"Sorry. I'm not as good in Albanian as you are in English."

"My father can't go by the Kanun because the

93

government doesn't recognize it as a law anymore. But he believes in it, yes."

"And what does that mean? To go by the Kanun."

"Like I told you before, women have no rights under the Kanun. They can't inherit property. Only males can inherit. And the only obligation a husband has to his wife is to provide her with food, clothing, and shoes."

"Shoes? That could get expensive in New York." Monica laughed.

"You have any sisters or brothers?" Conor asked.

Monica's mood was suddenly somber. "I had a sister. Her name was Besa."

Had? Was? Conor waited for an explanation.

Monica stared down at the table. "She died."

"I'm sorry."

They sat in silence for a long moment. Monica clearly didn't want to talk about it.

"Besa," Conor finally said. "That's a beautiful name."

"It means 'faith' in Albanian. She had a daughter. My niece, Olta. She's eight years old."

"Your niece live in Albania?"

"No. She was born here. She lives in the Bronx with my brother-in-law. I met her for the first time when I came to America five months ago."

"You hadn't ever seen her before?"

"No. Being young and unmarried, they wouldn't give me a visa. I think America is afraid all young, single Albanians will come here and not go back—

which is more or less true. Anyway, I got my work visa because of the bank. So while I've been here, I've spent as much time as I could with Olta. I saw her last night after Fatmir took her to see *The Lion King*."

"Fatmir? That's your brother-in-law?"

Monica nodded.

So the man and the little girl who met Monica at Thalia were her brother-in-law and niece. Now Conor felt really bad about checking up on her.

"How about you?" Monica asked. "You have family in the area?"

"My mother lives in Toms River."

"Toms River?"

"New Jersey. Near the shore. I was born there. A small town. Nothing much to it."

"How about your father?"

"He passed away a little over ten years ago."

"I'm sorry."

"Thanks."

"When did you learn to play guitar?" Monica asked.

"When I was nine I took some lessons. After that, I was hooked. Decided I would be a rock star when I grew up. I never meant to be a cop."

"Really? Then how . . ."

"After high school, I went to community college for two years. Then I formed a band. We appeared in clubs all over Jersey, but we didn't make much money. Anyway, one night I met this girl who had come to see us play. She was an NYPD cop. A rookie.

She made the job sound like the greatest thing in the world. Plus, I was twenty-one and I figured I was getting old."

Monica laughed. Conor continued.

"So, feeling old, I moved to New York, took the NYPD entrance exam, and here I am."

They spent the rest of the evening talking about music, Albanian history and culture, whatever wasn't too personal. After dinner, Conor offered to take her home or at least pay the taxi fare, but Monica declined both offers.

"I had a nice time," she said as she climbed into a cab.

"So did I," Conor agreed. "We'll have to do it again before you go back."

"I would like that," Monica said. "Good night."

Conor watched as the taxi pulled away from the curb. There was something special about Monica, something compelling, and Conor found himself drawn to her on many levels. She had taken care to keep her distance emotionally. He liked that somehow. He and Heather were in bed an hour after they met, and look where that led. Yet Monica's Eastern European sensuality beckoned. And wasn't that all he really wanted? Getting her between the sheets?

Even though he was dead tired, Conor couldn't sleep. All he could think about was returning the call to Tony Landis at East Coast Records. He grabbed his guitar and played songs until three then went to bed and thrashed around until seven. He got up, downed half a pot of coffee, took a shower, then headed for the precinct.

"Well, this is a first," Ralph said when he arrived at eight thirty and found Conor at his desk. "Beating me to work."

Conor told Ralph about the call from East Coast Records.

Ralph was genuinely thrilled. "That's great!"

"We'll see."

"Well, what are you waiting for? Call the guy back."

"It's eight thirty. Record companies don't usually open before ten."

Ralph clapped his hands together. "So what are we going to do for the next hour and a half? I'm too excited to work."

Ralph's phone rang. He picked it up.

"Kurtz."

"Hey, Kurtz. Guess what?" It was Brian.

"What?"

"You're not going to believe this but I managed to get a serial number off that gun."

Chapter Fifteen

Conor and Ralph walked into the NYPD forensics lab. Workstations, computers, microscopes, high-tech pieces of equipment, and all manner of things understood only by criminologists filled the room.

Brian pulled a cup of yogurt from a small counter-top refrigerator filled with petri dishes that appeared to have some sort of mold or bacteria growing inside them.

Conor frowned. "You keep *food* in there?"

"Sure. It's closer than the kitchen." Brian held up the yogurt. "Besides, it's the perfect temperature for the cultures in this stuff."

He placed the yogurt on a desk.

"Anyway, I thought I'd give it a try, and it worked."

"What worked?" Ralph wanted to know.

"The restoration of the serial number by ultra-sonically induced cavitation in water."

Conor and Ralph looked at each other. *What the hell is he talking about?*

"You mind explaining what you just said?" Ralph asked.

"I submerged the gun in water and induced cavitation by a piezoelectric transducer."

"Well, that explains it," Conor said.

"Okay. In layman's terms, cavitation is the formation of bubbles. Like in a soft drink or champagne." Brian was uncharacteristically excited. "With a piezoelectric transducer I was able to manipulate bubbles of gas so that they gathered under the compressed metal where the serial number had been filed off. You see, serial numbers are stamped, creating grooves. When you file the surface, some of the metal is compressed into those grooves. The pressure of the gas bubbles under the compressed metal forces it to lift. In some cases, cavitation can even restore the numbers below the depth of the stamped grooves. Understand?"

Conor understood one thing. The case that had seemed destined for the deep freeze was now suddenly thawing out.

It was ten fifteen when Conor and Ralph got back to the precinct.

"All right," Ralph said. "Call the guy at the record company."

Conor dropped into his chair, picked up the phone, dialed.

"East Coast Records," a pleasant female voice said.

"Tony Landis, please."

"Who's calling him?"

"Conor Bard."

"Does he know what this is regarding?" The voice was now flat.

"I'm returning his call."

"One moment."

Conor looked at Ralph. "I'm on hold."

And then: "Conor!" Tony Landis sounded as if he had known Conor all his life. "How *are* you?"

"I'm fine, Mr. Landis."

"My *father's* name is Mr. Landis. *Please*. Call me Tony."

"Okay, Tony."

"So I listened to your songs. Very interesting."

"Thank you."

"Tell him I'll call him back!" Tony yelled to someone, then turned his attention back to Conor. "Sorry. It's frantic around here. How's next Monday at eleven? That good for you?"

"Great."

"We're at 810 Seventh Avenue. Twenty-eighth floor. Look, gotta run. See you Monday."

"See you then."

"Ciao."

Conor hung up the phone and smiled at Ralph. "I'm meeting him next Monday."

"Perfect," Ralph said. "That's the night of my retirement party."

"Maybe we'll both have something to celebrate."

"You celebrate," Ralph said. "I'll mourn."

* * *

Conor and Ralph began the process of determining the origin of the .22. Conor wasn't a political animal but he found himself wishing there were a national gun registry. In fact, most cops were conflicted about the concept. On the one hand, it would make tracking criminals much easier. On the other hand, it would infringe on the privacy of those who believed it was their birthright, or at least their constitutional right, to bear arms without anyone looking over their shoulder. As it was, Conor would have to contact Beretta and track down the retailer who ordered the gun, then the person who bought it. That would take time, which in a homicide investigation was a precious commodity.

At least he had the Gun Control Act of 1968 on his side. That's when serial numbering of all firearms was first required by law. Conor was also comforted by the fact that there was NIBIN, the National Integrated Ballistics Information Network, formed in the mid-nineties when the FBI and the ATF adopted the same imaging protocol. Prior to that, the FBI's system, dubbed Drugfire, and the ATF's IBIS (Integrated Ballistic Identification System) database were incompatible. Now, at least, images of fired bullets and spent shell casings from crime scenes resided under one searchable roof. If there was physical evidence in the records that the weapon retrieved from the river had been used in another crime, they would get a hit.

Meanwhile, Beretta was reluctantly cooperative. It wasn't that the company didn't want to be helpful, it was just that it wasn't overly enthusiastic about divulging information regarding its customers. Nonetheless, Beretta came through in a couple of hours. The gun had been sent to the Blue Ridge Gun Shop in Grundy, Virginia. Conor wasn't surprised. The majority of the guns confiscated at crime scenes in New York began their violent journey in Virginia.

"Let's put in a call to Grundy PD," Ralph said. "Have them go over to the shop and pull the paperwork. Although I don't think it's going to do any good."

Conor agreed. "It's not like those gun shops do much of a background check. Besides, whoever bought it probably lied about their personal information."

The officer from Grundy PD who Ralph finally got on the phone had a Southern drawl so thick Ralph was having a hard time understanding what he said.

"What?" Ralph said. "Could you repeat that?"

"Sed, ahl hedonovah layda."

Ralph finally figured out that the officer was saying he'd "head on over later."

"The sooner, the better," Ralph said.

"Awl rat. Ahl give you a hollah inna bit."

Ralph hung up the phone and looked at Conor.

"They speak another language down there."

Amanda materialized in front of them. The expression on her face foretold some sort of disaster.

Ralph frowned. "Hey, Conor. Looks like the sarge has some bad news."

"Doesn't she always?"

Amanda stared at Conor, then held out a piece of paper.

"I'm supposed to deliver this fax to you immediately."

"What is it?" Conor asked.

"Take it," Amanda commanded.

Conor took the piece of paper and read for a few seconds. He frowned, confused.

Ralph leaned in on Conor. "What does it say?"

"It says," Amanda intoned, "that a disciplinary hearing has been scheduled regarding the incident at the Rhythm Bar. Monday morning at ten thirty."

Conor shook his head. "I can't be there."

"It's not an invitation, Bard," Amanda said. "The only RSVP allowed is: I *will* attend."

Conor rubbed his eyes.

"I'm sorry," Amanda said. Then she walked away.

Conor looked at Ralph. "The meeting with East Coast Records."

Ralph grimaced. "I know."

Conor ran his hands through his hair. "Fucking Reynolds."

"He's really got a hard-on for you, doesn't he?"

"Yeah. And I have no idea why."

"He's up for deputy inspector," Ralph said. "Maybe he's looking to make a few sacrifices to the gods. Starting with you."

"Yeah, but it feels like more than that." Conor reached for the phone. "So now I have to reschedule the meeting at East Coast Records. What else can I do?"

"You could resign from the job," Ralph offered.

"Believe me, I'm tempted."

Conor dialed. The cheerful receptionist answered. "East Coast Records."

"Yes. Tony Landis, please."

"Who's calling him?"

"Conor Bard. I spoke with him this morning and—"

"Mr. Landis is in a meeting. Would you like to leave a message?"

"Yes. I set up an appointment with him next Monday at eleven and I was wondering if we could make it later that day."

Conor was met with silence on the other end of the phone.

"Hello?" he said.

"Please hold."

While Conor was on hold, Ralph got up and poured himself a coffee. He stood by the machine and watched Conor from across the room.

Finally . . .

"Mr. Bard?" The receptionist's voice was devoid of humanity.

"Yes?"

"Mr. Landis is jammed all day on Monday."

"What about Tuesday? Or Wednesday. Actually,

anytime next week is good." Conor was doing his best not to sound too desperate.

"We're going to have to get back to you," the receptionist said.

"When do you think—"

"We'll let you know."

The line went dead. Conor stared at the phone. Apparently canceling an appointment with Tony Landis wasn't such a great idea.

Chapter Sixteen

Conor tried to shake the sinking feeling that his music career had been dealt a fatal blow, but it wouldn't go away. Worse yet, all he and Ralph were doing at the moment was waiting. Waiting for a ballistics match. Waiting for Grundy PD. Waiting, waiting, waiting.

"We ought to be doing something besides waiting," Conor said, his frustration evident.

"Like what?"

"Why don't we take a look at the photos of the footprints?"

"I took them home last night." Ralph shrugged. "They're footprints, that's all."

"We could apply for a warrant, poke around in Zeffri's closet, see if his shoes were at the scene."

"Without anything to link Zeffri to this," Ralph said, "no judge is going to give us a warrant."

They sat without speaking for a long moment.

"The Dirt Doctor," Conor said, breaking the silence.

"The Dirt Doctor?"

"Yeah. What's his name? The forensic geology guy at John Jay. Teaches geographic profiling."

"Oh, yeah," Ralph recalled. "*That* guy. Wagner, something like that."

"No. Rugner. That's it. Gerard Rugner."

"Yeah. Rugner. So?"

"So we stop by John Jay and ask him to do a workup on the soil in the lot."

Ralph nodded. "Beats waiting around."

John Jay College of Criminal Justice was located on Fifty-eighth Street and Tenth Avenue, just five blocks from the precinct. Conor and Ralph decided to walk. When they arrived at the office of Professor Gerard Rugner, he was happy to see them. Most of his time was spent talking about soil in the abstract, in scientific terms. But then in walk Conor and Ralph, and with them, an opportunity to take his expertise out of the classroom and into the real world.

"Geographic locations have unique soil characteristics," Rugner explained with a professor's enthusiasm. "Like a fingerprint."

"What we'd like," Ralph said, "is to compare the dirt on, let's say, a pair of shoes, to the soil from the crime scene. So to start with, we want an analysis of the soil from the lot."

"When do you need it?" Rugner asked.

"Yesterday," Conor said.

Rugner was eager to get started. "I'll collect samples immediately. But it will take some time to give you a thorough analysis."

"How long?" Ralph wanted to know.

"A couple days," Rugner replied. "I'll get it to you as fast as I can."

Great, Conor thought. *More waiting.*

Back at the precinct, Conor decided to call Monica, set another date to get together. But before he had a chance to call her, his cell phone rang. He checked the caller ID. It was Monica.

"Hello, Monica."

"Hi, Conor."

"I was just going to call you."

"Really?" Monica sounded appreciative. "I wanted to thank you for dinner."

"Thank *you* for joining me."

After a moment of awkward silence, Conor said, "Look. I know you're only here for a week, and you probably have a lot of people to see, but—"

"I'd love to get together again."

"How about tonight?"

"Sure."

"How's eight?"

"Okay."

"Let's make it easy," Conor said. "Meet me at Maria Pia. Then we can either stay there or go somewhere else."

"Okay. Eight o'clock. Maria Pia."

And just like that, the sick feeling in the pit of Conor's stomach about East Coast Records was replaced with an almost adolescent anticipation.

Grundy PD finally called in. "Ah tawked to Homer ovah at the gun stawe."

By now, Ralph was able to translate most of the drawl into English.

"Did you get the bill of sale?" he wanted to know.

"No, suh."

"Why not?"

"Seems they had a far lass summah."

A *far*? *What the hell's a far?* And then Ralph realized what a "far" was.

"A fire?" Ralph's voice was filled with incredulity.

"Yes, suh. A real baad far."

The records, of course, had been destroyed.

Ralph hung up and looked at Conor, who had gotten the gist of the conversation from hearing Ralph's responses.

"So we've got a pile of ashes," Conor surmised.

"A *fire*? Give me a break." Ralph pointed at the phone. "What I'd really like to do is send an arson squad to Grundy and close that gun shop down."

Amanda walked toward them.

"Please," Conor said as she approached. "I can't take any more bad news."

"Oh, ye of little faith. This time I've got good

news. I just received a call from Otisville. A prisoner up there says he has information about your case."

"His name's not Sidorov, is it?" Ralph asked.

"No. Thomas Carlson. He won't talk to you at Otisville though. Insists he be transferred down here. They've got a detail waiting to escort him."

"Bring him on," Ralph said.

Conor checked his watch. It was four fifteen. Otisville was at least an hour and a half away. That would put the prisoner in the precinct at six or later. Conor wondered if he should cancel his date with Monica. He decided to wait, play it by ear.

There was a lot of traffic on the way from Otisville and by six thirty the prisoner still hadn't arrived. Conor was pissed off. The guy probably knew nothing and just wanted a trip to the city. A little fresh air, a cigarette, some real food. Anger and frustration welled up inside him. He wasn't about to let the job derail both his music career *and* personal life in the same day. *Hell,* Conor thought, *I don't even want to be a cop.* He was seeing Monica even if he had to walk out in the middle of an interview. Remembering what a stickler she was for being on time, he dialed her number and got her voice mail.

"Monica. I'm running a little late. Call me when you get to Maria Pia. *Or,* if you want, you can meet me at the precinct."

* * *

Two Otisville guards finally arrived at seven fifteen with Thomas Carlson in tow. Carlson's rap sheet had indicated he was a career criminal with a long list of petty crimes. His face revealed the hard reality of that life. He was thirty-eight but looked far older. White, cracked-limestone skin. Vacant inkwell eyes.

As the guards helped themselves to the meager contents of the detectives' refrigerator, Conor and Ralph took Carlson into an interview room and, after polite introductions, got down to the business at hand.

"You have a nice trip, Tommy?" Ralph sometimes liked to use a perp's name in every question, every sentence—particularly when he was seeking information.

"Yeah."

"Bet it was nice to get out of Otisville for a while, right, Tommy?" Ralph's voice was filled with empathy.

"Real nice." Carlson smiled, exposing his rotting teeth.

Ralph tapped a file folder. "Been arrested a lot of times, Tommy."

"Yeah," Carlson said. "I know."

"Ever occur to you, Tommy, you're not very good at being a criminal. Maybe you ought to get into another line of work."

"When I get out this time," Carlson insisted, "I'm going to get an honest job."

"Good to hear that, Tommy," Ralph said.

Carlson rocked in the chair. "Can I have a cigarette?"

"As soon as you tell us what you know about the murder of Walter Lawton," Conor shot back, tired of the preliminaries.

Nicotine craving always expedited an interview.

"I know who killed that lawyer," Carlson said. "So, if I give this guy up, can you guys get me an early release?"

"Well, Tommy," Ralph said, his delivery sincere, "we're going to do whatever we can for you. But *first* you have to tell us what you know."

Carlson hesitated then leaned over the desk. "I was talking to this guy and he told me he had a lawyer down in New York City whacked a couple days ago."

"Who told you this, Tommy?" Ralph asked.

"This guy in D block." Carlson paused, stared at Ralph.

"Come *on*." Conor slapped the table with his open palm. "We don't have all night."

Ralph looked at Conor. *Take it easy. We're almost there*.

"What's his name, Tommy?" Ralph asked gently.

"Anatoli," Carlson said. "Anatoli Sidorov."

Chapter Seventeen

There were, of course, two possibilities. One, Sidorov actually did tell Carlson he ordered a hit on Lawton. Two, Carlson had made up the whole thing.

Ralph stared at Carlson. "Wait a minute, Tommy. I remember you. When we were up at Otisville. I saw you in the hall."

It was a total fabrication. Ralph had not seen Carlson, but he wondered if Carlson had seen him. After all, when a cop visits a prison, he stands out like a zebra in a horse corral.

Carlson fidgeted, then said, "Yeah. I saw you."

"Will you excuse us a minute, Tommy?" Ralph asked politely.

"Sure."

Conor and Ralph walked out of the interview room.

"Don't you find it strange," Ralph began, "that a couple days after we're at Otisville interviewing Anatoli Sidorov, this clown shows up and says Sidorov confessed to killing Lawton?"

"No," Conor said. "Not strange. Predictable. When he heard cell-block talk that we were questioning Sidorov about the murder of Walter Lawton, Carlson probably figured he'd come up with a story that might get some time knocked off his sentence."

"But what if Sidorov *did* tell this vermin he had Lawton hit?" Ralph wondered aloud.

Conor looked through the glass at Carlson. "What's Sidorov got to lose? He's already in for life, no chance of parole."

Ralph thought for a moment. There *was* another possibility. "Okay. What if Sidorov tells this guy he had Lawton hit but really had nothing to do with Lawton's murder?"

Conor saw immediately where Ralph was going. "But by taking credit for it, Sidorov gains respect in the yard and generates fear among the inmates."

"So which is it?" Ralph wondered aloud. "Sidorov *did* say he whacked Lawton or he didn't say it? And if he said it, did he do it or didn't he?" He frowned. "If this was an exacta, I'd box it. Cover all the combinations."

Conor and Ralph started toward the interview room. Conor grabbed Ralph's shoulder. They stopped just outside the door.

"Listen, Ralph. Enough with the Tommy this, Tommy that. You're giving me a headache."

They walked back into the interview room.

"All right, Tommy," Ralph said. "We're going to take your statement and have you sign it."

Conor sighed. *Tommy, Tommy, Tommy*. The name was driving him crazy.

"So this is good stuff," Carlson said, squirming in his chair. "Right?"

"And we want you to take a lie detector test." Ralph stopped himself from saying Tommy.

Carlson grew agitated. "Hey, man! I'm not lying! You guys think I'm lying?"

"No," Ralph reassured him. "We believe you. We just need you to pass the test so we can use it to help reduce your sentence."

Carlson's eyes darted nervously, like a trapped animal—or at least like someone who knew there was no way he was conning a polygraph.

"Can I have a cigarette now?"

"Sure, Tommy," Ralph said. "We'll get you a whole pack."

Conor and Ralph arranged for Carlson to be held over at the Tombs so they could administer the lie detector test the next day. Conor checked his watch. It was ten after eight.

"You got somewhere to be?" Ralph asked.

"Yeah. I'm meeting someone."

"Someone?"

"Her name's Monica."

"Really? When did this happen?"

"The other day," Conor said.

"I hope she's not like the last one."

"No. Thank God."

"Have fun. I'll take care of the DD5 on Carlson."

"Leave it," Conor said. "I'll do it in the morning."

"No. I really want to do it. It's my last week. And I'm already getting nostalgic about the paperwork."

Conor scanned the precinct, checking to see if Monica had found her way there. She hadn't. He walked briskly out the door. As he neared Eighth Avenue, the figure of a woman approached him.

"Conor!"

The voice was familiar—too familiar. Conor was stunned to see Heather rushing toward him. He had to admit, as she moved under the streetlight, that she looked as crazy gorgeous as she always did. She was wearing a midnight blue jacket, a chalk white blouse, and a tight, smoky gray skirt; high-heeled knee-length black leather boots, lace-pattern panty hose peeking out of the top of them; cherry red lip gloss that accentuated her full mouth; long auburn hair shining like a model in a Clairol commercial; and her hazel eyes made outrageous promises they would never keep.

"Conor!" She stopped directly in front of him, inches away.

The smell of her, the perfume, the shampoo, her

pheromones, filled his nostrils. He fought off the narcotic effect of it all.

"Heather?"

But why was he surprised? Heather had a proclivity for just showing up. In all the time he had known her, she hardly ever called. She would just appear.

"Oh, Conor," Heather sighed.

Conor didn't want any part of her drama. Not tonight. Not ever.

"Look, Heather. I'm meeting someone. And I'm running late. What's up?"

"My boyfriend . . ."

Conor flinched. *Boyfriend? What boyfriend?*

"Well, he *was* my boyfriend until about an hour ago," Heather continued. "But after what he did . . ."

She left the rest of the story hanging, an annoying trait she had fully mastered. It forced you to ask questions. This time, Conor didn't bite.

"Heather. I really have to go. Let's talk about this tomorrow. I'll give you a call and—"

"I tried to tell you about him on the phone, but . . ." Heather sighed. "I'm sorry. I'm so sorry."

Conor braced himself. *Sorry? For what? What has the crazy bitch done this time?*

"He's so jealous of you," Heather whimpered. "*Insanely* jealous."

Now she had cast him as a character in whatever upheaval was going on in her life, luring him into her emotional chaos. And, like always, it worked.

117

"Heather. What do you mean, jealous of *me*? Who?"

"Maybe it was my fault. Maybe I talked about you too much." Heather placed her hand on her forehead. "I knew it made him jealous. But I didn't know he was going to actually *do* something to you."

"To *me*? Heather! For God's sake, spit it out!"

"Frank gets crazy whenever I bring you up."

"Frank? Frank *who*?"

"Frank Reynolds."

Conor was stunned, confused. "*Captain* Frank Reynolds?"

Heather nodded, tears forming in her eyes. "And now he's filed some kind of complaint against you. I feel so terrible."

Conor felt needles pricking tiny holes in his entire body. His head filled with searing heat. *Screwing someone inside my fraternity?* Even for a cold-blooded specimen like Heather, this was beyond the pale. Did she realize she had put his entire career in jeopardy with her wanton lack of boundaries?

"Oh, Conor! I'm so sorry. Please forgive me."

Heather wrapped her arms around Conor and buried her head into his chest. He would have felt more comfortable in the embrace of a boa constrictor. As rage began to build within him, the thought crossed his mind that he should just kill her right there, right then. Grab her lovely neck and strangle her. He tensed his muscles, ready to push her away, get her off of him. But before he could disentangle himself from her clinging arms, he looked over her shoulder and saw the only thing that could make the moment worse.

Monica was standing in the middle of the street, frozen there, not sure what to do, an expression of embarrassment and betrayal washing across her face.

Chapter Eighteen

Conor quickly extricated himself from Heather, who turned, raising her eyebrows. Monica stood rooted to the asphalt. And so there they were, three people locked in an odd triangular configuration, each waiting for someone else to make a move.

"Monica." Conor finally broke the silence, not sure what to say after that. He walked to the curb and stopped.

"Monica," he repeated, then motioned toward the sidewalk. "This is Heather."

Heather smiled. Drama. Her favorite pastime.

"Hi, Monica." Heather spoke in a condescending tone.

"Hello, Heather," Monica replied, seeming to grow smaller as she said it.

Conor wanted to walk over and wrap his arms around Monica, protect her from the predatory female stalking a few feet away.

"Heather's an old friend," Conor said purpose-fully, as if he were describing a casual acquaintance. "She's having trouble in a relationship."

Heather blanched at Conor's detached, dismissive delivery, then smiled. "Yes, Monica. Conor and I are old friends."

Monica took a step backward. "If you'd rather we get together another time . . . ," she offered, shrinking even more.

Conor looked at Heather. "Sorry. We've got to go. We have a dinner reservation. And we're late."

We've got to go. We have a dinner reservation. We're late. The collective pronouns ripped into Heather just as Conor knew they would. It wasn't that Heather was by nature jealous, she was posses-sive. In her mind, she owned people. Forever. With Conor and Monica a *we*, Heather felt robbed of a possession.

"Don't let me keep you," Heather managed to reply.

"I hope everything works out," Monica said to Heather, surprising Conor with her subtle yet effec-tive parry. "Nice to meet you," she added, her voice now strong and sweet, her aim true.

"Nice to meet you, too," Heather replied, strug-gling for the upper hand.

"Good night, Heather," Conor said.

"Good night, Conor." Heather forced a smile, then turned and walked away.

"Is she going to be all right?" Monica asked with

the air of a compassionate conquerer. "She seemed very upset."

Conor took a swig of his martini. Monica worked her tongue against the inside of her cheek.

Heather was an ex-girlfriend, Conor explained. He and Heather stayed in touch, but there was nothing between them anymore.

Monica sipped her wine, considered Conor's monologue. The silence pressed against Conor's chest.

"That's pretty much all there is to it," he concluded. Of course, there was much more to tell but this wasn't the time or place. Even though it was difficult to keep from venting about Heather, screaming obscenities, calling her every name he could muster, he contained himself. One look across the table and he could see he had already lost ground with Monica, at least on the trust issue.

"How's your case going?" Monica asked, signaling she was over the ex-girlfriend portion of the evening.

"Like wading through seaweed."

"Seaweed? Is there seaweed in the Hudson River?"

Conor laughed. "Wading through seaweed. That's an expression. What I mean is, it's very slow going. I'm not much further along than I was Sunday night." He paused, did a quick inventory in his head. "Although I do have the murder weapon. That's good. And I have a witness who may have seen the shooter over by the river."

"Sounds like you're making progress."

"Yeah, I guess you could say that."

"Can the witness identify the person?" Monica wondered.

"Unfortunately not. It was too dark."

Conor realized he was breaking a cardinal rule by talking about an open investigation. He rationalized his temporary lapse in judgment by reasoning that he was so relieved to get past Heather's intrusion into his life, he would have talked about anything.

The appetizers arrived. Conor waved his hand, trying to look and sound Italian. *"Mangia, mangia."*

Monica was surprised. "You speak Italian?"

"No. Not really. Just a few words. How about you?"

"Si. I learned it when I was a child."

"Well, you're neighbors with Italy. I guess that would be like me learning to speak Connecticut."

Monica laughed. "At the closest point, between Vlorë and Brindisi, we're only forty kilometers across the Adriatic."

Vlorë and Brindisi? Conor had no idea which city was in which country.

"You speak any other language?" Monica asked.

"Me? I barely speak English."

"I noticed that," Monica said, exhibiting a previously absent sense of humor.

"Thanks. But just because you speak Albanian, English, and Italian, don't think—"

"Actually," she cut in, "I speak Russian, too."

"Well, I'm glad you speak English. Otherwise we wouldn't have much to say to each other."

"It wasn't easy learning English." Monica leaned over the table. "I mean—you told me you were hoping for a ree-cording contract? How come you don't pronounce *record* like that? 'Ree-cord.'"

"Good question."

"And what about b-u-s-h? You say 'bush,' right?"

"Right."

"But h-u-s-h is pronounced 'hush.' And r-o-u-g-h is 'rough.' But t-h-o-u-g-h is 'though.'"

"How about *bear* and *hear*? Or *womb* and *bomb*?"

"You see! Why *shouldn't* you pronounce *bomb*, 'boom'? That's the noise it makes when it goes off." Monica shook her head. "Everything is confusing in America. To me, *soccer* is 'football.' Not the game *you* play." She shrugged. "You call it *foot*ball but all you use is your hands."

The conversation segued to music, a universal language that needs little interpretation. Conor had always felt you could tell a great deal about someone by asking them to name their favorite songs. As it happened, Monica preferred rhythm and blues. Whenever she named a song, Conor would sing a few bars.

"What time is it?" Monica's question broke the spell.

"Twelve thirty," Conor said as he glanced at his watch then looked at Monica's wrists.

"You don't wear a watch?"

"I don't like wearing jewelry. When I need to know what time it is, I look at my cell phone."

Conor smiled. *A woman who doesn't like jewelry?* A perfect complement to a cop's salary.

"How about dessert?" he asked.

"I'd love to, but I have to be at work early tomorrow morning."

Conor nodded. "I hope we can see each other again before you leave."

"Let's see, tomorrow night my coworkers at the bank are taking me out. And Friday I promised my cousins in New Jersey I'd have dinner with them. How about Saturday?"

Conor was disappointed but tried not to show it. "Saturday would be great."

The grand seduction would have to wait.

Conor watched Monica's taxi weave into Hell's Kitchen's after-theater traffic and walked very slowly in the direction of his apartment. As he continued down Eighth Avenue, his mind wandered randomly. The call from East Coast Records. Heather turning up outside the precinct. Monica leaving in a few days. Bits of conclusions and speculations filled his mind. And then, in the midst of all his mental meanderings, it occurred to him what he was doing wrong. Always digging into the past or chasing the future, he never allowed himself to fully experience the present. Instead of dwelling on yesterday or waiting for tomorrow, he should be taking life one day at a time. Like AA. He had always felt that Alcoholics Anonymous had a great twelve-step program. It was spiritual, rational, and made sense. Except for the part about not drinking.

Conor spun around and headed back toward Maria Pia. He would have a nightcap and forget about Heather, forget about a recording contract, forget that Monica was going back to Albania, and simply savor the fact that he had even met Monica at all. A song by Elvin Bishop echoed in his head.

I must have been through about a million girls, I'd love 'em and I'd leave 'em alone . . .

Conor replayed the events of the evening. Somehow, what Heather had done was actually a relief, providing an absolute end to their relationship, leaving no possibility of reconciliation. Heather was truly history now. And the finality of it had a soothing effect.

Conor thought about the looming disciplinary hearing. What could they really do to him? Suspend him from the force? Good. He didn't seem to have the courage to quit and go after a music career. A suspension would propel him in that direction. Put him behind a desk? No problem. At least he'd have a regular schedule. Pushing paper nine to five would allow him to schedule his gigs without some major case pulling him from the stage. He smiled. *Every cloud has a silver lining.*

And every glass was half full.

"Give me the usual," Conor said as he walked into Maria Pia and approached the bar.

Chapter Nineteen

Conor slept soundly for the first time since he had stood over the body of Walter Lawton.

"You look well rested," Ralph teased as Conor walked into the precinct. "Guess nothing happened last night."

"You know, Ralph, your powers of observation haven't left you, even in your later years."

"Don't worry, kid," Ralph fired back. "You'll be as old as I am one day. If you're lucky."

"I ran into Heather last night," Conor said abruptly.

Ralph frowned. "Oh, Lord."

Conor related the details of his encounter with Heather.

Ralph shook his head. "Boy, you can sure pick 'em."

"Tell me about it."

Ralph thought for a moment. "You can blast Reynolds out of the water with this. It shows he had a personal agenda in pressing for a disciplinary hearing."

"Yeah. You're right."

"Of *course* I'm right. Matter of fact, if I were you, I'd confront the bastard before the hearing. Get the whole thing dropped. No way he'll proceed if he knows you're going to expose his sick mind to the entire department."

Conor considered his options for a moment. "I'll figure it out. I just don't want to think about it right now."

Ralph pointed at a *New York Post* lying on his desk. "Lawton's funeral. Three this afternoon. Let's head over there. See who shows up."

It was generally a good idea to stake out the funeral of a murder victim. The behavior of the mourners sometimes offered up a clue. But the first order of business was the administration of a polygraph to Thomas Carlson.

Carlson failed miserably. Watkins, the polygraph operator, pointed at a graph and deciphered the peaks and valleys that corresponded to Carlson's responses.

"The subject is being deceptive here. *And* here. And also here."

Conor and Ralph walked back to their desks.

"He's a lying little prick," Ralph observed. "But we already knew that, didn't we?"

"Yeah. We did. The question is: What else do we know?"

"Not much."

"By the way," Conor said as he dropped into his chair, "what's going on with the ballistics? Did they match the gun to other crimes or not?"

"Yeah. They should have called us with something by now. Even if they came up empty."

Ralph picked up the phone, dialed.

"Cobb," Brian answered.

"Brian. It's Ralph. You hear anything on the gun?"

"Looks like we've got a hit."

"When were you planning to share this tidbit of information?" Ralph asked, clearly irritated.

"NIBIN just got it to me. I took it under the scope to confirm the match."

A computer wasn't as precise as a human, not in this instance, anyway. Even when the software identified a possible correlation, someone, a person, had to compare the striations on the two bullets with a microscope before the result could be deemed conclusive.

"Get your ass moving," Ralph said. "Meet us at the Cosmic."

Conor and Ralph sat in a booth at the Cosmic Diner, on the corner of Fifty-third Street and Eighth Avenue. Conor ordered orange juice and a bagel. He wasn't much of a breakfast person. Ralph had his usual bacon and eggs.

"Don't you worry about cholesterol?" Conor asked.

"Too late for that," Ralph replied as he buttered his toast.

Brian arrived, file folder tucked under his arm.

"Hey, guys," he said as he folded himself into the booth next to Ralph.

"Lay it on us," Ralph said.

"Let me order something first. I'm starved."

Ralph flagged down a waiter who was walking past. "Another order of bacon and eggs."

"No," Brian called out as the waiter walked away. "Make that a lox-and-onion omelet. Egg whites." He looked down at Ralph's plate.

"Don't you worry about cholesterol?" Brian asked.

"Let's hear it," Conor said.

Brian opened the folder and spread out a series of photographs and documents.

"It seems your gun was used in a convenience store robbery a year ago. The gun was never recovered, but based on fingerprints at the scene and tape from a security camera, a suspect was arrested a week later. He was subsequently convicted. So this guy can't be your shooter. He's serving time at Riker's."

"What's his name?" Conor asked.

Brian referred to the file. "Conrado Rivera."

"Gangbanger?" Ralph wanted to know.

"Ethnic profiling is illegal," Brian scolded.

"So he's a gangbanger," Ralph shot back.

"Mara Salvatrucha," Brian replied.

Mara Salvatrucha, or MS-13 as it was known, was considered by law enforcement to be one of the most dangerous gangs in America. Formed in Los Angeles in the 1980s by Salvadorans, its membership had grown over the years to include other Latino nationalities.

Conor pondered what he had just heard. "MS-Thirteen, huh?"

"Yeah," Brian said. "Good luck getting *this* guy to talk."

Brian's egg-white omelet arrived. Ralph frowned at the plate.

"What?" Brian asked.

"It's yellow."

"So?"

"So egg whites are white," Ralph said. "Otherwise they'd call them egg yellows."

"They put cornmeal in them," Brian explained. "To make them look like real eggs."

"I know," Ralph retorted. "But I'd rather eat things that don't need stuff added to them in order to make them look like what they're supposed to look like even though they really aren't what they look like."

Brian frowned. "That didn't make sense."

"Neither do yellow egg whites," Ralph countered.

Conor wasn't listening to the banter between Ralph and Brian. He was already wondering how they were going to get Conrado Rivera, a gangbanger who would be signing his own death warrant if he said anything at all, to tell them what happened to the gun.

Chapter Twenty

Conor and Ralph headed down the hall inside Riker's. "Got it!" Ralph said, clapping his hands.

"Got what?"

"How we're going to loosen up Rivera." Ralph smiled smugly. " 'The Corbomite Maneuver.' "

"Sounds great. But what the hell is it?"

"The episode where Captain Kirk bluffed an alien named Balok into believing the *Enterprise* had a doomsday weapon called Corbomite."

"So who am I? Spock or Sulu?"

"Just follow my lead," Ralph said, "and we'll know where that gun went in under a minute."

"A minute?"

"Want to make a wager?"

"No, thanks."

Conrado Rivera was not afforded the same respect that had been given Anatoli Sidorov at Otisville.

Accompanied by a burly guard carrying about 250 pounds of solid muscle, Rivera was led into the interview room in leg shackles and handcuffs.

"Hey, Conrado," Ralph began. "How you doing?"

Rivera stared coldly at Ralph.

Ralph looked at the guard. "Give us a minute alone."

"You're wasting your time," the guard said.

"A minute," Ralph said. "That's all. One minute."

The guard shrugged, left the room, shut the door behind him. Ralph looked at Conor. "Time this, will you?"

Rivera frowned, confused. Conor held his wrist in front of his face.

"Go," Ralph said to Conor, then stepped closer to Rivera.

"Okay, Conrado. Here's the story. You used a gun in a robbery. When they arrested you, the gun was gone. I want to know where the gun went."

Rivera continued to stare silently at Ralph.

Ralph looked at Conor. "How am I doing on time?"

"Seven seconds."

"Good," Ralph said, then faced Rivera again.

"If we're in here more than say, one minute, your roommates are going to wonder what you said. So just tell me what you did with the gun and we're out of here. No one ever knows you told us anything."

Rivera smirked.

"Time?" Ralph said.

"Seventeen seconds," Conor replied.

Ralph went back to work. "All right. When I walk out of here, I'm going to act like a happy man. Make sure everyone sees I'm in a good mood. Then I'm going to go to the DA and ask him to knock some time off your sentence. You know, because you've been so cooperative."

Rivera's jaw clenched.

"Time?" Ralph called out.

"Twenty-nine seconds."

"I'm not bluffing, Conrado. You don't tell me what I want to know, I'll make you look like the biggest canary since Sammy the Bull."

Rivera seemed nervous but remained tight-lipped.

Ralph looked at Conor. "All right. Let's go. And don't forget to smile because Conrado here was nice enough to give up his buddies."

Conor and Ralph started for the door.

"Wait!" Rivera shouted.

Conor and Ralph stopped.

"I sold it."

"To who?" Ralph wanted to know.

"Fat Albert."

"Fat Albert? You sold your gun to a cartoon character?"

"No. This guy. Everybody calls him Fat Albert."

"What's he look like? Red sweater? Blue pants?"

"Let me go back to my cell," Rivera pleaded. "I told you about the gun."

"What's he look like?"

"Big fat white guy. Works Washington Heights." Rivera was squirming. "Come on, man. That's all I know."

"Time?" Ralph asked.

"Fifty-seven seconds."

Ralph tapped on the door. The guard opened it.

"Look, punk," Ralph said to Rivera. "You're never getting out of here if I have anything to say about it."

The guard was smug. "I told you."

Ralph let out a heavy sigh then left the room.

Conor looked at the guard. "It's sad, you know? My partner used to be the best interrogator in the business. Poor guy. When he got old, he just lost it."

Conor glared at Rivera, then walked out and joined Ralph in the hall. They headed for the exit.

"You should've bet," Ralph said.

"I would've lost."

"Fifty-seven seconds. I cut it pretty close. Would've been more exciting for you if you had a little money riding on it."

"Don't worry. It was exciting enough."

They went through security and walked across the parking lot.

"Big fat white guy named Fat Albert?" Ralph said. "In *Washington Heights*?"

"Shouldn't be too hard to find."

"I hope not," Ralph said wistfully. "We find Fat Albert, we track the gun, maybe we can close this case before I retire."

"Hey, hey, hey," Conor said.

Chapter Twenty-one

Conor and Ralph parked the car at 181st Street and Fort Washington Avenue, near the center of Washington Heights, which extended from 155th Street to 200th Street and spanned the entire width of Manhattan, from the Hudson River to the East River. It was a huge area to canvass.

"I forgot to ask Rivera *where* in Washington Heights," Ralph groused as they walked along Fort Washington Avenue.

"Maybe next time you should take a minute and a half," Conor suggested.

They stopped on the corner and surveyed the endless line of apartment buildings and storefronts.

"Don't we have a CI up here somewhere?" Ralph said.

"Yeah. That guy Jimmy."

"Right. Jimmy."

Conor never liked using confidential informants. They played new cops like a violin. Even veteran detectives were sometimes taken in by their verbal shell game.

"Think it'll be easier to find Jimmy than Fat Albert?" Ralph wondered aloud.

"Didn't Jimmy used to hang out at St. Nick's Pub? The jazz joint on Saint Nicholas Avenue and a Hundred and Forty-ninth Street."

They got back in the car and drove thirty blocks south. Jimmy wasn't there, but the manager who was setting up the club for the night told them Jimmy had stopped by and said he was going to get something to eat at Esther's Soul Kitchen, a small take-out place at 179th Street, two blocks from where Conor and Ralph had started. So it was back in the car and thirty blocks north.

Jimmy was placing an order when Conor and Ralph entered. "Yeah, give me an order of them wings. And some collard greens. Macaroni and cheese."

"Make that three orders," Ralph said.

Jimmy turned. He was happy to see them. "Hey, Detectives. Where you guys been lately?"

Jimmy was a wiry little guy of indeterminate age, maybe around thirty-five, although he could've been much older or much younger. His genealogy was equally hard to pinpoint. Black. White. Latino. Jimmy seemed to be a combination of all and yet none of these groups.

"Got a minute?" Conor asked.

"For you guys? I got all day."

Conor, Ralph, and Jimmy walked to a corner of the small storefront.

"You know somebody named Fat Albert?" Conor asked.

Jimmy smiled. "Hey, hey, hey."

"Not the cartoon character, Jimmy," Ralph said.

Conor rolled his eyes. Every other word out of Ralph's mouth was going to be *Jimmy*.

Jimmy leaned in on Ralph. "Listen, Detective. I'm embarrassed to say this, but I'm a little short."

Conor was annoyed. "Yeah, I know. Talk to God about that, not us."

"Don't mind my partner, Jimmy," Ralph said, pulling a twenty out of his pocket. "He's having a bad day."

Jimmy reached for the twenty. Ralph held it away from him.

"Fat Albert, Jimmy? Know where we can find him?"

"Sure. I can find him for you."

Ralph creased the twenty in half. "I didn't ask *you* to find him, Jimmy. I asked if you knew where *we* could find him."

Jimmy eyed the twenty. "He hangs out at a Hundred and Fifty-ninth and Broadway."

"On the *street*?" Conor frowned.

"All I know, you want to do business with Fat Albert, you go to a Hundred and Fifty-ninth and Broadway."

Ralph thought for a moment, then handed the twenty to Jimmy.

The African-American woman behind the counter shouted at them. "Three orders of wings, collard greens, and macaroni and cheese."

Conor, Ralph, and Jimmy walked over to the counter.

"You guys got this?" Jimmy asked.

"Sure, Jimmy," Ralph said.

Conor and Ralph sat in the car at the corner of 159th and Broadway.

"I've got to tell you," Conor said as he gnawed on a chicken wing, "I hate it when you use some guy's name over and over. It drives me crazy."

"Well, I'll be gone in a few days. You won't have to deal with it."

"Yeah, but I've put up with it for twelve years."

"You're a saint." Ralph dug into the collard greens. "These collard greens are fantastic."

"And another thing," Conor said. "You gave Jimmy twenty dollars *and* bought him lunch. These guys will say anything for a buck. So now we're sitting here at a Hundred and Fifty-ninth and Broadway for what? You really think Fat Albert's going to show."

"Yeah," Ralph said. "I do."

"When?"

"*That*, I don't know." Ralph scooped up a plastic spoonful of macaroni and cheese. "This is great stuff," he said as he chewed. "We oughta come up here more often."

* * *

Almost two hours later and Fat Albert was still nowhere in sight. Conor wasn't happy. "Jimmy conned us."

"Look on the bright side," Ralph said. "We had a good lunch."

Conor checked his watch. "It's two thirty. We better head over to the cemetery."

Walter Lawton was being interred at St. John's Cemetery on Long Island, in the town of Hempstead. Considering Lawton's clientele, it was fitting that St. John's was also the final resting place for a number of Mafia capos: Vito "Don George" Genovese; Joseph Columbo; Carlo Gambino; Carmine Galante. Even the iconic gangster Charles "Lucky" Luciano was spending eternity there.

"Let's go see the Catholics," Ralph said as he started the engine. It was a nice way to put it.

Chapter Twenty-two

They obviously weren't invited guests, so Ralph parked the car on a hill about a hundred yards from the proceedings. Conor pulled a pair of high-powered binoculars from the glove compartment and focused on the somber crowd.

"See anybody interesting?" Ralph wanted to know.

"Looks like the cast of *The Sopranos* out there," Conor replied. He slowly panned across the gathering. "The wife looks spectacular."

"Even in black?"

"She's wearing blue."

"Give me those," Ralph said.

Conor handed Ralph the binoculars. Ralph held them up to his eyes.

"That's not blue, that's purple. What are you, color-blind?"

"Yeah."

Ralph lowered the binoculars. "All these years and you never said anything?"

"I can see colors."

"But you just said you were color-blind."

"It's called red-green color blindness," Conor explained. "I can see colors. Only sometimes I think brown is green or red is brown."

"Or purple is blue."

"That's why I never told you. I knew you'd give me a hard time."

Ralph raised the binoculars to his eyes again. "You're right. The wife looks great."

Conor reached over and pushed Ralph's head a couple inches to the left. "Stop looking at the wife."

Ralph lowered the binoculars. "You know what? There are about thirty guys out there that could have popped Lawton for some reason."

"Like what?"

"Like they got pissed off at the size of the bill?"

"I don't think these guys really need a reason."

"Me neither," Ralph agreed.

"So some goon goes to his usually reliable source for untraceable firearms . . ."

"Which, let's say, was Fat Albert."

"But Fat Albert screws up. Sells them a gun that wasn't clean. Used before in a previous crime."

They sat and contemplated the possibilities.

"So now we've got another theory," Conor pointed out. "Sanctioned mob hit."

"Carried out by one of these guys."

"Or by Zeffri."

"If this was a sanctioned job," Ralph said, "and the

mob hears we're on the trail of the gun, Fat Albert's going to be Dead Albert."

Conor stared out at the expanse of the mourners. "We ought to snap some photos, ID them when we get back to the house."

"Good idea."

"Where's the camera?" Conor asked.

Ralph frowned. "I thought you put it in the car."

"I thought *you* did."

Back at the precinct, Conor and Ralph sat at their desks in silence, both thinking the same thing. The whole case hung on the gun and what Fat Albert did with it after he got it from Rivera. Of course, Fat Albert *could* have been the shooter but they both dismissed the idea. He sounded more like a vendor than a killer.

"Fat Albert's got some nerve," Ralph said.

"Yeah. Selling a gun used in a crime."

"No," Ralph countered. "Calling himself Fat Albert. I mean, *Fat Albert and the Cosby Kids* was a great cartoon. I used to watch it all the time."

Conor frowned, thought for a moment. "How come we never heard of this guy?"

"I was wondering that myself," Ralph replied. "Sounds like Fat Albert's the wheeler-dealer of Washington Heights. But he never came up on our radar."

"We should call someone up in the Three Four."

A phone call to a detective at the 34th Precinct

revealed that Fat Albert was a shadowy figure who appeared and disappeared like an overweight ghost. He was something of a legend in the Heights. Cops would see him here and there, knew he was up to no good, but never found a reason to collar him. As far as a name or address, the detective had no clue.

"In this PC world we live in," the detective said, "we can't ask people for an ID anymore unless we have a good excuse. Thank the ACLU for that."

"I know what you mean," Ralph said.

"He hangs out on Broadway," the detective continued, confirming what Jimmy had told them. "A Hundred and Fifty-ninth."

"We need to talk to him about a homicide," Ralph said. "Tell your guys, they see him, call us immediately."

As Conor and Ralph considered their next move, Amanda walked up to them.

"Aren't you looking at someone named Salvatore Zeffri in the Lawton homicide?"

"Yes," Conor said. "Why?"

"The Queens DA just announced he's going to retry Zeffri for a contract killing a couple years ago."

"Thanks for the heads-up," Ralph said.

Amanda walked away.

"Without the great Walter Lawton to defend Zeffri," Ralph said, "the Queens DA has to figure he's got a better shot at conviction."

"That's not good news."

"You're telling *me*?"

They both knew that Zeffri would adopt a bunkerlike mentality, making him even more defensive than he already was. Further access to him regarding the Lawton homicide had been rendered virtually impossible.

"I hate lawyers," Ralph said.

"What's that got to do with anything?"

"If Lawton hadn't gotten Zeffri off in the first place," Ralph said, "we wouldn't even be talking about him right now."

"Good point," Conor agreed.

Ralph's observation conjured up another "what if?" in a case already filled with them. What if Lawton had kept his own killer out of jail? Wouldn't *that* be ironic.

Chapter Twenty-three

Ralph went home. Conor wondered what he was going to do with himself. He thought about Monica. It would be nice to see her but he'd have to wait until Saturday for that. He needed to eat something. The problem was, where? Maria Pia? He wasn't in the mood for a restaurant. Fu Ying? No, not Chinese.

Twenty minutes later he was at Esther's Soul Kitchen. The woman who'd taken his order that afternoon recognized him right away.

"Wings, collard greens, and macaroni and cheese, right?" she said.

"That's me," Conor replied. "But you can just call me 'wings.'"

The woman didn't laugh. "What can I get you?"

"Same thing."

She walked away and began putting together the order.

* * *

Conor drove down Broadway and parked near 159th Street. He didn't like having the car. He would've taken the subway but standing on the street made him too conspicuous. As it was, any perp worth his salt would spot the unmarked sedan in a heartbeat.

Conor dined from the cardboard container using fine plastic cutlery, hoping he might kill two birds with one stone. He could have dinner and, at the same time, see if Fat Albert turned up.

The corner was full of activity. Various men and women would congregate there for a few minutes then move on. One man, who stood by the curb for half an hour, seemed to be waiting for someone. Fat Albert, maybe? The man finally gave up and walked away. Conor even watched a drug deal go down. Somebody was selling what appeared to be a crack vial. He could have jumped out of the car and made a collar, which he would have done when he first joined the detective squad twelve years ago, but there were three good reasons he didn't. One, he wasn't in narcotics. Two, making an arrest on the corner would jeopardize his main objective, which was finding Fat Albert. And three, he had a box of food in his lap.

Conor thought about the upcoming disciplinary hearing and how he was going to handle Reynolds's jealousy-fueled attack. Despite the fact that he had previously expressed apathy regarding the outcome, he realized that he wouldn't want to end his years on the job with a suspension. So maybe the best thing, like Ralph said, would be to confront Reynolds before the hearing, which might get the whole thing dropped. But Conor decided he would wait until the hearing itself, hit Reynolds with the Heather connection in front of the NYPD brass. Yes, Conor liked that idea. He wanted to see Reynolds's face when that bit of information was introduced into the proceedings.

Boredom was really setting in now, so Conor switched on the radio. As Al Green's classic song "Tired of Being Alone" floated out of the speakers, it made him long for the funky little stage at the Rhythm Bar. And it made him think about the aborted meeting with East Coast Records.

Conor turned off the radio.

At one point, six men in hooded sweatshirts materialized from the shadows. They swarmed around the back of the car and whispered to one another. Conor placed his hand on his gun and kept an eye on them through the rearview mirror. Three were black, two white, one Latino. They were very young, which worried Conor. At their age, maybe they weren't savvy enough to realize they were standing next to an unmarked NYPD vehicle.

The Latino sauntered slowly to the driver's door and peered in at Conor. Suddenly, the situation had escalated. Conor's next move would either ignite a potentially deadly encounter or defuse one.

Conor rolled down the window.

"Got a cigarette?" the Latino asked.

"Not at these prices," Conor replied.

"How about a little money?" the man pressed, his tone menacing.

"How about you and your friends move along." Conor slipped his shield from his pocket and held it up. "I don't want to have to shoot you."

The Latino recoiled from the badge like Dracula from sunlight. He backed away from the car fast, walked to his friends.

"That guy's a pig," Conor heard the Latino say. Then they all ran up Broadway as if they were being chased by the Devil.

Conor smiled. So what if the NYPD didn't have the greatest reputation in Washington Heights? *At least that kid really believed I would shoot him.* Of course, if the gang had attempted to rob him, he would've had no choice but to draw his weapon. Anyway, it didn't happen.

After two hours of watching people come and go, Conor had had enough. He drove toward Midtown. It was only ten fifteen, too early to go home. He'd stop somewhere and have a drink. But where? As he ran a series of bars through his head, his cell phone rang. He pulled it out of his pocket and checked the caller ID. He recognized the number.

"Hello, Mrs. Lawton."

"Detective Bard. I'm sorry to bother you."

"It's all right."

"I need to talk to you."

"Sure. When?"

"Right now. If that's possible."

Conor remembered the last time he was with her. Draped on the couch, robe falling open, her perfectly toned body exposed. If he found himself in that position again, what would he do? *I'd walk away just like the last time*, he told himself, but he didn't want to take the chance.

"Where are you?"

"I'm at Coals Steak House."

Coals Steak House, located on East Fifty-third Street just off Second Avenue, had arguably the best steaks in Manhattan. At least the Mafia thought so. It was in front of Coals where an ambitious underboss gunned down a crime family capo as he headed in for a sirloin. The incident sparked a chaotic struggle for control that was more effective in weakening the mob than even the most persistent efforts by the federal government.

"After the funeral," Holly said, "we all came here for dinner."

Bury a Mafia lawyer, have dinner at the Mafia's favorite restaurant. It made perfect sense. At least Conor was relieved he would be meeting Holly in a public place. Besides, it solved the problem of where to have a drink.

Chapter Twenty-four

Conor entered Coals and was met by the maître d', who was attired in a tuxedo.

"May I help you?"

"I'm meeting someone," Conor said. He scanned the restaurant. It was a large place, filled with diners, but he finally spotted Holly sitting at the head of a table with about twenty men and women, mostly men. She looked up, saw Conor, then said something to the others. Several of the men twisted in their chairs and looked at him. Their collective stare was filled with suspicion and infused with a macho challenge. *Nice dinner guests*, Conor thought. If it hadn't been for the fact that Holly, a woman, was seated in the place of honor, Conor would've guessed this was a mob sit-down.

Holly stood. So did all the men, who also bowed slightly in reverence and respect.

"Hello, Conor," Holly said as she approached.

He was somewhat taken aback by her informality,

and definitely taken in by how ravishing she looked in her purple or blue or whatever-the-hell-color dress it was.

She motioned to the bar, which was empty. "Let's sit over here. Where we can talk."

"So, Mrs. Lawton," Conor said as he pulled up two bar stools. "What did you want to talk to me about?"

Holly took his hand. "Oh, Conor, *please*. Call me Holly."

"Okay, Holly." He felt uncomfortable. She was trying to force some sort of false familiarity.

"I'm so glad you're here," she said, squeezing his hand. "It's been such an awful day."

A bartender walked over. "Something to drink, Mrs. Lawton?" He glanced at their intertwined hands.

Conor was certain he saw disapproval in the bartender's eyes. Holly was obviously known there and Conor didn't want anyone to get surly with him because they thought he was somehow defiling the widow Lawton. He slowly pulled his hand out from Holly's grasp.

"I'll have Glenfiddich, please, Lirim."

Lirim looked at Conor. "And you, sir?"

"Ketel One martini. Up. With a twist. Very dry. No vermouth."

"I don't use vermouth," Lirim said flatly, then walked away.

Conor recognized Lirim's accent but couldn't place it. He watched him as he set about making the martini. He was a big man, around fifty, Conor guessed, like Anatoli Sidorov. But no, Sidorov's accent was different. And Lirim didn't sound like a Russian name. Then Conor realized that Lirim's intonation sounded very much like Monica's. *Maybe Lirim is Albanian.*

"Conor," Holly said. "Forgive me if I'm a little tipsy but, fuck, I put my husband in the ground this afternoon. I think you can understand."

"I do."

Holly narrowed her eyes. "The Queens district attorney is going to try Sal again."

"I know," Conor said. "I heard."

"I don't care what happens in *that* trial. I only care that Sal doesn't get away with killing my husband."

"Whoever killed your husband—"

"There was something I didn't tell you," she interrupted.

Holly checked to make sure Lirim wasn't listening, then leaned in on Conor. "The night Walter was killed, Sal had a gun."

"How do you know? Did you see it?"

"Yes. He was wearing a shoulder holster. One time, when he reached for his cell phone, his jacket opened up. I think he did it on purpose, opened his jacket, to scare me."

"Do you know what kind of gun it was?"

"A twenty-two."

The fact that Lawton was killed with a twenty-two had never been made public. So either Zeffri actually happened to have a twenty-two that night and Holly saw it, or Holly's sources at the DA's office had leaked information to her again.

Conor tried to read her, determine if she was lying. "How do you know it was a twenty-two?"

Holly looked caught. Lirim appeared with the drinks, allowing Holly to consider her response. He placed a scotch in front of her. "Here you are, Mrs. Lawton." He pushed a martini across the bar. "And for you, sir."

"Thanks." Conor waited for Lirim to walk away, then leaned closer to Holly. "How do you know it was a twenty-two?"

"It must've been," Holly said, not sounding so convincing. "Sal told me one time he liked twenty-twos."

Conor didn't believe Zeffri had told her any such thing. On the contrary, he was reasonably certain that Holly was only saying this because she already knew a .22 had killed her husband. And because she was determined to put Zeffri behind bars one way or another.

"Can you describe the gun to me?" Conor asked.

Holly didn't respond.

"Can you tell me what it looked like?"

"Like a gun," she said, annoyed. "Black. Metal. You *know*, a gun." She covered her ears with her hands as if she were blocking out noise. "Sal needs to pay for what he did to Walter. That's all I'm saying." Her face became suddenly ashen. She swayed.

"Are you all right?" Conor asked.

"I think I'd better go home," she whispered, suddenly aware that all the alcohol she had consumed was finally hitting her brain. "Will you walk me to the car?"

Conor stood, helped Holly to her feet, turned to Lirim. "I'll be right back."

They walked out to a waiting limousine. Conor opened the door. Holly slipped her arms around him.

"Thank you, Conor." She kissed his cheek. "When this is all over, I'd like to take you to dinner."

Holly slowly removed her arms from Conor's waist, steadied herself by grabbing the door of the limousine. She struck a pose, head tilted to the side, stared at Conor demurely. Beautiful. Sexy. Crazy. And drunk. *What a combination*, Conor thought. *This is like a scene from a movie*. Only he didn't allow himself to imagine for a moment that he was the leading man. He was playing a supporting role to Holly's dazzling performance.

"Good night, Conor." She kissed his other cheek then climbed slowly into the backseat, casting a provocative glance at the same time.

As he watched the limousine pull away from the curb, Conor tried to comprehend Holly's bizarre behavior, to find some rational explanation for her actions, but it seemed that everything about her defied logic.

Conor headed back into Coals. Maybe a martini would help sort it all out.

Chapter Twenty-five

Conor returned to the bar, picked up his martini, and savored the icy vodka. What had Holly hoped to accomplish by asking him to see her tonight? Why was she intimating that a sexual reward was waiting for him? A reward for what? Nailing Zeffri? Did she hate Zeffri that much? Did Zeffri really kill Lawton?

Lirim drifted over to him. "How's the martini?"

"Perfect," Conor replied. "Thank you."

Lirim looked around at the empty bar stools. "Quiet night. Usually have a full bar."

"Where are you from?" Conor asked.

"Guess."

"Albania."

Lirim was surprised. "Nobody ever gets it right. They always say Russia. But maybe that's because you're a cop."

Now it was Conor who was surprised. "How do you know I'm a cop?"

"You're in this business, you become a good judge

of people," Lirim said. "Besides, in this place, a cop stands out. Know what I mean?"

Four of Holly's dinner guests walked out of the dining room. They gave Conor long, penetrating stares before exiting the restaurant.

"Yeah. I know what you mean." Conor took a sip of his martini. "I'm working the Walter Lawton homicide."

"I know."

Conor frowned.

"Another thing you learn in this business," Lirim explained, "is how to pick up a conversation from across a room."

Bartenders were a breed unto themselves. Men, women, young, old, it didn't matter. Something happened to ordinary people when they stepped behind a bar. They instantly developed keener powers of observation and photographic memories. Conor had often thought that if he ever retired and started a private investigation firm, he would hire bartenders.

"I hope you find the guy who did it," Lirim said.

"Oh, I will," Conor replied. "I will." He repeated it to convince himself.

"So how did you know I was Albanian?"

"Not because I'm a cop. I just met an Albanian woman the other day."

"You're very lucky. Albanian women are the best. They care about the home and that's important."

"And they're beautiful, too. At least this one is."

"What's her name?"

"Monica."

"Last name?"

"Kodra. Monica Kodra."

Lirim nodded. "Kodra. Sure. I know that family."

"You wouldn't happen to know *Monica*, would you?"

"No. I don't know a Monica Kodra. But I know a Kodra family from the north. That's where I'm from. The mountains."

"Monica's from the north."

"I probably know her cousins. There aren't that many of us Albanians. Three and a half million. And the country is only the size of Massachusetts. So everybody knows everybody else. How old is Monica?"

"Thirty-five, thirty-six."

"Then she's living in Tirana."

"How did you know?"

"Her generation, they left the mountains a long time ago to go to the city. Young people want new adventures, not old customs."

"Monica was telling me about the Kanun."

Lirim frowned. "The Kanun? What did she say about it?"

"She said it's an ancient set of laws where women have no rights. And only men can inherit property."

Lirim grew agitated. "What does that matter to me? My ancestors are as poor as they have always been. What do I inherit? Dust?"

"Anyway, she said it was banned by the government. Nobody practices it anymore."

"That is not true," Lirim said sharply. "I am here

because of that stupid law. And because of my brother, who is even more stupid."

"What do you mean?"

"Three years ago, my brother killed someone. With a knife in the heart. Over what? Some small thing."

"Was he arrested?"

Lirim snickered. "Arrested? No, he ran away to hide like rat."

"Guess he didn't want to go to jail," Conor offered.

"Jail? He would be lucky to go to jail. He ran away because of the taking of the blood."

"Taking of the blood?"

"It's called *Gjakmarrja*. When a member of your family kills someone, then a member of *that* family must take the blood from *your* family. So the family of the man my brother killed, by the law of Kanun, must now kill my brother. They cannot find my brother. But they still want to take the blood. And you know what that means?"

"No."

"It means they have the right to kill a man in my family. And that man is me." Lirim massaged his forehead, as if he had a headache. "My father is dead and I have no brothers. I have two sisters. But, according to the Kanun, you do not kill women or children. It's between men, these things. So being the only male in my family, they came for me. To take the blood." He leaned over the bar and looked at Conor. "I barely escaped with my life. I would have been killed if I stayed there."

"You feel you are safe in New York?"

Lirim looked away. "I just don't want to think about that."

Conor took a sip of his martini. "Sounds like the Mafia."

"It's worse," Lirim said. "But maybe that's why so many Albanians now run Italian restaurants. We understand the Italian vendetta better than they do." He motioned toward two waiters who were crossing into the dining room. "Albanians. All Albanians. I think the Italians and the Americans don't want to work anymore. So we are happy to take their jobs."

Funny, Conor thought, how you can go from not knowing a single Albanian to all of a sudden being in the middle of an Albanian crowd.

Lirim looked at Conor. "Nino's. You ever been there?"

"No. But I've heard they have great pasta."

"Nino. He's Albanian. And his brother Bruno also has a restaurant."

"Nino's? Bruno's? I always thought those places were Italian."

"Nino and Bruno? I know their family in Albania. Selimaj. Their last name is Selimaj. Does that sound Italian to you?"

"I don't think so." Conor drained his martini.

"Would you like another one?" Lirim asked.

"I would love another one, but no, thanks."

Conor stood, reached in his pocket, pulled out some cash. "How much I owe you?"

Lirim waved him off. "It's on me. I enjoyed the conversation."

Conor started to leave a tip.

"I said it was on me," Lirim insisted.

Conor stuck the money back in his pocket, looked toward the dining room. "Maybe I'll bring Monica in for dinner on Saturday."

"Better make a reservation," Lirim cautioned. "It's a mob scene in here on Saturday night."

Conor almost laughed out loud. *Yeah, it's a mob scene all right.*

Conor walked to the car and climbed behind the wheel. As he drove toward the precinct, he snapped on the radio, which was tuned to all-news WINS. A sports announcer finished giving the scores and then the station ID filled the speakers.

"Ten Ten WINS. Give us twenty-two minutes and we'll give you the world."

"Murder at a Queens dog kennel," a news anchor intoned.

Conor squinted at the radio in disbelief. *Did I hear that right?*

"A Queens man was found murdered this hour at the Canine Care Kennels in Hillside, Queens," the anchor continued. "His name is being withheld pending notification of kin."

Zeffri? Can't be. Conor hit the lights and siren, stepped on the gas, then pointed the car in the direction of the Midtown Tunnel. He made the fourteen-mile trip to Hillside in twelve minutes. The kennels were a hive of police activity.

Conor walked up to a uniformed cop on the perimeter of the crime scene and flashed his shield.

"Who's in charge?" Conor wanted to know.

"Detective Morton." The cop pointed to a man near the entrance to the kennels.

Conor walked over to Morton. He was a newly minted gold shield. Thirty-two years old at the most. If Conor had to guess, he'd say it was Morton's first homicide. "Detective Morton?"

"Yes?"

"Detective Bard. One Eight."

"What can I do for you, Detective?" Morton was very official.

"I need an ID on the victim."

"We're awaiting notification of next of kin before we release that information."

It was a new-detective kind of thing to say.

Conor smiled. "Don't worry. I won't tell anybody."

Morton hesitated. Conor slipped off the kid gloves.

"That information may be vital to an ongoing homicide investigation in Manhattan. I want that ID. *Now*."

Morton looked nervous, not sure what to do.

"Is there a duty captain here?" Conor demanded.

"Okay," Morton said, afraid he might get into trouble by holding back. "The name of the deceased is Zeffri. Salvatore Zeffri."

Conor rubbed his hands through his hair. He'd known it, of course, had a strong feeling it was Zeffri, but the confirmation was still a sledgehammer.

Who did this? And why? Was Holly Lawton involved? Was it retribution for her husband's murder? Is that what the dinner at Coals was all about? Did she have Zeffri taken care of so he couldn't point an accusing finger at *her* like she was doing to him?

Of course, some of the people enjoying a steak with Holly may have wanted Zeffri silenced for their own reasons. And the rubout of Zeffri had all the earmarks of a preemptive strike by the mob to keep him from making a deal with the Queens DA and turning state's evidence.

But what really stood out to Conor was the chain of events that had all occurred on the same day. Lawton's funeral. The announcement that Zeffri would face a new trial. An apparent sit-down at Coals. Zeffri whacked.

The sequence was as linear as it gets. All Conor had to do now was connect the dots.

Chapter Twenty-six

Conor stepped away from the crime scene and called Ralph.

"You've *got* to be kidding me," Ralph said when he heard the news.

"I wish I was."

Ralph sighed. "All right. Let's get on this early. Say six thirty."

"See you at six thirty," Conor replied. Just the thought of having to get out of bed in time to be at the precinct that early would keep him up all night.

In fact, he did have trouble sleeping. Of course, his prime suspect in a homicide had just become a victim of one. But that wasn't the only thing that kept him staring at the ceiling.

It occurred to him he missed being on a stage, playing music, singing, but there was no slumber-inducing solace in recalling that state of affairs. He had shortchanged his musical career by becoming a cop. Why hadn't he just hung tough, kept plugging away when he was twenty years younger? *Let's don't go there*, he told himself.

Holly Lawton.

Why did a part of him still find her so strangely alluring? She might be a murderer or an accomplice to murder. Yet there was something about her that stirred a desire in him. It was crazy. He knew it. But he couldn't deny it. The only rationale he could come up with was that maybe after meeting Monica, who offered real possibilities and to whom he was genuinely attracted, his sense of freedom was threatened. What better way to sabotage himself than with such a sexy co-saboteur like Holly?

Thinking back, he realized that every relationship he had ever embarked upon had emotional safety as its main appeal. Heather, for example. He knew from the beginning that it was a limited run. On the other hand, his attraction to Monica had the potential to become more perilous in the sense that he couldn't seem to look at her as merely a diversion. That bothered him.

Why was he so afraid of feeling something for her? After all, he hadn't really been hurt by anyone. Sure, he'd had his share of bad breakups, suffered the hollowness of rejection on more than one occasion, but the pain he had experienced probably had more to do with his ego than his emotions. He had *felt* heartbroken before, but his heart had never been broken. There was a huge difference. He recalled Kenny, a percussionist he hired once in a while, who was more in love than anyone he had ever seen. Sandra was his soul mate, Kenny often said, the best thing that ever happened to him. One day Sandra walked out and Kenny was in palpable agony for months. Hell, it had been six years and Kenny still walked around like the living dead. And what about Ralph? When he lost his beloved Laura, Ralph just shut down, the spirit sucked right out of him.

Conor rolled out of bed, walked to the kitchen, and poured himself half a water glass full of vodka, then headed into the living room and dropped onto the couch. What was the point of getting too close to someone when it was destined to end someday, one way or another? He decided to confront the question like he would a case, look at the evidence, start with the known facts.

He was forty-two. Never married. Oldest of three children. Now *there* was a clue. Oldest child. But how did that affect him? His father, a stone alcoholic, died of liver failure at age fifty-eight. And having an alcoholic father meant he had a father who was never really there, forcing Conor to pick up the slack at a very early age. So what? He had made out okay. But wasn't he sitting there with a water glass of vodka in his hand in the middle of the night? Was *that* okay?

Conor stared at the glass, then raised it in a toast. "Thanks, Dad."

Dredging up his parents was the easy way out. But no matter how hard he tried to affix the blame on them, he couldn't accept their complicity in his aversion to romantic commitment. There had to be something else.

How did he interact with women? He had been a football star in high school—a quintessential jock. Being the hero in a town where high school sports took on an exaggerated importance, girls were easy to come by.

Then what happened? He formed a band. Again, there was no scarcity of willing women. All he had to do was stroll backstage and they were waiting.

Okay, he wasn't Brett Favre or Bruce Springsteen. Didn't matter. He had been a big fish in a small pond, so the result was the same. The fact was, jocks and musicians attract women. And when you're eighteen or twenty-something or even thirty-something and there are beauties swarming around you, the last thing you want to do is settle for just one of them.

So somewhere along the line he had become a player. And what does a player do? Treats women like objects and then seeks out the object of least resistance. That observation led to another question. What does that kind of behavior do to the psyche?

Conor downed most of the vodka. A line from the Eagles song "Take It to the Limit" filled his head.

You can spend all your love making time.

Is that what he'd done? Spent all his love making time?

And then a line from another Eagles song, "Desperado."

These things that are pleasin' you can hurt you somehow.

He had avoided falling in love for so long, he had become afraid of it. The lyrics of "Walk Away from Love," a David Ruffin song he often performed on stage, came to mind.

This time I'm playin' it smart . . . I'm gonna walk away from love before love breaks my heart.

Conor took a deep breath. He had identified the problem. Granted, he hadn't come up with a solution but getting to the source of one's issues usually takes years of therapy. He had done it in ten minutes.

Forget Freud. Analysis by song lyrics is the path to mental health. He got up and poured another vodka. *Who needs a shrink? I'm fine.*

The alarm sounded at five thirty and Conor willed himself to get up. He made a pot of coffee, showered quickly, threw on his clothes, and found himself walking into the precinct at six fifteen. Ralph was already there. He held up a copy of the *New York Post*. There was a photo of a bloody Zeffri sprawled out on the kennel floor, cages of terrified dogs visible around him. The headline blared *Murdered Among the Mutts.*

"I can't believe they let somebody take that picture," Conor said.

"I can't believe they let somebody write that headline," Ralph countered.

"The media don't have a sense of decency." Conor sat behind his desk.

"Look on the bright side," Ralph pointed out. "Zeffri bought it in Queens. It's not our case."

"He's still our suspect. Especially after last night."

"How so?"

"I saw Holly Lawton."

"Again? This is getting to be a regular thing with you two. If I didn't know better, I'd be suspicious."

"She was having dinner at Coals," Conor said. "With a few friends of the family."

"I don't suppose you're talking about the Lawton family."

"No. I'm not."

Conor recounted the details of his rendezvous with Holly.

"Head of the table?" Ralph said when Conor had finished. "The seat of honor."

"I know. And for a woman to be at the head of the table . . ."

Ralph turned slowly and looked at Conor. "You know what I'm thinking?"

"Yeah," Conor replied. "Maybe Walter Lawton was more than a mob lawyer."

"Maybe," Ralph finally said, verbalizing what they both now suspected, "Walter Lawton was consigliere."

Chapter Twenty-seven

Amanda paced back and forth behind her desk, rubbing her temples as if she had a headache. Conor and Ralph shifted in their chairs.

"If there is even a hint that Lawton was mob connected," Amanda began, "other than as a defense lawyer, every single case he ever tried is going to be looked at, probably appealed, maybe even thrown out completely. And since you can't retry someone after an acquittal, unfortunately that little inconvenient thing called double jeopardy gets in the way, the only people who could conceivably be helped by a revelation like this are the scum who managed to lose even with Lawton at their side." She looked at Ralph. "When you start your new job, you want somebody to say to the DA, your boss, 'Oh yeah, this is Ralph Kurtz. He's the reason defense lawyers are lining up outside your door.'"

"You don't have to tell me about lawyers," Ralph said. "They're all vermin as far as I'm concerned."

"You know, Ralph," Conor teased, "the DA's a lawyer too."

"At least he's on the right side."

Amanda sat on the edge of her desk. "So why don't we keep this between us for now. We don't want to start a landslide that buries the Appellate Court."

Conor and Ralph nodded their assent.

"Good." Amanda looked at Conor. "By the way, Robert Willis, the guy you collared at that bar?"

"Yeah?"

"Pleaded not guilty."

"*What?* Eyewitnesses. Blood. DNA. Surveillance video. I've never seen a stronger case."

"What can I tell you? His lawyer—"

"Goddam lawyers," Ralph muttered.

"What's the deal on Mike Boyd?" Conor wanted to know.

"Nothing's changed. DA's taking the case in front of the grand jury next Wednesday. Murder one."

Conor sighed in frustration.

"You think he didn't do it?" Amanda said. "Then it's your responsibility to find out who did."

Yes, Conor thought, *it is*. Unfortunately, he was running out of time.

Conor and Ralph walked out of Amanda's office.

"A professional gun broker?" Conor said. "A dead wiseguy? Where does an amateur like Boyd fit in?"

They looked at each other and made a tacit decision. And then they strode out of the precinct like men on a mission.

Conor and Ralph entered an office with three desks. Ralph walked over and tapped one of them.

"This is where I'll be," he said.

Conor looked around the room, then stepped to the window, overlooking Centre Street. "Nice view."

"Yeah," Ralph said. His face grew somber, the reality of the move to the DA squad setting in.

"Sorry to keep you waiting." The voice belonged to Sharon Bocca, who swept into the room carrying an armload of files. An assistant district attorney, she was twenty-seven, just out of law school, had auburn hair and was attractive. She wore a conservative blue skirt with matching blouse and blazer. Her hair was tousled and she seemed to be having a rough day. "My caseload is ridiculous," she said as she dropped the files on one of the desks.

"Which one of you is Kurtz?" Sharon asked.

"That would be me," Ralph said.

"I understand you'll be joining us."

Ralph nodded.

"We finally got rid of him," Conor said.

"My partner, Conor Bard. Don't pay any attention to him."

Sharon's eyes wandered over Conor's body. She smiled. Conor smiled. *I haven't had a twenty-something in a while*, Conor thought as his libido switched into autopilot.

Ralph watched the mutual appreciation for a

moment, then: "So, Ms. Bocca . . . ," Ralph began.

"Michael Boyd," Sharon cut in, shifting back to work mode. She leaned over the desk and began searching for the right folder. She finally found it. "Here it is." She looked at Conor and Ralph. "I've been meaning to call you guys. But every time I reach for the phone—"

Sharon's cell phone began playing the *Sex and the City* theme. "See what I mean?" She hit the volume button to silence it. "So what's the deal? You got anything else on Boyd?"

"Nothing," Conor said.

"Nothing?" Sharon was alarmed. "We're taking this in front of the grand jury next week."

Conor played into her concern. "You don't think you have enough for an indictment?"

"For an indictment?" Sharon frowned, confused. "I *think* so. If I'm not mistaken, he was apprehended driving the guy's car. Right?"

"That's true," Ralph said. "But we have reason to believe he was not the shooter. Just at the wrong place at the wrong time."

Sharon sighed. "I wish somebody had told me this before."

"The thing is, Ms. Bocca," Conor interjected quickly, "we *are* going to be arresting someone in the murder of Walter Lawton, and it won't be Mike Boyd."

"It *won't*?" Sharon reacted as if she had been slapped.

"I'm sure you're very talented," Ralph said. "And I have no doubt you could push through an indictment with no problem. But . . ."

Ralph let the word *but* hang like a dark cloud.

Sharon was starting to panic. "But what?"

Ralph looked around to make sure no one was listening. "All I'm saying is, when we arrest the person who killed Lawton, you could wind up with egg on your face."

Ralph spoke like her father. Softly. A mix of wisdom and warning. "Which might have a negative impact on your career," he pointed out. "And we wouldn't want to see that happen to a bright young woman like yourself."

"So what should I do?"

"I'd start by giving Boyd a polygraph," Ralph suggested.

"Right," Sharon said. "We *were* going to do that." She flipped nervously through Boyd's file. "*Did* we do that?"

"Well, if you haven't, I'd do it right away," Ralph added.

"My guess is he'll pass," Conor said.

Sharon wrinkled her nose. "And if he does?"

"Get him to plead guilty to grand theft auto," Ralph replied, "in exchange for dropping the murder-one charge."

"And then?" Sharon wanted to know.

Conor smiled. "And then you'll have one less case."

* * *

Conor and Ralph headed back uptown. Ralph, as always, was driving.

"There's a lot I've got to fix when I get in that office," he huffed. "Young kids like that holding people's lives in their hands? Somebody's got to teach them a thing or two."

"And you're just the man for the job."

"Damn right, I am."

Once back at the precinct, Ralph made a beeline for the coffee machine. Conor sat at his desk. It was Friday. Ralph officially retired on Monday. Monica was flying back to Albania on Tuesday. Which meant he had to say goodbye to a partner of twelve years and attempt to sort out whatever he felt or didn't feel for Monica, all in the next three days.

Ralph returned with his coffee.

"Let's break this down to the lowest common denominator," Ralph said. "Salvatore Zeffri. Mob associate. Lawton's client. An affair with the wife. Now that he's dead, we've either got to nail him or clear him." He took a sip of coffee. "Or we could just let sleeping dogs lie."

"Very funny," Conor said, unamused. "What I think we need to do is get a court order, go to Zeffri's house, and take every pair of shoes he has out of the closet. Then compare the shoes with the prints left at the scene."

Conor started moving papers around on his cluttered desk.

"What are you looking for?" Ralph asked.

"The photographs of the shoe print impressions."

"They're at my house."

Conor looked up at Ralph.

"I told you," Ralph said. "I took them home the other night."

Conor remembered. "Oh, yeah. You did say that."

"I'll bring them in tomorrow."

"Or we could just call Brian and get another set."

"I'll bring them in tomorrow. Don't worry, no way a judge is going to give us a court order anytime today."

"And another thing we have to do," Conor said with conviction, "is call the Dirt Doctor. See if he's done with the soil analysis."

Ralph frowned. "Boy, you're on fire today, aren't you?"

"I want to close the case before you leave me here alone with this mess. You retire on Monday."

"Technically, today is my last day. But don't worry, I'm working right up until my party Monday night. Besides, when I go to the DA's office, you'll have my number. It's not like I'm going to the moon."

Ralph's phone rang. He picked it up. "Kurtz."

"Detective," the voice said. "We've got Fat Albert for you."

Chapter Twenty-eight

Two uniformed cops were waiting for Conor and Ralph inside Laszlo's Coffee Shop, an old-style luncheonette on Broadway and 157th Street.

"He's in the back," one of the officers said.

Conor looked down the length of the narrow room. Fat Albert was ensconced at a table near the kitchen door, which was swinging open and shut from the constant flow of waiters and busboys. A whale of a man around fifty, he had a shaved head, a neatly trimmed goatee, and a triple chin. He was, as might be expected, eating.

Conor and Ralph walked to the table.

"Albert?" Conor said.

Fat Albert looked up. "Yes?" He stuffed another forkful of something into his mouth.

"I'm Detective Bard. This is Detective Kurtz. We'd like to ask you a few questions."

Conor and Ralph sat across from Fat Albert, who chewed and stared at them. He swallowed. "About what?"

"About a gun," Ralph said.

"Shoot," Fat Albert replied, then burst into hysterical laughter. Rolls of fat jiggled from his spontaneous explosion of joviality. Even Conor and Ralph had to laugh.

A busboy swept past them and pushed into the kitchen. The door swung back and forth like a metronome marking time.

"We have reliable information that you purchased a weapon," Ralph said. "A twenty-two-caliber handgun."

"I do not recall," Fat Albert said, then wiped his mouth with a napkin.

"Let me refresh your memory," Conor said. "A year ago—"

"A year ago?" Fat Albert cut in. "I can't remember yesterday."

"That's too bad, Albert," Ralph said. "Because the problem is that someone got shot with this weapon. And we know it was in your hands at some point. So if you don't tell us what you did with it, we might start thinking you were the shooter."

Fat Albert was unimpressed. "Who did I kill?"

Conor was rapidly losing patience. "Look. My partner may be okay with playing this game but—"

"Good cop, bad cop?" Fat Albert yawned. "*Please*. Detectives. Give me a little credit, will you?"

"This particular gun killed somebody," Ralph said. "If you sold it . . ."

"So?" Fat Albert said, waving his arms. "If a car

salesman sells somebody a car and the car runs over somebody, you going to hassle the salesman?"

"Selling cars is legal," Conor said. "If you sold that gun, you committed a crime."

Fat Albert looked at Ralph. "Is he serious?"

Ralph looked at Conor. "Are you serious?"

"Dead serious," Conor replied.

Fat Albert stared at Conor and Ralph. "Look. I get it, okay? I *get* it. You're going to make my life miserable unless I spill my guts. But if I tell you I brokered an illegal firearm, you guys will have to lock me up. No choice, right? It's a felony. Then I have to get a lawyer to say you entrapped me or beat a confession out of me or never read me my rights or whatever works. I'll be back on the street in an hour but that's beside the point." He leaned over the table. "So how you want to play this?"

Conor and Ralph looked at each other. They both knew the options well. Lock up a gun dealer or trade off for information that could lead to a killer. Conor often wondered what people would think if they knew the reality of his job. It wasn't black and white, right or wrong. It was always the lesser of two evils. You never got anything without giving up something else.

Conor turned and faced Fat Albert. "You didn't happen to *hear* anything about a twenty-two-caliber gun being sold on the street last year, did you?"

"Now we're talking." Fat Albert smiled. "But I need more details."

"What do you want to know?" Conor asked.

"At least give me something to go on," Fat Albert said. "Your informant. The guy who falsely implicated me. Was he white? Black? Chinese? Indian? What?"

"Hispanic," Ralph said.

"Latino," Fat Albert corrected him. "You're not supposed to use the word *Hispanic* anymore. It's not PC."

"Sorry," Ralph said. "I'm not really a PC kind of guy."

Fat Albert began thinking out loud. "Latino . . . a lot of Latinos . . . twenty-two-caliber . . . not too many on the street . . . everybody wants cannons these days." A lightbulb went off behind his eyes. "You're not talking about that little gangbanger Conrado, are you?"

"What if we were?" Conor asked.

A waitress walked by. Fat Albert held up a finger to Conor and called out to her. "Hey, Nora, honey. Bring me my usual sandwich, will you?"

Nora nodded, headed into the kitchen. Back and forth went the door. Fat Albert looked at Conor and Ralph. "You want one? On me. It's really good. Made it up myself. Pastrami, roast beef, Swiss, a fried egg, bacon, coleslaw, tomato, slice of onion, on pumpernickel with plenty of mayo."

Conor stared at him. "The *gun*?"

"Right. The gun." Fat Albert rubbed his face with both hands. "The reason I remember it is because right after I bought—I mean, right after I *heard* somebody bought it off him—I read in the *Post* where they pinched Conrado for a holdup. Whoever bought it should've known right then the gun was trouble and should've just thrown it in the sewer." He slapped himself in the face. Hard. "So what I *hear* happened is that somebody put the twenty-two in a drawer, you know, to let it cool off. Then a couple weeks ago along comes some guy who's looking for a twenty-two and the dumb fuck who should have thrown the gun in the sewer *sells* him the gun."

"Who?" Conor asked.

"You want to know who bought the gun?" Fat Albert replied. "There are conditions."

"Like *what*?" Conor was annoyed.

"Let me put it this way," Fat Albert began. "If we're talking about the same gun, the guy who I *hear* bought it is not going to talk. No way."

Ralph smiled. "We'll see about that."

Fat Albert frowned. "What? You get Conrado to cry like a baby and now you think you're Eliot Ness? You probably told him that if he *didn't* cooperate you'd make it look like he *did* cooperate. Am I right?"

Ralph's face flushed. "Yeah, well . . ."

Fat Albert burst into another bout of uncontrollable laughter. "That's the oldest trick in the book. But that kind of crap won't work with this guy."

"Who are we talking about?" Conor pressed.

"I'll tell you what I *heard*," Fat Albert said. "But if you go straight to this guy and ask him about the gun, that could cause a problem for me. So all I'm asking you is: be creative. Rough him up about something else—parking ticket, jaywalking, spitting on the sidewalk, doesn't matter what it is—and *then* get around to the gun thing."

"We'll do our best," Conor said.

"Not good enough," Fat Albert fired back. "I want you to guarantee that no way this guy's ever going to know we had this conversation."

"Okay," Ralph said. "I personally guarantee it."

"I should believe you?" Fat Albert shook his head. "You gave up Conrado."

"We didn't give him up," Conor retorted.

"Exactly my point," Fat Albert said. "You let me figure it out. You have to be smarter with this guy than you were with me."

Conor smiled. "We'll try not to be so dumb next time."

Fat Albert looked toward the kitchen door. "What's happening with my sandwich?" He turned back toward Conor and Ralph. "You screw this up and I'm going to have to move to East L.A." He rolled his head around on his tree-trunk neck, working out a kink. "I could probably make a good living out there, but then again it's still L.A. Know what I'm saying?"

The kitchen door swung open. Nora exited with Fat Albert's monstrous sandwich. She placed it on the table.

"Thanks, honey," he said. Nora walked away.

"The guy you're looking for? His name is Bregu. A card-carrying member of A.M. The Albanian Mafia."

"Albanian, huh?" Ralph pointed toward Conor. "His girlfriend's Albanian."

"She's not my girlfriend," Conor protested.

"Bregu?" Ralph asked. "That a first name or last name?"

"How the hell should I know? Do I look Albanian to you?" Fat Albert leaned over the table. "The Albanians buy a lot of guns. Of course, the Italians aren't so shabby either. Anyway, the Albanians are ruthless. They make the Italians look like Boy Scouts. I'm fearless and they scare *me*." Fat Albert looked at Conor. "All due respect to your girlfriend."

"When was the last time you saw this guy, Bregu?" Ralph wanted to know.

"Me?" Fat Albert acted shocked. "I never saw him. I'm just telling you what I heard. I'm trying to cooperate here."

"Let me rephrase that," Ralph said.

"Please."

"When was the last time you *heard* he was in this neighborhood?"

"That's better." Fat Albert smiled. "I heard he comes around once in a while. Last time was two days ago. Looking for a Glock."

"Where can we locate him?" Ralph asked.

Fat Albert opened his arms. "Shouldn't be so hard to find him. How many Albanians can there be in New York?"

"That's what *I* was just wondering," Conor said.

"Somebody told me he was working at a garage in the Bronx," Fat Albert said. "Mundy's, Mendy's, something like that. Which is really a chop shop. But you guys are so smart, you probably already figured that out."

"Speaking of finding someone," Ralph said. "What's *your* address, Albert?"

"My address?" Fat Albert thought about it for a moment. "I just decided. Starting tomorrow, it's East L.A."

He picked up the mammoth sandwich, opened his jaws wide, and somehow managed to get it into his mouth. He closed his eyes in ecstasy, chewed slowly for a moment, swallowed, then looked at Ralph. "You oughta have one of these."

Ralph cleared his throat. "Yeah. Maybe I'll get one to go."

Chapter Twenty-nine

Ralph was driving. Conor was in the passenger seat, thinking he should have driven because Ralph was trying to steer and, at the same time, eat a Fat Albert special sandwich. Consequently, the car was taking a serpentine route down Broadway.

"Pull over," Conor said with a sigh. "I'll drive."

"You hate to drive," Ralph said as he chewed.

"I also hate to be DOA."

"Relax. I'll get us there in one piece."

Conor gave Ralph a look. "You had to get that sandwich, didn't you?"

Ralph took another bite. "It's unbelievable. You want some?"

"No, thanks."

"It's strange," Ralph said as he chewed.

"What's strange?"

"Albanians are everywhere all of a sudden."

"Seems that way," Conor said.

"You turn up with an Albanian girlfriend—"

"She's not my girlfriend."

"—and from what I hear, Albanians are taking over the restaurants."

"I know. When I was at Coals, the bartender was Albanian. And most of the other staff was Albanian."

Ralph thought about that for a moment. "Which is interesting because the Italians used to run all those joints. Now here come the Albanians. Either the Italians and the Albanians got something going on together or the Albanians are more dangerous than I thought."

Conor's cell phone rang. He answered it. "Bard."

"Yeah, Detective," the voice said. "It's DeBellis."

John DeBellis handled research at the precinct. If you needed a phone number or address, names of family members, places of employment, whatever, you went to DeBellis. Conor had asked him to do a run on the name Bregu.

"What'd you get?" Conor asked.

"Two Bregus," DeBellis said. "One named Fitim, the other Besnik. Besnik Bregu lives in Detroit. So I guess your guy is Fitim Bregu."

"What's his story?"

"Won the green-card lottery and immigrated in 1995. Moved around a lot since then. Last known address is 1578 Gerard Avenue."

"You run him through the database?"

"Nothing on Fitim Bregu. Clean as a whistle."

"What about the garage?"

"Closest match I found was Mandi's Auto Repair.

That's M-a-n-d-i-apostrophe-s. Located at 360 Grand Concourse."

"Thanks."

Conor hung up the phone and looked at Ralph. "He found two Bregus."

"Two Bregus? Sounds like a galactic currency."

"Turn around," Conor said. "We're going to the Bronx."

Conor and Ralph arrived at 1578 Gerard Avenue. It was a boarded-up six-story apartment building. A quick canvass of nearby shops and they learned that some developer had bought the property. A new high-rise was going up. Another piece of New York history was going down.

A visit to Mandi's Auto Repair wasn't any more fruitful. Mandi, a nervous little Albanian man, told Conor and Ralph that Fitim Bregu had not been there for a week.

Another trade-off, Conor thought. *Close down a chop shop or locate a murder suspect.*

"Don't worry, Mandi," Conor assured him. "Grand theft auto isn't our thing. We just want you to call us if he turns up."

As to where Fitim was living, Mandi said Fitim was staying with a cousin somewhere but he didn't know the address.

Conor and Ralph stopped by the precinct covering that area of the Bronx and gave the detectives there everything they had on Fitim Bregu. The detectives said they'd shake the trees, see if Fitim Bregu fell out. Then Conor and Ralph headed back downtown.

"The good news," Ralph said as he steered the car onto the West Side Highway, "is that he's Albanian. And you've got an Albanian girlfriend."

"I told you before. She's not my girlfriend."

"Whatever she is, maybe she can give us some insight into this guy."

"She doesn't know anything about people like Fitim Bregu."

Ralph reached down on the seat and retrieved his half-eaten sandwich. He took a bite. Pieces of tomato and pastrami fell into his lap. "I know a lot of Italians. *You* know a lot of Italians. I love Italians. I even wish I had been born in Italy."

"What's your point?"

"All groups have their boundaries. Now, I know *profiling* is a bad word these days, but I think I have an idea how far the Italians will go. Whether we're talking about a Mafia capo or the guy who landscaped my yard or the cop on the beat, they have this inner Italian thing going on. There's a line they won't cross no matter what. But I've never spent any time with an Albanian. So I have no idea where they draw the line."

"Ralph. She's a young woman. She works for a bank."

"We're grasping at straws here. Are we grasping

at straws or not? You never know what she might say that could help us."

Ralph was right. Cultural differences could be significant.

"I'm seeing her tomorrow," Conor said.

"How romantic," Ralph said. "But that's tomorrow. We're in the middle of a case here."

Chapter Thirty

The application for a warrant to search Zeffri's house went smoothly up until a judge decided he'd need to "take it under consideration." They would have to wait at least another day.

"The only people as bad as lawyers," Ralph said in disgust as they left the courthouse, "are judges."

"Judges are lawyers," Conor reminded him.

"Crocodiles, alligators, what's the difference?"

They stopped at the car. Ralph leaned on the hood. "So what's the connection between Bregu and Zeffri?"

"Bregu gave Zeffri the gun?"

"*Or*," Ralph said, "Bregu gave the gun to someone who gave the gun to someone *else* who gave the gun to the shooter? It's a hot potato. It was burning Bregu's hands somewhere along the line. Whether he used it himself and passed it along . . ." Ralph held up a finger. "*That* is the question."

"Should I call you Shakespeare?"

"You can call me William."

Ralph opened the car door. "Shakespeare had a point."

"About what?"

"About lawyers," Ralph replied. "The line he wrote in *Henry the Sixth*. 'The first thing we do, let's kill all the lawyers.'"

Conor was mildly surprised. "You been reading Shakespeare?"

"Had a lot of long nights the past two years."

At least they now had a timeline on the murder weapon: used in a robbery last year; purchased by Fitim Bregu a couple of weeks ago; fished out of the Hudson River on Tuesday. That's what they knew. What they needed to find out was whether Bregu passed the gun along or used it himself.

They climbed in the car. "There has to be a connection between Bregu and Zeffri. Or else Zeffri's not the shooter. Which means Bregu could be the shooter. But what's his motive?"

"Maybe he had one," Conor said. "The Maybach."

"Mandi's chop shop?"

"Right."

"But what about that kid Boyd?"

"Try this out," Conor offered. "Bregu was in the process of carjacking the Maybach. Takes Lawton into the empty lot to kill him. Along comes Boyd.

Sees a Maybach with the engine running. He jumps in, drives off."

"Double carjacking?"

"Why not?"

Ralph started the engine. "How many theories we going to have on this case?"

"As many as it takes," Conor replied.

Once back at the precinct, Conor called Monica.

"Hi, Conor," she said.

"You're not going to believe this," Conor began, "but my case has an Albanian connection all of a sudden."

There was no response.

"Monica?"

"Did you say an *Albanian* connection?"

"Yes. It's a long story. Look. I know you had something to do tonight—"

"I'm seeing my cousins in New Jersey."

"Yes. I know. You told me. But do you have some time before that? For a coffee? I'd just like to pick your brain about Albanians."

"Really?"

"And it gives me a good excuse to see you."

"I could switch my cousins to Sunday instead." Monica sounded eager.

"If you can, that would be great."

They made plans to meet at Pongsri, a small Thai place on Forty-eighth Street between Eighth Avenue and Broadway. Just as Conor hung up, Ralph walked in holding a photograph.

"This is what DeBellis pulled from INS. Bregu's green-card photo." He handed it to Conor. "I told DeBellis to circulate it to precincts in all five boroughs."

Conor studied Bregu's face for a moment. Black hair. Dark, close-set eyes. An emotionless expression. "We should send out an alert. In case he tries to leave the country."

"I already talked to the sergeant," Ralph said. "She's putting it in the works right now. Across the board. All federal agencies."

"Good." Conor gave the photo back to Ralph.

"You call your Albanian girlfriend?" Ralph asked.

"How many times I have to tell you—"

"I know, I know. She's not your girlfriend. Did you call her?"

"I'm seeing her tonight."

"Great. Where are we going?"

Conor frowned. "*We?*"

"Yeah. Can't wait to meet her. Besides, it's my last day on the job."

Conor frowned, hesitated. Ralph looked hurt. "What? You don't want to take your partner of twelve years to dinner on his last day?"

"You said you were working right up until the party."

"I am. But this is my last *official* day."

Conor was caught. "Sure. Why not."

Ralph slapped Conor's shoulder. "I'm just busting your chops. Won't be able to do that after Monday."

"Detective Bard."

A uniformed officer walked up to him.

"There's a Miss Lawton here to see you," the officer said.

Conor was surprised. "All right. Send her back."

The officer walked away.

Ralph frowned. "You *sure* there's nothing going on between you and the merry widow?"

"Didn't I tell you? We're having a wild fling."

"You wish."

"Detective Bard?"

They turned to see a woman walking toward them. She was in her late forties, petite, with strong facial features framed by short brown hair. Her eyes were puffy and red. She wore a blue pinstriped jacket and skirt, pale blue blouse. A diamond Rolex watch. Conor had a feeling he had seen her somewhere before but couldn't place her.

"I'm Detective Bard."

"Linda Lawton. Walter's sister."

Conor realized where he had seen her. He had caught a glimpse of her through the binoculars when they staked out Lawton's funeral.

"This is my partner, Detective Kurtz."

"Pleased to meet you," Ralph said.

"Holly told me you're in charge of the investigation into Walter's murder."

"Yes, we are," Conor said.

"Would you mind filling me in on where you are at this point?"

"Not at all."

Ralph motioned across the room. "Why don't we grab the conference room? We'll be more comfortable there."

They started walking.

"I'm sure this is a very difficult time for you," Ralph said.

"Yes. Very." Her face was etched with pain. "I was in Dubai when Holly called."

"Dubai?" Conor wondered why she'd been there.

"I have business interests in Dubai," Linda explained. "My mother had just arrived for a visit." She shook her head. "Twelve hours on a plane. It's not easy for a woman of eighty-one. And then to have to get right *back* on a plane . . ."

They reached the conference room, entered, and took seats at a table.

"Anyway," Linda said. "I got the call at ten in the morning Dubai time, one in the morning here. Got back to New York Tuesday. And my poor mother. Our father just died three months ago. And now? To lose a son . . ."

Linda looked down, her eyes filled with tears.

At least someone cares about Lawton, Conor thought.

"When was the last time you spoke with your brother?" Conor asked.

Linda took a breath, composed herself. "In fact, he called me the day he was killed."

Conor and Ralph leaned in, interested.

"It was midnight in Dubai," Linda continued, "which was three in the afternoon here. Walter was in the Hamptons." She smiled from the recollection. "He was there by himself and he sounded happy for a change. He was always happy when he wasn't with that greedy gold digger." Her jaw tightened. "Hearing about Walter was bad enough. But to get the news from *that* bitch . . ." She shook her head. "What a mistake marrying her. I was beside myself at the wedding."

"Did you ever voice your concerns to your brother?" Ralph asked. "About Holly?"

"Voice my concerns? I was a thorn in Walter's side. I tried everything I could to talk him out of it but he just wouldn't listen. He didn't want to see what everybody else around him saw. That she was a master manipulator, that she was marrying him for his money. At least I was able to convince him to execute an airtight prenuptial agreement. Thank God for that."

"Do you have a copy of that agreement?" Conor asked.

"No. But when I leave here I'm going over to the law firm. I'll get you a copy if you like."

"Just for the file," Ralph said. "If you don't mind." Linda nodded.

"Did your brother have a will?" Conor asked.

Linda smiled a thin smile. "He was a *lawyer*, Detective. Of course."

"Do you know what his intentions were?" Conor pressed. "With the will, I mean?"

Linda crossed her arms. "I haven't had a chance to review it. But I assume I am the beneficiary, along with my mother."

Clearly, Linda didn't want to discuss the details. She was rapidly adopting a defensive posture. Conor tried a different tack and cast himself as a sympathetic ally. "So Holly was not the best choice your brother could have made in a wife."

Linda uncrossed her arms. "*Please!* She was running around behind his back from the moment they tied the knot." She sighed sadly. "And the shame of it all is that Walter had finally figured out what a lying slut she really was. He was just about to file for divorce."

Holly left out that little detail, Conor thought as he leaned back in his chair. Then again, it wasn't in her best interest to say anything. "So when you spoke to your brother that day . . ."

"He was happy. Really upbeat. He told me he was heading into the city early. He had a dinner date."

Conor was interested. "A date?"

"Why not? At least he waited until the marriage was over."

"Did Holly know he was seeing other women?"

"A couple weeks ago she caught him having a drink with someone. According to Walter, the woman was just a friend. But Holly still created a big scene in the bar. Can you imagine? That cheating little whore having the gall to confront Walter in a public place?"

"Do you know who your brother was meeting last Sunday night?" Ralph asked. "Did he mention a name?"

"No. I'm sorry. But I *do* know one thing for sure."

"What's that, Miss Lawton?" Conor asked.

"Holly had something to do with Walter's murder. I'm certain of it. I hope you're looking at her."

"Oh, yeah," Ralph said as he exchanged a glance with Conor. "We're *looking* at her, all right."

Conor mulled over Linda's revelation that a divorce was in the works. Taken in the context of a murdered husband, a pending divorce was a sticky thing for a wife with a prenup. If the divorce was to proceed, a living, breathing, *lawyer* husband would be particularly inconvenient were Holly to contest the terms of the prenup in court as wives often do. And what if the prenup covered divorce but not demise? Then Holly had a clear shot at the estate pending probate of the will, which she could also contest.

Either way, it would be less troublesome for her without Walter sitting across a table, which provided a strong motive. And it swung the pendulum of guilt right back at Holly Lawton's lovely blond head.

But what if Holly had indeed manipulated Zeffri into gunning down her husband then convinced her mobster pals to dispense with her husband's killer? Could anyone possibly navigate the labyrinth of lies and find the one path that led to Holly Lawton's guilt?

Conor was suddenly struck with the notion that

he could have avoided all this. If he hadn't jumped off the stage at the Rhythm Bar and collared Robert Willis, he wouldn't have been at the precinct filling out a DD5, and he wouldn't have caught the case in the first place.

Next time, he told himself, *I'm finishing the song*.

Chapter Thirty-one

"**S**o Lawton had a date the night he died," Ralph said as he watched Linda leave the squad room. "We need to get his credit card receipts."

"We should have done that before," Conor retorted.

"I know. So why didn't you think of it?"

"Hey, you're the senior partner. You should've been all over that."

"Plus, we need to talk to the wife about the divorce and the prenup," Ralph said.

"Right. And I wonder how she feels about Zeffri being whacked." Conor reached for the phone.

"No," Ralph said. "Let's just take a ride over there. Catch her off guard."

Holly appeared at the door wearing full riding regalia—a short red jacket, a frilly ascot attached to her gallery-white blouse with a gold pin, and shiny black boots. She had a dark gray helmet tucked under her arm. But the pièce de résistance was the pair of tight-fitting cream-colored jodhpurs replete with a brown suede seat that accented that part of her exquisite anatomy. Not to mention the fact she was holding a whip in her hand.

"Good afternoon, Conor," Holly said, her voice warm and inviting.

Conor had seen women in all manner of dress and undress but the image of Holly standing there in that outfit was like nothing he had ever witnessed or even imagined—it seemed half real, half fantasy.

"Hello, Holly," he said.

Conor and Holly locked eyes. Ralph cleared his throat.

"Mrs. Lawton," Ralph said. "May we come in?"

Holly broke off her silent repartee with Conor, turned toward Ralph. "Of course, Detective. Please."

Holly led them through the house.

"I wish you had called," she said, shaking out her blond locks. "If I had known you were coming I would have had a chance to change."

Conor's eyes soaked up Holly's equestrian elegance. So incongruous in the middle of Manhattan. So unexpectedly alluring. *I'm glad we didn't call.*

They followed her into a large kitchen with a center island surrounded by bar stools. "I went for a ride in Central Park," Holly explained. "It's so relaxing to be up on a horse." The sexual connotation was barely concealed.

She motioned to the stools. "Please, have a seat."

Conor and Ralph sat down. Holly walked to a cabinet and opened it. "I'm going to have a tea. Would anyone like one?" She pulled a silver tea ball from the cabinet. "How about you, Conor? A tea?"

"No, thanks."

Holly removed more items and placed them on the counter. A can of loose tea. A china teapot. A miniature loaf of bread. She walked over and opened the refrigerator. "I usually have a small sandwich and some cakes at four o'clock."

Holly took out a brick of country pâté. "It's called high tea in England. And it's a good idea. That way I'm not so ravenous when I go out to dinner."

Conor watched Holly as she filled a kettle with water, placed it on the stove, then set about preparing her afternoon snack. *Horseback riding through the park? High tea? This woman is unbelievable.*

Ralph looked at Conor and opened his arms wide, palms up, as if to say *What the hell are we doing? We're here to question her. Not to attend a tea party.*

"Holly?" Conor said.

Holly, a mini piece of bread in her hand, looked up at Conor. "Yes, Conor?"

"We need to talk to you about something."

Holly placed the bread on the counter. "Okay."

Ralph, done with the gentle tone of the conversation, stepped in. "Did you hear about Salvatore Zeffri?"

Holly smiled. "*Murdered Among the Mutts*. I found that rather appropriate."

Conor was taken aback by her apparent lack of compassion for a man with whom she had shared a bed. Holly noticed his reaction. She tilted her head and looked at Conor.

"How am I supposed to feel, Conor? He killed Walter."

"How do you know that?" Ralph asked.

"I don't *know* that," Holly retorted. "But I'm sure he did. So Sal got what he deserved."

Ralph kept up the pressure. "You were having an affair with Mr. Zeffri, weren't you?"

Holly blushed slightly, something that Conor found fascinating. "I already told Conor. It was a mistake. A terrible mistake. And I will never forgive myself."

Ralph's frustration was evident. "Mrs. Lawton. From what we can tell, it is possible that Mr. Zeffri was the victim of a mob hit. Which is interesting since Detective Bard tells me that you had dinner last night with a table full of known Mafia associates."

Holly frowned. "Known Mafia associates? To me, they were Walter's clients showing their respect."

Conor watched Holly carefully. She was unflappable. A study in grace under fire.

Ralph was now beyond frustrated, he was annoyed. All his years of interrogation kicked in. "Did you know that the night your husband died, he had plans to meet a woman for dinner?"

"It doesn't surprise me," Holly said without rancor.

Ralph was relentless. "Maybe he took her to a place where you and your husband go all the time. That would be embarrassing, wouldn't it?"

"Yes," Holly said simply.

Conor was mesmerized by the tug-of-war between Ralph and Holly. He stayed out of it, wondering if Ralph would be able to get anywhere with her.

"You have any idea where your husband might have taken his lover?" Ralph's tone was now bordering on mean.

"No. I don't."

"We're in the process of getting his credit card records. So when we find out where he likes to wine and dine his female dinner companions, we'll let you know."

Holly laughed. Ralph frowned. "You find that funny, Mrs. Lawton?"

"Walter always paid cash in a restaurant."

"Why?"

"I really have no idea."

"Well, do you have any idea where he got all this cash?"

Holly twitched her nose, looked at Conor. "Conor, what is he getting at?"

Ralph refused to let up. "We understand you and your husband were about to get a divorce."

"Who told you that?" There was a sudden crack in her attitude. An almost imperceptible change but a change nonetheless.

"Is it true?" Ralph pressed.

Holly placed her hands on her hips. "Linda told you that, didn't she?"

Conor and Ralph didn't respond.

"Of course she did." Holly sighed. "Linda never liked me. I guess she thought I was taking her precious brother away from her, so she wouldn't give me a chance." She stared at Conor and Ralph. "She probably tried to implicate me in the death of my husband. Right?"

Holly turned her back on them and began filling the tea ball. Conor couldn't help himself. He stared at the suede seat of her jodhpurs.

"If you want to arrest me, at least let me call a lawyer."

"We're not here to arrest you," Conor said. "We're just trying to—"

"To accuse me of something horrible." Holly whipped around. "What do I have to do to make you understand that I had nothing to do with Walter's murder?"

Conor studied Holly. For the first time since he had met her, there was a hint of fear in her eyes.

"What do you want me to say?" she asked. "That I killed Walter?"

"We just want the truth," Ralph said.

Holly seemed to be unraveling. She walked over to the center island.

"I married Walter for his money."

Conor and Ralph were surprised to hear her admit that.

"You said you wanted the truth," Holly continued. "That's the truth."

She picked up a paper napkin and began twisting it in her hands.

"I had three skirts the whole time I was in high school. Every sweater I ever wore when I was a teenager was handed down. We never had any money when I was growing up. Never. I didn't go to college because my parents couldn't afford it and I wasn't smart enough to get a scholarship."

Holly stared off, swimming into the past. "Guys were always all over me. But I knew they didn't want *me*. They just wanted to fuck me. I got fired five different times from dumb jobs because I wouldn't screw the boss. And the one time when I *did* sleep with the owner of the company, he fired me anyway because his wife found out."

The paper napkin in Holly's hands was now in shreds. "So I was broke. Totally depressed by all that stuff." Her eyes misted. She swallowed hard. "Then along came Walter. He was so nice. He listened to me. Sent me flowers. Told me every single day how wonderful I was. Begged me to marry him. So I did."

Holly let go of the tattered napkin, picked up a knife, and cut a thin slice of pâté.

"But I was never in love with him. And you know what? I don't think Walter was in love with me, either. I mean, can someone *really* love me? What do I have to offer? I'm not that smart. I'm not witty. Or creative. Or *anything*. So what else is there? My *looks*? Maybe that's *all* I have."

Holly placed the knife on the counter.

"No, it wasn't love that brought Walter and me together, not even for him. He wanted a trophy wife. I wanted his money. We both got what we wanted."

The whistle on the kettle sounded. Holly ignored it.

"So, to answer your question, yes, Walter was planning to divorce me. And I told him I wouldn't ask for any more than what was in the prenup. Which is quite enough."

She walked to the stove and turned off the burner under the kettle. The whistle slowly faded.

"I get a ten-million-dollar lump-sum payment," Holly said as she walked back to the island. "And fifty-thousand-a-month maintenance for ten years, which is how long we were married. I will never be broke again. And I will never have to depend on a man for anything as long as I live."

Holly wiped a tear from her eye. "Now, if you're not going to arrest me, would you please leave?"

She glanced intensely at Conor for an instant, then quickly turned away.

Chapter Thirty-two

Conor and Ralph walked a block down the street without speaking, each of them wondering what to make of Holly's monologue.

"I've got to hand it to her," Ralph finally said. "That was one hell of a performance. She should get an Oscar." He laughed derisively. "'I'm not that smart.' You hear her say that? She said, 'I'm not that smart.' Believe me, that woman is as smart as they come."

They climbed into the car, Ralph behind the wheel.

"And *another* thing." There was an edge in Ralph's voice. "The way you two looked at each other when we got there? What was *that* about?"

Conor didn't offer an answer. He simply didn't have one that was rational.

"You were thinking with the wrong head," Ralph said.

"What can I say?" Conor replied.

"You can say you're not going to let some rich bitch cloud your judgment."

"I'm not going to let some rich bitch cloud my judgment," Conor said dutifully. "Let's change the subject, all right?"

"What do you want to talk about?"

"Dirt," Conor replied.

Conor and Ralph met Rugner in the lab where he had conducted the tests on the soil.

"The samples I collected from the crime scene have characteristics that are geologically common all along the river," Rugner said as he held up a test tube.

Conor and Ralph couldn't hide their disappointment.

Rugner waved the test tube. *"But!"* He paused like an infomercial host ready to say: But if you order *right now* . . .

"The samples from the crime scene contain trace chemicals that are unique to that particular site." Rugner cradled the test tube like a newborn baby. "My research has revealed that the area encompassing the crime scene was once used by the City of New York to store an experimental salt compound manufactured in Minnesota. The compound was intended as a snow-and-ice-melting agent designed to quickly clear the city streets. The ratio of sodium and—"

"In other words," Ralph interjected, "the soil at the scene is different."

Rugner was almost hyperventilating. There he was in the midst of a genuine homicide investigation with two flesh-and-blood detectives.

"Yes!" he shouted.

Conor and Ralph exited John Jay College and stopped in front of the building.

"So we've got salt that *only* comes from the scene," Conor observed. "That's good."

"Yeah. What are the odds? But if I had been standing in that muddy lot and shot Lawton, the first thing I'd do is get rid of my shoes."

"Criminals aren't that smart."

"Some of them are. The ones we never caught."

They began walking toward the precinct.

"What time you want to start tomorrow?" Ralph asked.

"Not too early."

"Oh, that's right. You've got a hot date. Me? I'll be home alone like always."

"Look. Ralph. I wasn't even supposed to see Monica until tomorrow. You're the one who pushed me to see her tonight."

"Which is because an Albanian suddenly popped up in the middle of our case. So your assignment is to get a crash course on all things Albanian."

"I got it. All things Albanian."

"Just remember that after your third martini."

"How do you know I'm going to have a third martini?"

"How do I know the sun's going to come up tomorrow?"

Conor was happy to arrive at Pongsri fifteen minutes early. The carved teak artwork hanging on the walls always had a soothing effect on him, inducing a certain serenity. After spending an evening there, Conor always vowed he would try to be more Zen about things. But then he'd walk out onto the city streets and would realize that achieving a meditative state in Manhattan required more than a mantra.

Tina, the manager, greeted him. She was Thai, petite, with classic features. As always, she was wearing traditional garb. Tonight she had chosen a red silk dress with a floral pattern.

"*Sawatdee kaa*," Tina said. It was the way women said hello in Thai.

"*Sawatdee khrab*," Conor replied, using the masculine form, *khrab* instead of *kaa*. It was also one of only two Thai expressions in his vocabulary.

"Are you by yourself?" Tina asked.

"I'm meeting someone."

"Man or woman?"

"Woman."

Tina smiled. "Then I'll give you the lucky table."

"Good. I'm going to need all the luck I can get."

Tina led Conor to a table in the back, just to the left of the service bar. It was the most private corner in the restaurant.

"The usual?" Tina asked.

"The usual," Conor replied.

Tina walked the few steps to the service bar. The bartender, a Thai woman, looked past Tina, waved at Conor, then pointed at the bar. There was a martini waiting.

"I saw Mr. Conor come in," she explained to Tina, who carried the martini to Conor.

"*Chai yo,*" he said, raising the glass. That was the other Thai expression he knew: cheers.

"*Chai yo,*" Tina said, then walked away.

Conor recapped the events of the day. A lot had happened, but he wondered if he was any closer to finding Lawton's killer than he was when he'd crawled out of bed that morning. In the middle of running down the list of possible suspects, he looked up and saw Monica entering the restaurant. As she made her way across the room, Conor imagined she was a Mediterranean princess sailing slowly toward him on an ocean breeze, which should have been the start of a romantic evening. But after a fleeting fascination with Monica's exotic appeal, the next thought that entered Conor's mind was *Can she help me find Fitim Bregu?*

Chapter Thirty-three

"**A**m I late?" Monica asked as she reached the table. Conor stood to greet her. "No. You're right on time."

He kissed her cheek. Monica pointed to her other cheek. "Two kisses. That's how we do it in Europe."

Conor smiled. "I don't mind that at all." He kissed her again. "You look beautiful tonight."

"Thank you."

She slipped off the dark gray canvas coat she was wearing to reveal a red V-neck top and black skirt. Neither was designed to be particularly sexy, rather casually elegant, but the way her curves filled the fabric evoked a certain understated sensuality.

Conor took her coat, laid it over a chair. They settled in at the table, across from each other. Monica smiled. Maybe it was his imagination but it seemed to Conor that she had warmed to him in the last two days. Or was it he who had allowed himself to edge into the warmth that had been there from the beginning?

"A glass of wine?" Conor asked.

"Yes, please."

Conor motioned toward Tina. She stepped over to the table.

"A glass of Monsoon Valley red, please," Conor said.

"One Monsoon Valley red," Tina repeated. She looked at Monica.

"This is Monica," Conor explained. "Monica, this is Tina."

"*Sawatdee kaa,*" Monica said, her voice rising and falling in perfect tonal Thai.

"*Sawatdee kaa,*" Tina said, then walked away.

Conor looked at Monica quizzically. "Don't tell me you speak Thai."

"Not a bit. When I joined the bank, they had us learn how to say *hello, thank you, please,* those kinds of things, in several different languages. Actually, I'd forgotten. So before I came here, I looked it up on the Web."

Conor found it interesting that Monica would take the time to relearn the Thai greeting. It wasn't a major effort, probably took her two minutes. But then again, little things reveal much more about someone than grandiose gestures.

"How was your day?" Conor asked.

"Busy," Monica replied. "I have to wrap up six months of work before I leave."

"I had a killer day myself," Conor said. "And like I told you on the phone, now there's an Albanian in the middle of my case."

A waiter delivered the Monsoon Valley red. Monica picked it up, held it toward Conor.

"*Chai yo,*" Monica said, beating Conor to the traditional Thai toast.

Conor raised his martini glass. "*Chai yo.*"

They touched glasses.

"It doesn't surprise me there might be an Albanian involved," Monica said sadly. "There are so many desperate people leaving Albania for a better life. Unfortunately, desperate people do desperate things."

Conor found Monica's compassion admirable, but because they had come from such disparate backgrounds, the way she felt was perhaps beyond his understanding. He was more cynical, less forgiving. Bad people do bad things. *Desperate* bad people do even worse things.

"A lot of immigrants had problems when they first came to America," Conor allowed. "The Italians, the Irish. Things will change for Albanians, too."

"I hope so," Monica said.

Tina approached the table. "Are you ready to order?"

Conor was happy that Tina appeared at that moment. It gave him time to decide just how much he should tell Monica about the case. On the one hand, it was an open investigation. On the other, if he had any hope of finding Fitim Bregu or gaining any significant edge in solving Lawton's murder, he would probably need to tell her most of what he knew.

"May I order for you?" Conor asked Monica.

"Sure."

"We'll start with shrimp dumplings," Conor said. "Then a Pad Prik-Yolk with pork. And a chicken with red curry."

Tina walked away to fill the order.

"I'm not supposed to eat pork," Monica said.

"Oh. I'm sorry." Conor scanned the room for Tina.

"No. It's all right. I love pork. I was just saying, as a Muslim, I'm not supposed to eat pork."

Religion had never come up. Hearing Monica say she was Muslim seemed an incongruous proclamation. She looked Mediterranean, sounded European. Of course, not all Muslims were Arabs, but given headlines these days, it was easy to forget that.

"I'm not a practicing Muslim," Monica explained. "It was forced on us by the Turks in the fifteenth century. As a matter of fact, I've never even been inside a mosque. And most of my ancestors are Catholic." She looked at Conor. "How about you? I take it you're not Muslim."

Conor laughed. "No. Not exactly." He glanced up at a teak carving hanging on the wall. "I'm thinking about becoming a Buddhist."

"You're kidding."

"Yes. I'm kidding. I'm Christian. But I haven't been to church since I was nine. Except for midnight mass at Holy Cross."

"So you're Catholic?"

"No. I'm Protestant. I go to midnight mass

because Father Peter is a friend of mine. And because it's Christmas Eve."

"Okay. We got religion out of the way. Now, what about the Albanian connection in your case?"

"I don't want to bore you with details, but—"

"You won't bore me," Monica insisted. "All I've watched on television since I got here is *FBI Files*, *The First 48*, Dominick Dunne's *Power, Privilege and Justice*. Dominick Dunne is my favorite. I love the narrator." She sat up straight, made a serious face, and tried to mimic the voice-over. "But then, police found the one piece of evidence that could put the suspect behind bars forever. And it was a *shocking* discovery."

"Not a bad impression."

"But that's what I mean. Everything is *shocking*. *Shocking* evidence. *Shocking* confession. *Shocking* revelation. No way you can turn those shows off when you hear something like that."

"Well," Conor said, "I hate to tell you this, but the reality of police work is not so earth-shattering. It's pretty mundane."

"Oh, come on, Conor," Monica said as she leaned over the table. "Tell me something *shocking*."

Chapter Thirty-four

Conor pondered where to begin and how he could tell Monica enough to elicit useful information while keeping the details at a minimum.

"One of our suspects is a man named Fitim Bregu," Conor finally said.

There was a glint of recognition in Monica's eyes. Conor frowned. "You *know* him?"

"No," Monica replied. "I don't know a Fitim Bregu, but there was a Bregu family in Shkodra. Near where I grew up. I wouldn't say it's a common name, but there are quite a few Bregus living in Albania."

"Well, there's at least one Bregu living in New York right now. From what I've been able to find out, he works at an auto repair place in the Bronx."

"There's an Albanian community up there," Monica noted. "It's where my brother-in-law and niece have their apartment."

"Unfortunately, the last known address for Fitim

Bregu is a boarded-up building on Gerard Avenue. And so far, we can't find a phone number listed in his name."

"He's probably staying with a relative. If he has a cell phone, it's in the name of a relative too. Family is important to Albanians. Everybody stays in touch."

Conor realized that finding Bregu was going to be much more difficult than he thought. Bregu had an entire extended family in America in which to find refuge. How many cousins? How many different last names?

"Albanians are coming to this country without a plan," Monica continued. "Fitim Bregu? You're looking for a shadow. And, like a shadow, if you shine a light on him, he will disappear."

A shadow in America. That was a good way to put it. With no verifiable address or phone, Bregu was virtually a nonperson. Funny, Conor thought, how numbers determined who a person was. Street numbers, phone numbers, credit card numbers, Social Security numbers. At least Bregu had a green-card number.

"If I wanted to find someone like Fitim Bregu, how would I go about it?" Conor asked.

"Albanians are very social. I know my brother-in-law likes to hang out at a restaurant called Gurra Café on Arthur Avenue. There are a lot of places like that in the Bronx, where Albanians congregate. Find Fitim Bregu? I wouldn't know where to begin.

Unless . . ." Monica squinted her eyes, concentrated on something.

"Unless what?"

"He might be a member of a *besa* club."

"Besa?" Conor was confused. "Isn't that your sister's name?"

"Yes. It's a popular name in Albania. When used as a name, it means 'faith.'"

"Yes. You told me that before."

"But it's also a word that translates into English as 'trust' or 'honor.' It's in the Kanun a lot. What it really means is 'to keep the promise.' And to be a man of *besa* is to command respect. My father considers himself a man of *besa*. Which is why he chose to name his first daughter Besa."

"You know," Conor said, "the more I hear about the Kanun and now *besa*, the more it sounds like the Italian Mafia."

"They're similar," Monica replied. "Men who are bound together by a common belief. In Sicily, La Cosa Nostra was originally created by native Sicilians to protect themselves from conquering armies. The same with *besa*."

"You said Bregu might be a member of a *besa* club?"

"There are *besa* clubs all over north Albania. And there's an Albanian club in the Bronx called Besa." Monica paused, thought for a moment. "*Shqiptarët vdesin dhe besën nuk e shkelin*. Which translates as 'Albanians would rather die than break *besa*.' Or they say, *Shqiptari kur jep fjalën therr djalën.* 'An Albanian can sacrifice his own son for besa.' His own *son*? That's the *besa* mentality. In the north, where respect is valued above all else, *besa* is practically a religion."

Respect. How many times had Conor heard that word spew out of the mouth of an Italian mobster or a black or Latino gang member as a justification for murder? The *besa* lead was definitely worth following up. He had already circulated Fitim Bregu's photo. Now he would call detectives in the Bronx and ask them to check out the Besa club connection.

The shrimp dumplings arrived.

"Just put it in the middle," Conor said.

The waiter set a plate and small bowl on the table then walked away. Conor pointed at the bowl. "That's plum sauce. You dip the dumpling in it."

Monica picked up a fork, speared a dumpling, dipped it in the plum sauce, then took a bite. "Mmmm. That's really good."

"What's the first thing you're going to do when you get back to Albania?" Conor asked.

"Sleep," Monica said with a sigh. "This last week at the bank was crazy. I'm totally exhausted."

Conor decided he had spent too much time talking about work so they spent dinner discussing tourism in Albania. The nightlife in Tirana. The beaches in the south. Conor found himself planning a trip in his head.

"We still on for tomorrow?" Monica asked as a busboy cleared the table.

"Absolutely."

"I'm looking forward to it."

Conor could see that Monica was tired, and by mentioning their date the next night, she was signaling an end to the evening.

"What time is it?" Monica asked.

Conor checked his watch. "Ten fifteen."

Monica reached over and took Conor's hand. "I don't want to go but I think I should. Get a good night's rest."

Conor looked toward Tina and motioned for the check. Monica picked up her pocketbook. "This is on me."

"Absolutely not."

"Please, Conor. I want to take you out tonight."

"I can't let you do that."

"What? A woman can't take you to dinner?" Monica frowned. "You've been reading the Kanun, haven't you?"

Conor laughed. "All right. Just this once."

Monica paid the check. They walked outside onto Forty-eighth Street.

"At least let me take you home."

"Not tonight," Monica said apologetically. "Tomorrow night you can take me home, okay?"

"Okay," Conor said.

Conor raised his hand. A taxi slowed to a stop. He opened the back door. Monica put her arms around his waist and kissed him. *Not* on the cheek. It was a tender kiss, filled more with promise than passion.

"Good night, Conor."

"Good night, Monica."

Monica slid inside the taxi and, in an instant, she was gone. Conor missed her immediately. And for the first time he could remember, he felt very much alone.

Chapter Thirty-five

Conor entered his apartment and sat in front of his computer. He Googled the Besa club and got the address: 400 East 198th Street. Then he searched the Web for the Gurra Café. It was located at 2325 Arthur Avenue. He mapped the addresses and discovered they were both near Fordham University, twelve blocks from each other. That would be the 47th Precinct. He stood and walked to the refrigerator where he had a card with all the precinct phone numbers attached to the door with an NYPD insignia magnet. He dialed the number for the 47th Precinct and, after being transferred around a few times, he finally got a detective named Gersh on the phone. Conor explained that he'd like someone to stake out both places and anywhere else that was a popular watering hole for Albanians.

"We sent a photo of Bregu to all precincts in the city," Conor said. "It was marked 'unusual.'"

Tagging something "unusual" was the way NYPD

made sure it didn't get thrown into some in-box of ordinary paperwork.

"Yeah," Gersh replied. "I remember seeing it."

"I appreciate this," Conor said.

"No problem."

"Let me know if Bregu surfaces."

"Will do. And you can call me here all day tomorrow. Got two guys out sick and one on vacation. Pulling a double."

"Yeah. I know how *that* is."

Conor hung up and went straight to bed. He slept well. Too well. He woke up late. Ten fifteen. He blasted through a shower and headed to the precinct.

When Conor arrived, Amanda was waiting for him. She was holding several sheets of paper.

"You working Saturdays now?" Conor asked.

"Saturdays, Sundays, Mondays, what's the difference?" She handed him the sheets of paper. "Lawton's credit card records."

"That was fast."

"I know the head of the fraud department at Visa, American Express, MasterCard . . ." Amanda paused for effect. "*And* Discover."

"Thanks."

"You're welcome. So maybe you'll take me to dinner sometime."

"Anytime."

"Just keep your hands to yourself."

"I'll try."

Amanda walked away. Conor sat at his desk and

went over the listing of Lawton's charges. The night of his murder, nothing. Not a single purchase anywhere. He tossed the credit card records on his desk.

"What's that?"

Conor turned to see Ralph walking up to him.

"Lawton's credit card records," Conor replied.

"And?"

"And nothing. If he had dinner with someone, he didn't pay with a credit card."

"Like the wife said. Always paid cash in a restaurant."

Conor frowned. "I mean, he could deduct dinners as a business expense. Wouldn't it be easier to document the transaction using plastic?"

"Maybe he was so rich, he didn't care about the tax break."

"Or had cash he didn't want to report to the IRS."

"Or maybe he didn't want his whereabouts being tracked." Ralph dropped into a chair behind his desk. "So how'd you make out last night?"

"I had a nice time."

"I'm happy for you."

"As far as the Albanian crash course, there wasn't much she was able to tell me. About the only thing worth checking out is a club called Besa."

"Besa?"

Before Conor could explain, Amanda walked back into the room. "I just got a call from Judge Harrison's clerk. Your warrant to search Salvatore Zeffri's premises is ready."

"Excellent," Ralph said.

They both stood and headed toward the door.

"You bring the photos of the shoe prints?" Conor asked.

"Damn!" Ralph sighed. "I put them out on the table so I wouldn't forget them."

"All right. Never mind. Brian can get us another set."

Brian and the Crime Scene Unit were outside Zeffri's house when Conor and Ralph arrived.

"Hey, Brian," Conor said. "What's up?"

"There's a little problem," Brian replied.

Suddenly, a small man, no more than five feet four inches tall, around seventy-five, ran from the house.

"Bastards!" he shouted in a thick Italian accent. "Get offa my son's property!"

"His name is Patrizio Zeffri," Brian said. "Salvatore's father."

Conor looked at Ralph. "You want to take this?"

Ralph walked toward Patrizio. "Mr. Zeffri?"

"*Va fa un culo!*" Patrizio screamed, waving his arms like a wounded duck.

"Mr. Zeffri," Ralph said. "I'm sorry. I know you lost your son. But we have a warrant. And—"

"My son did nothing! Why you do this? You have no respect for my dead boy."

Conor motioned to Brian and the three members of the Crime Scene Unit. "Let's go."

As the entourage headed for the house, Patrizio turned to go after them. Ralph blocked his path.

"Mr. Zeffri," Ralph said, careful not to be too confrontational. "We have to do this. Please."

Once inside the house, Conor looked at Brian. "We need all the shoes. And while you're at it, take the suits and jackets."

Brian reached into the closet and picked up a shoe. He frowned. Conor noticed.

"What's the matter?" Conor asked.

"Size nine. B width."

"So?"

"So there were no size nine men's shoes at the scene."

"You sure?"

"Positive. I did a statistical analysis of the shoe prints. See, most men wear between a size ten and twelve. C width. Women run from six to nine. You find a print that fits those parameters, you're looking at eighty, eighty-five percent of the population. Men's size nine? Small shoe like that would've caught my attention."

Conor sighed. Did that mean Zeffri wasn't the shooter?

"What do you want to do?" Brian asked.

"Take the shoes anyway. Check for soil residue."

Brian shrugged. "Hey, that's your call."

Forty-five minutes later Brian and his unit drove away. Conor walked up to Ralph, who was standing next to the car. Patrizio was in the backseat, staring blankly out the window.

"How'd you calm him down?" Conor asked.

"I didn't. He just started crying. So I put him in the car."

"Poor guy," Conor said.

"Yeah, well, you lose a child . . ."

Ralph open the back door of the car. "Mr. Zeffri?"

Patrizio just sat there.

"Mr. Zeffri?" Ralph repeated.

Patrizio slowly climbed out of the car, walked to the house without a word, then disappeared inside.

"So what's the story on the shoes?" Ralph asked.

"Not too promising."

"What do you mean?"

"According to Brian, they're not a match."

"So Sal may not be our guy?"

"Brian said to meet him back at his office in two hours. We'll see what the situation is then."

Ralph checked his watch. "Want to have lunch?"

"Yeah. Why not? Where you want to go?"

They climbed into the car, Ralph, as usual, behind the wheel.

"You know what I have a craving for?" Ralph said.

"What's that?"

"One of those sandwiches."

"What sandwiches?"

"You know. That sandwich we had uptown."

"Where uptown?"

"*Uptown*," Ralph said as if Conor should know where he meant. "With Fat Albert."

Conor was incredulous. "You want to go all the way up there just for a sandwich?"

"It's a great sandwich. Besides, maybe we can lean on Fat Albert a little more while we're at it."

Conor and Ralph entered Laszlo's Coffee Shop. Nora greeted them at the door and led them to a table.

"You guys were in here yesterday," Nora recalled. "Sat in the back with Fat Albert."

"Fat Albert been in here today?" Conor wanted to know.

"Yeah," Nora said. "You just missed him."

"He coming back?" Ralph asked.

"No."

"You sound sure of that," Conor said.

"He's moving to L.A.," Nora explained. "He stopped by and gave me five hundred dollars. Real nice thing to do. Said it was for all the times I waited on him." She looked away, seemingly remembering every day Fat Albert took a table. "I'm going to miss that big fat guy." She looked at Conor and Ralph. "I'm a little worried about him."

"Why's that?" Conor asked.

"He looked scared," Nora said. "Kept staring at the door. I've never seen Fat Albert scared of anything."

Conor remembered what Fat Albert had said. *The Albanians are ruthless. They make the Italians look like Boy Scouts. I'm fearless and they scare* me.

The possibility of Fitim Bregu seeking revenge had frightened Fat Albert enough to skip town. So who *was* Bregu? Obviously not someone to be taken lightly. And now that it appeared Zeffri may not have been the shooter, Bregu, a man who once held the murder weapon in his hands, was beginning to look more and more like a killer.

Conor reached in his jacket pocket and produced the green-card photograph of Fitim Bregu. He held it so Nora could see it.

"Have you seen this man?" Conor asked.

Nora took Bregu's photo and studied it for a long moment, then handed it back to Conor.

"No," she said, "I'm sorry. I've never seen him before." She started to walk away. "I'll be right back with menus."

Ralph called after her. "I don't need a menu. Just bring me one of those Fat Albert special sandwiches."

Nora looked at Conor. "You want one too?"

"I'll have a tuna on rye."

Nora pushed through the swinging door into the kitchen.

Conor stared at the photo of Bregu. "We really need to find this guy."

"I'm with you on that. As soon as I get my sandwich, we're out of here."

Chapter Thirty-six

Conor and Ralph walked into the 47th Precinct. The place was filled with the usual suspects. Pimps. Prostitutes. Drug dealers. Gang members. A cacophony of voices fought to be heard.

Conor looked at Ralph's chest. "You've got coleslaw on your shirt."

Ralph flicked off the coleslaw. "Believe it or not, I could eat another one of those."

They located Detective Richard Gersh and followed him to a small office just off the squad room. Gersh was slightly built, over sixty, nearing retirement. He wore a cheap brown polyester-blend suit and a lime green tie which was knotted too short, the point of it hitting him five or six inches above his belt line.

"So I sent a dozen guys out last night looking for your suspect, Fitim Bregu," Gersh said. "They came up empty."

"You have anything local on him?" Conor asked.

"Nothing. Not even a parking ticket. Which doesn't mean he's an innocent bystander. More like we haven't caught him yet."

Gersh sat behind his desk. Conor and Ralph pulled up two chairs.

"Albanian crime is way up," Gersh was eager to point out. "Twenty years ago, I wouldn't even know what you meant if you said Albanian. Nowadays, these crazy bastards are all over the place."

"They haven't hit Midtown yet," Ralph pointed out.

"Don't worry, they will." Gersh leaned back in his chair. "Just like the Westies did a few years back."

"The Irish wound up doing the dirty work for the Italians," Ralph observed. "The killing, the collections, the enforcement."

"But *now*," Gersh said, gesturing with his hands, "the rules have changed. The Albanians are not only in business for themselves, they're shaking down the *Italians*. *That* takes balls." Gersh folded his arms. "Let me tell you a story. A couple months ago, the Albanians decided they liked this restaurant over on Jerome Avenue. This little Italian joint. So you know what they did? They moved in. Took over the place."

Ralph shrugged. "Everybody loves pasta."

Gersh continued. "Of course, the neighborhood capo wasn't too happy about that. So he demanded a sit-down. The Albanians say, 'Okay. Meet us at the gas station around the corner from the restaurant.' The capo shows up with an army. Guess who's there to meet him? Two Albanians. Two guys. That's all.

Can you believe it? So the capo says, 'Stay the fuck out of my restaurant.' And the Albanian says, 'It's our restaurant now. *You* stay the fuck out.' Well, the capo just smiles, waves his hand around the parking lot at all his soldiers surrounding the gas station, and says to the Albanian, 'I don't think you understand who you're dealing with.' The Albanian pulls out a gun, points it at a gas pump, and says, 'No, *you're* the one who doesn't understand who you're dealing with. If you and your crew aren't out of here in ten seconds, I'm going to blow up this whole fucking block.'"

"So what happened?" Conor asked.

"The capo and his crew got the hell out of there. And now that little restaurant is controlled by the Albanians." Gersh leaned in on Conor to emphasize what he was about to say. "I've been on the job up here thirty-eight years and I have never seen anybody as vicious as the Albanians. They don't have boundaries. And they're not above killing cops. Even the Sicilians wouldn't do *that*."

Conor and Ralph exited the precinct and stopped at the car. Ralph stood next to the driver's side and swallowed, made a face.

"I don't feel so hot," Ralph said.

"Why don't you have another sandwich?" Conor teased.

"You mind driving?"

Conor walked to the driver's side and got behind

the wheel. Ralph dropped like a dead weight into the passenger seat.

"Stop at Duane Reade, will you?" Ralph said. "I think I need an antacid."

Brian was waiting for them in his office. He looked at Ralph's face, which was drained of color and dotted with beads of sweat. "You don't look so good. You all right?"

"He ate a Fat Albert special," Conor explained.

"What's that?"

"You don't want to know," Conor said. "So where are we with the shoes?"

"Plenty of dog doo-doo," Brian said. "And I sent soil samples over to the Dirt Doctor at John Jay. But I'm ninety-nine percent certain the residue on these shoes will not match the characteristics of the samples from the scene. Zeffri wears size nine, B width, and there were no impressions that size in the lot by the river. Now, I don't want to step on your toes . . ."

Brian laughed. Conor and Ralph didn't.

"That was a joke," Brian said. "Get it? Shoe prints? Step on your toes? Anyway, what I was going to say was, unless Salvatore Zeffri knew how to levitate, no way I can place him at the scene." Brian tapped a loose-leaf binder of shoe-print photos that was lying open on his desk. "We haven't talked about women's shoes."

"Women's shoes?" Conor frowned.

Ralph looked at Conor. "Sorry. I know how fond of the wife you are." Ralph turned toward Brian. "My partner here thinks the wife is innocent."

"I *know* she's not innocent," Conor said. "Whether she killed her husband is another thing."

Brian leafed through pages. "Let's see. Size six Nike tennis shoe. And here's a size eight casual shoe that's been identified as being manufactured by Nine West." He flipped a page. "Size six and a half Steve Madden flat shoe." He turned another page. "But this one's interesting." Brian rotated the photo so Conor and Ralph could see it. "Size seven high heel. Not your average dog-walking shoe. In a muddy field, the point of the heel's going to sink right in."

Conor rubbed the back of his neck. "A woman comes home from a night out, dog's going crazy, maybe she doesn't bother to change shoes."

"Could be," Brian said. "But if your shooter *was* a woman, wearing *these* shoes, there are two other problems."

"Like what?" Ralph asked.

"Well, first of all, there's no sole pattern, so identifying a manufacturer is almost impossible. I *could* take the exact measurement of the sole, right down to a millimeter, and then compare that with all women's shoes on the market. That could take weeks and we still might not ID the shoe."

Conor studied the photo of the shoe impression. "You said two problems."

"That's a size seven medium width," Brian

explained. "Forty-six percent of the women in America wear that size."

"So we're nowhere with that shoe," Ralph said.

"Not necessarily." Brian pointed at the page. "There are unique signs of wear on the sole. You know, you step on a pebble, a piece of glass, a nail, whatever, it makes a mark. So if you bring me the actual shoe, I can match it to this print."

Ralph looked at Conor. "Your mistress wouldn't be dumb enough to hang on to a pair of muddy shoes."

"I don't think so," Conor agreed.

"Mistress?" Brian was confused.

"In his mind," Ralph said.

Brian shrugged, flipped through the book. "Now, I told you before, any size outside of normal parameters narrows things down. Not much. But it takes us into a smaller segment of the population. Doesn't mean he or she is the shooter. Just means that if you have a suspect who wears an unusual shoe size, and that shoe size is at the scene, you could make a stronger case."

Brian found the photo he was looking for. "Right here. Size thirteen, triple-E width. That's a big, wide shoe."

They all looked at the photo. Then, slowly, all six eyes wandered down to Ralph's feet.

"That's my size," Ralph said. "I feel sorry for the guy. These are really hard to find."

Conor was well aware of Ralph's disdain for lawyers. In fact, every observation Ralph made about lawyers during the Lawton case was tinged with disgust.

When Lawton turned up dead by the river. *A dead lawyer? What's the big deal? You know how I feel about lawyers.*

When they met the young woman attorney at Lawton's office. *She's a lawyer. What do you expect?*

When Zeffri remarked that Lawton's death was a terrible tragedy, Ralph had said, *Not so terrible.*

When Anatoli Sidorov told them he was planning to appeal his conviction. *We bust our ass, risk our lives, then some mook with a law degree in his hand puts these scum back on the street. And you wonder why I can't stand lawyers.*

And the capper, when Ralph quoted Shakespeare: *The first thing we do, let's kill all the lawyers.*

Ralph frowned at Conor and Brian, who were still staring at his shoes.

"What are you guys thinking?"

Conor looked at Ralph. "You have the right to remain silent. Anything you say can and *will* be held against you in a court of law."

Chapter Thirty-seven

"**Y**ou have the right to an attorney," Conor continued. "If you can't afford an attorney—"

"Attorney?" Ralph frowned at Conor. "Are you *crazy*?"

"What's the matter, Ralph?" Conor pressed. "You don't like lawyers?"

"I hate lawyers."

"That's right! You hate lawyers. A lawyer winds up dead. Your footprints are next to his body."

"Not *my* footprints."

"Oh, *really*?" Brian added accusingly. "My research indicates that less than one percent of the population wears that size. And they're all cops."

Conor and Brian began to laugh.

"Not funny," Ralph said.

"All kidding aside," Brian said, "where *do* you buy your shoes?"

"They're hard to find," Ralph replied. "Usually I get them on the Internet. But there are a few places that stock them. A store down on Church Street has them sometimes. Rochester Big and Tall on Sixth Avenue. Harry's Shoes up on Broadway."

Conor and Ralph decided to start with places in closest proximity to the crime scene then work their way outward. But Rochester Big & Tall, which was only a few blocks from where Lawton was killed, wasn't much help. Being more of a clothing store than a shoe store, the salesman didn't recall anyone who had purchased a size 13 triple E, although he did offer to research recent shoe sales.

Conor and Ralph headed up Broadway to Harry's. Conor was driving. They weren't speaking.

"You look better," Conor finally said.

"I can't believe you even thought something like that," Ralph groused. "You really thought that for a minute. Admit it."

"No, Ralph. I honestly didn't. I'm sure there's another guy in New York who wears size thirteen triple E." Conor feigned concern. "At least I hope so. For your sake."

"You're a real pal, you know that?"

"All right," Conor said. "Let's be serious."

"Please."

"Looks like we have to start thinking about eliminating Zeffri as a suspect," Conor noted. "*You*, on the other hand . . ."

Ralph smiled sarcastically. Conor had a good laugh.

* * *

They parked the car in front of Harry's, on Broadway and Eighty-third Street.

"Wouldn't it be something if Bregu wears a size thirteen triple E?" Conor said as they climbed out of the car and walked toward the shoe store. "That would get you off the hook."

"You're loving this, aren't you?"

"Yes, I am."

"So what if I really *did* kill Lawton? I bet that would wipe the grin off your face."

"Did you?"

"Yes. I killed the son of a bitch."

Conor patted Ralph on the shoulder. "Don't worry. Just get yourself a good lawyer and you can plead it down to jaywalking."

Ralph sneered. They entered Harry's and were immediately approached by Larry the shoe sales-man.

"Detective," Larry said with a fake smile. "How are you?"

"Just wonderful, Larry," Ralph replied.

"What are we looking for today?" Larry asked, his goofy smile plastered to his face.

"A killer," Ralph said.

Larry continued to smile, even though he wasn't sure if he had heard Ralph correctly.

"What color?" Larry asked, his smile intact.

"Black," Ralph said. "Or white. Or Hispanic. Indian. Chinese. Doesn't matter."

"Lace-up or slip-on?" Larry asked, still smiling.

Conor leaned in on him. "We're not looking for shoes, Larry."

"Oh," was all Larry could say. His smile faded.

"You know my size," Ralph said.

"Thirteen triple E," Larry answered without hesitation.

"Who else buys thirteen triple E?" Conor asked.

"Not too many people," Larry pointed out.

"We're glad to hear that," Conor said. "Now, what we need is a list of people who buy thirteen triple E."

"It's a short list," Larry said.

"That's good news," Ralph observed.

"I know who buys thirteen triple E," Larry beamed. "In this store, I'm the expert on big feet."

Conor stifled a laugh. Ralph gritted his teeth.

"There's Mr. Andrews," Larry said. "And there's Mr. Leslie. And Mr. Naskret." Larry frowned. "I think that's it."

"You sure?" Conor asked.

Larry nodded. "Mr. Andrews was just here yesterday. Very nice man. He comes in with his dog."

Conor reacted. "He has a dog?"

"Yes. An English bulldog."

Conor and Ralph found Donald Andrews working at a Chase bank on Columbus Avenue and Seventy-second Street. He was a broad man, not fat but wide. He was neatly dressed in a charcoal pinstriped suit accented by a red tie, and he was wearing highly polished black shoes. Size thirteen triple E.

"Yes," Andrews said. "I walk Euro there almost every night."

"Your dog's name is Euro?" Ralph asked.

"That's right," Andrews replied. "Because he's more valuable than dollars."

Conor and Ralph exchanged a glance. *He's definitely a banker.*

"I live on Fifty-second Street," Andrews explained, "so I like to take Euro down to the empty lot on Forty-third sometimes and let him run."

"How about last Sunday?" Conor wanted to know.

"Last Sunday?" Andrews repeated as they crossed the lobby of the bank. "Are you talking about the night that lawyer was killed?"

"Yes," Ralph said.

"I was there last Sunday," Andrews said. "I was walking Euro." Andrews puffed out his cheeks and exhaled audibly. "I couldn't believe it when I woke up and read the paper. I got chills. I could have been a witness to a murder."

"Were you?" Conor pressed.

"No. And thank God I wasn't."

"What time did you walk Euro?" Ralph asked.

"Eight thirty. I always walk Euro at eight thirty."

Conor's cell phone rang. He checked the caller ID. The number was unfamiliar. He answered the phone. "Bard."

"Detective Bard. It's Linda Lawton."

"Hello, Miss Lawton."

Conor held up a hand. *Be right back*. He drifted a few feet away from Ralph and Andrews.

"I need to see you right away," Linda said.

"Okay. What time?"

"As soon as possible."

"What's this about, Miss Lawton?"

"Please, Detective. It's urgent."

"Where are you?"

"I'm at the Sherry-Netherland Hotel. Just tell the concierge you're there to see me, and they'll direct you to my suite."

"All right, Miss Lawton. We'll be there in a few minutes."

Conor snapped his phone shut and walked back to Ralph and Andrews. Ralph looked at Conor. "Mr. Andrews was just telling me he had a young lady visit him at nine o'clock on Sunday. They were together until midnight."

"And the young lady will confirm this?" Conor asked Andrews.

"Yes," Andrews said, his eyes darting.

"Erotic Elegance Escorts," Ralph added. "Mr. Andrews paid with a credit card."

"I don't usually do things like that," Andrews insisted, both fear and embarrassment evident on his face. "Am I in trouble?" He stared down at his feet. So did Ralph.

"Nice shoes," Ralph said.

*   *   *

Conor and Ralph exited the bank.

"The wife called you?" Ralph asked.

"No," Conor replied. "That was the sister."

"What's wrong with me?" Ralph said mockingly. "I should have realized it was the sister. You and the wife are on a first-name basis."

Conor and Ralph arrived at the Sherry-Netherland, on the corner of Fifth Avenue and Fifty-ninth Street. They took the elevator up to the tenth floor and knocked on the door of the corner suite where the concierge said Linda Lawton was staying. The door opened quickly, as if Linda had been standing just inside. She was dolled up: designer dress, full complement of jewelry. Obviously she had been somewhere that required making an impression.

"Come in," Linda said. She stood aside so they could enter.

The place was opulent. A wall of windows overlooked the majesty that was Central Park.

"I can't believe Walter could be so careless." Linda sighed. She remained standing in the foyer. "It's like the shoemaker's children who go without shoes."

"Miss Lawton," Conor said. "You want to tell us what you're talking about?"

Linda was stricken. "The *will*. We had the reading of the will this morning."

"Was it what you expected?" Conor asked.

"No," Linda almost shrieked. "Walter never

changed his will. He prepared the divorce papers but he *never changed his will.*" She placed her hand on her forehead. "He was the best lawyer in the world but when it came to his own estate, he was totally negligent."

"What did the will say?" Ralph wanted to know.

Linda slammed the door shut. "That bitch is getting two hundred million dollars."

Conor and Ralph looked at each other. *No wonder she's pissed off.*

Chapter Thirty-eight

L inda walked into the living room of the suite. Conor and Ralph followed. Conor looked around. It would take a week's salary, maybe more, just to pay for one night in the place. Another reminder that the rich were different.

"I've been in meetings all day at Walter's law firm," Linda said. "No way she's getting a dime from the estate."

Another thing Linda had been doing all day was drinking. She picked up a glass of something on the rocks. Dark amber in color. Scotch or bourbon. Although the way she downed it, it wouldn't have mattered what it was.

"Miss Lawton," Conor said. "I can see you're upset. And I understand. But may I ask why you wanted to see us?"

"*Why?*" Linda was jumping out of her skin. "Don't you see? When Holly found out Walter was about to divorce her, she killed him before he had a chance to change the will."

CHARLES KIPPS

"Do you have any evidence to support this?" Ralph asked.

"Evidence?" Linda threw her hands in the air. "It's so clear what happened."

"Your sister-in-law does appear to have a motive," Conor said. "But without supporting evidence, there's nothing we can do."

"Well, there's something *I* can do," Linda said. "I've got a team of lawyers filing motions with the probate court. My position is that Walter's wishes were clear when he prepared the divorce papers. If that blond piece of shit gets anything at all, it will be over my dead body." She walked up close to Conor. "She didn't even come to the reading of the will this morning. You know why? Because she already knew what it said. She knew Walter hadn't changed it. She *knew*. And now she's sitting in my brother's house waiting for the check to arrive. That gold-digging bitch! Well, she won't be sitting there much longer, because I'm going to get a court order and throw her in the street." Linda tightened her lips, clenched her fists. "I'll kill that whore with my own hands before I'll let her lavish away two hundred million dollars of Walter's hard-earned money."

Conor and Ralph were happy to escape Linda's suite. They walked toward the car.

"How much you think that place costs a night?" Ralph wondered aloud.

"I don't know, but I'm pretty sure neither of us will be staying there anytime soon."

They turned the corner onto Fifty-ninth Street.

"The question is," Ralph said, "why do people kill?"

"Jealousy. Revenge. Money."

"The wife knows her husband is cheating, puts on her little size-seven stilettos, blows him away, and collects two hundred million dollars. That covers all three motives."

"I can't picture her shooting somebody."

"You *are* thinking with the wrong head."

"I'm not saying she didn't have anything to do with it," Conor protested. "All I'm saying is that she doesn't seem the type to look somebody in the eye and pull a trigger. And besides, if she *did* shoot her husband, what were they doing standing in the middle of a muddy lot? How did they get there? What made him pull over? Seems to me the only way he parks the car on the side of the highway and walks to the river is at gunpoint."

Ralph shrugged. "The wife pulls a gun from her purse. Orders Lawton to stop the car. Takes him to the lot. *Bam!* One dead lawyer, two hundred million dead presidents."

"So what do we do now? Clean out Holly Lawton's closet? Like you said, if she *was* the shooter, she's too smart to hang on to the shoes."

"And we know she didn't hang on to the gun either." Ralph laughed. "Remember that line in *The Godfather*? 'Leave the gun, take the cannolis.'"

"So what about the weapon?" Conor wondered aloud. "We know it was in Fitim Bregu's hands at one point. How did it find its way to Holly Lawton?"

Ralph thought about Conor's question for a moment.

"The wife is well known at Coals Steak House, right?"

Conor nodded.

"More than well known," Ralph added. "They treat her like a Mafia princess."

Conor nodded again.

"And most of the staff at Coals are what?" Ralph asked, already knowing the answer.

"Albanian."

"Bregu is what?"

"Albanian."

"So let me ask you this. If Holly Lawton really wanted a gun, who would she ask? Why not an Albanian waiter? Or she could ask one of her husband's clients, who might then go to *his* source, who just happens to be an Albanian by the name of Bregu."

They stopped at the car, Ralph on the driver's side, Conor by the passenger door. Ralph looked over the roof at Conor.

"Now, I don't know if the wife really did any of this," Ralph said. "But I do know one thing. Whoever did it was holding that twenty-two. So we follow the gun." He looked at his watch. It was four thirty. "You know what? I think I'm going to head home. Nothing else we can do today anyway. Unless you can think of something." They climbed in the car. "What are *you* up to tonight?"

"I'm getting together with Monica. It's the last chance I'll have to see her before she leaves on Tuesday."

Ralph started the engine.

"You taking her somewhere nice?"

"Actually, we're going to Coals."

"Good boy."

"It's a date, Ralph. It's not about the case."

"You're a cop, kid. It's always about the case."

Conor entered the precinct and sat at his desk. He placed a blank piece of paper in front of him and picked up a pen. He scribbled *Walter Lawton* in the center then wrote *Holly* on the lower left corner of the paper and *Zeffri* on the lower right. He drew a line from Lawton to Holly, another line from Lawton to Zeffri, and finally a line between Holly and Zeffri. He studied the triangle for a moment, then added the words *Mafia*, *Albanians*, *murder weapon*, and *Bregu*.

More lines. Mafia to Zeffri. Mafia to Lawton. Bregu to Zeffri. Bregu to Mafia. Albanians to Bregu. Mafia to Albanians. Even Mafia to Holly. His hand pushed the pen along frenetically. Murder weapon to Bregu. Albanians to murder weapon. Murder weapon to Mafia. He stopped and stared at the crisscrossing connections. If he was ever going to unravel this tangled web of intersecting relationships, tonight was his best shot. He was on his way to the location where both murders, Zeffri's and Lawton's, may very well have been planned. He would need to remain vigilant, watch the tables closely for subtle signs of a sit-down in progress. Eyes might betray a hint of guilt, pursed lips could whisper an unspoken confession.

Conor was forced to admit Ralph was right. It's always about the case. Which was why he wasn't onstage at the Rhythm Bar. And why, later that night, he would likely squander a chance at having a life.

Romantic dinner with Monica? Forget about it.

Chapter Thirty-nine

Conor went home, showered, and dragged out his best suit, the one he never wore on the job. Italian-made, charcoal gray, it had been an expensive fortieth birthday present to himself. *Might as well look good when you start over the hill.* As he dressed, he realized he had worn the suit only twice in the past two years: when he celebrated that birthday with Heather, and when he attended a dinner hosted by the mayor at Gracie Mansion a few months ago. He had been invited by Victoria, a willowy brunette who worked in the New York City public relations department. They had a lusty little fling that lasted a couple weeks.

Conor pulled a red silk tie from the closet. Also Italian-made. He knotted it around the collar of his white shirt then checked himself in the mirror. Not bad. Gray, white, red. A nice combination. He had read somewhere that a man looks his best in solid colors.

* * *

Conor walked into Coals at seven fifteen, arriving forty-five minutes before he was to meet Monica. But he had an agenda. He wanted to sit at the bar and talk to Lirim, hoping that the bartender could shed some light on Fitim Bregu. Conor was well aware of the desperation inherent in such a thought, but these were desperate days. He had reached a point where the case would either be solved or boxed up and relegated to a warehouse full of abandoned investigations.

There were a few patrons at the bar. Lirim was busy at the service end filling a stream of drink orders flowing from the dining room. Conor took a seat near him and watched his hands moving deftly at hyperspeed. Pouring, mixing, shaking, stirring.

"Be with you in a minute," Lirim said, glancing at Conor then resuming his bartender's ballet. He popped the cap on a bottle of beer and placed it on a tray full of other libations. A waiter scooped up the tray and took off at a fast clip. Lirim stepped over to Conor.

"Good evening, Detective," Lirim said. "How are you doing tonight?"

"Not bad. You?"

"I haven't stopped moving since five thirty."

"Busy night, huh?"

"I told you. Saturdays are crazy. Dining room's packed. So I've got to fill *those* orders." Lirim motioned toward the half-full bar. "And I've got a few people now, but wait till eight thirty. Then it really gets interesting." He looked at Conor. "Where's your Albanian girlfriend?"

"She's on her way."

"Ketel One martini, straight up with a twist. Right?"

"You got it."

Lirim walked away to make the martini. Conor found it interesting that Lirim remembered what he drank. How many drinks had he served since Conor had last been there? Then again, how many cops sat at the bar?

As he waited for Lirim to put the finishing touches on the martini, Conor convinced himself that the Albanian community in New York was very small and Lirim could very well know something about Bregu. *It wouldn't be such a stretch if Lirim had at least heard of him*, Conor told himself.

Lirim stepped over and placed the martini in front of Conor.

"Cheers," he said.

Conor picked up the glass. "How do you say cheers in Albanian?"

"*Gezuar*," Lirim replied.

"*Gezuar*," Conor repeated. He took a sip. "Great. Now I can say cheers in seven languages."

"A useful word. But now you are with an Albanian woman, you must learn more of *her* language." Lirim leaned over the bar. "*Të dua*."

"*Të dua*," Conor said.

A waiter stopped at the service bar, looked at Conor, and frowned.

"What did I just say?" Conor asked.

"You told me you loved me."

Conor smiled. "Well, you *are* a very attractive man."

"I know. I get that all the time."

"Two gin and tonic," the waiter said, unamused.

"But the most important word you must know is *po*," Lirim said as he set about making the drinks.

"*Po*? What does that mean?"

"It means 'yes.'"

"I don't suppose I need to learn the Albanian word for no."

"*Jo*," Lirim said.

"*Jo?*"

"Never use it. It can cause big trouble. Just say *po* all the time no matter what she says. You understand?"

"*Po*."

They shared a knowing laugh. Lirim placed two gin and tonics on the waiter's tray. The waiter rushed into the dining room.

Conor seized upon their newfound camaraderie. "You wouldn't happen to know someone named Fitim Bregu, would you?" He was careful to keep his voice down.

Lirim wiped his hands with a towel and stepped back over to Conor.

"Sure," Lirim said. He glanced toward the people at the end of the bar, who didn't seem to be paying attention to their conversation. "The mechanic."

I'm definitely hiring bartenders as private investigators, Conor thought.

"If you know how to reach him," Conor said, "that would be very helpful."

"Why do you want to talk to him?" Lirim asked, suddenly suspicious.

Conor contemplated his response. If he wanted Lirim's help, he'd have to be careful.

"Actually," Conor said, "my car's been running a little rough lately. I think I might need a tune-up."

Lirim studied Conor for a long moment. They locked eyes. Conor could see that Lirim understood it wasn't about a car.

"We keep his number in the book in case anyone needs a mechanic," Lirim finally said. "You want me to get it for you?"

"*Po,*" Conor said.

Lirim hesitated for a moment, checked the bar patrons, then opened a large black address book on a shelf behind him. He leafed through it, found the number, then wrote it down on a notepad. He tore off the page and handed it to Conor.

"Fitim is a very good mechanic," Lirim said. "I'm sure he can fix your car."

They exchanged a glance, a tacit promise from Conor that no one would know where he got the number.

"How do you say thank you in Albanian?" Conor asked.

"*Faleminderit.*"

"*Faleminderit,*" Conor said as he stared at the piece of paper. 917-555-5240. He couldn't believe he had Fitim Bregu's number in his hands.

"Do you know him?" Conor asked.

"Not really. I've seen him a few times when he came to jump-start somebody's car or whatever he did. And he comes in for dinner once in a while. He sat at the bar the other night. First time I actually talked with him."

Conor frowned. "The other night?"

"Yes," Lirim said. "Let's see . . . it was Wednesday."

Wednesday night? *Where was I Wednesday night?* Then Conor remembered he had had dinner with Monica at Maria Pia. The next night, Thursday, was when Holly had asked him to meet her at Coals. The restaurant wasn't even on his radar until Holly had called. Which began to trouble Conor. Had it not been for Holly, Coals would not have been a place the investigation would have necessarily taken him. So if Holly had something to do with either the murder of her husband or the rubout of Zeffri, why would she have led him to a place where the plan may have been conceived? Was she that diabolical?

"Excuse me a minute," Conor said. He stood and walked out of the restaurant, moved half a block away from the entrance, and dialed Bregu's number. It went straight to voice mail.

"Hello, this is Fitim. Leave a message."

Conor hung up then speed-dialed the precinct.

"Eighteenth Precinct," an officer answered.

"Yeah. This is Detective Bard. Who's on duty tonight?"

"You mean . . ."

"I mean a sergeant."

"Sergeant Pitts is here," the officer said. "Would you like to speak with her?"

"*Po*— I mean, yes."

Conor was put on hold. Good old Amanda. Always ready to serve.

"Bard," Amanda said. "What's up?"

"I need you to run a number, a cell phone. It could be Lawton's killer."

"All right. What's the number?"

"917-555-5240."

"917-555-5240," Amanda repeated.

"That's it," Conor confirmed.

"Don't worry," Amanda assured him. "I know all the fraud guys at the phone companies."

"You know everybody, don't you?"

"Some of them biblically."

"That's too much information."

"Okay. I'll get back to you."

Conor hung up and walked back inside to the bar. The group that was sitting there had apparently gone in to dinner, leaving the bar momentarily empty. Lirim had made a fresh martini.

"Nothing worse than a warm martini," Lirim said. "*Faleminderit.*"

Lirim smiled. "You speak very well Albanian."

"*Faleminderit,*" Conor said again.

"You reach Fitim?" Lirim wanted to know.

"No."

"I'm thinking you'd rather he didn't know you were looking for him," Lirim said.

"You speak very well English." Conor took a card out of his pocket and handed it to Lirim. "Call me if he comes in again."

Conor detected uncertainty in Lirim's eyes. Which might mean that Lirim would have second thoughts in the event that Bregu wandered into the restaurant.

"Let's just say I'm a man of *besa*," Conor added.

Lirim raised his eyebrows. "You know about *besa*?"

"I know what it means. It means that if you see Fitim Bregu and call me, no way anyone knows. Nothing about you goes into the paperwork."

Lirim nodded, seemingly satisfied. Another waiter arrived at the service bar. Lirim turned, more drink orders to fill.

Conor felt two hands glide around his waist and soft tresses of perfumed hair fall onto the back of his neck. *Monica?* But when Conor turned, it was not Monica with her arms wrapped around him. Instead, he found himself staring into the lovely blue eyes of Holly Lawton.

Chapter Forty

"Hello, Conor," Holly said, her arms still around his waist.

"Hello, Holly."

She looked at him and smiled. "I can't hate you, Conor. I know you were just doing your job. So I forgive you for making those nasty accusations about me."

Conor twisted all the way around on the bar stool. Holly repositioned her arms accordingly. They were now face-to-face, chest against breast, lips inches apart. She was wearing the Manhattan ladies'-night-out uniform: a little black dress. Although Conor was no fashionista, it seemed the hemline was a little shorter and the neckline a little lower than the classic women's evening attire was supposed to be.

"I don't think I accused you of anything," Conor said.

"No, actually you didn't. It was that other detective who wasn't very nice."

"I'll have to speak to him about his attitude."

"What are you doing here, Conor?"

"I'm meeting someone."

"Someone?" She played with a strand of her hair. "You mean a woman?"

"Yes."

"That's too bad. I'm having dinner with a girl-friend. You could have joined us."

"Another time, maybe." At this point Conor wasn't even sure what he was saying. With Holly pressed up against him like she was, it wasn't easy to think.

"I didn't know you liked Coals," Holly said. "But who doesn't? The steaks are the best in town."

"I wouldn't know. I've never eaten here before."

"Never?" Holly's voice rose as if to say *That's impossible. Everybody eats at Coals.*

Holly looked at Lirim. "Isn't that cute, Lirim? A Coals virgin."

Lirim smiled weakly, clearly uncomfortable that Walter Lawton's wife was wrapped around a man so soon after her husband's death. So was Conor, especially in this place. He could feel eyes all over him. Curious eyes, angry eyes, jealous eyes. But what could he do? Holly was immediately in front of him, her arms on either side, the bar against his back.

She looked at Lirim. "The drink's on me." She raised her right arm and pointed at the martini. Conor used the opportunity to slide off the stool and stand. He quickly checked his watch. Quarter to eight. Fifteen minutes before Monica would arrive.

"Would you like a drink?" Conor asked, motioning to a bar stool. He actually did want her to stay for a moment. There was that little issue of the will—two hundred million little issues in fact. He had been planning to contact Holly anyway, follow up on what Linda Lawton had told him, so why not now?

Holly sat down. Conor took the stool next to her.

"What would you like?" he asked.

"Lirim knows."

"Mrs. Lawton always has a cosmopolitan before dinner," Lirim informed Conor as he walked away.

Holly took Conor's hand. She couldn't keep from touching him.

"I really meant it when I said I wanted to take you out sometime," she said.

"I appreciate the invitation, but with the case ongoing—"

"I knew you were going to say that." Holly pulled her hand away from his, a girlish pout forming on her lips. "If you really believe I had nothing to do with what happened to Walter, what's wrong with us having dinner?"

Conor wasn't sure how to respond. He almost said *Okay, so you didn't kill your husband. Did you kill your lover?*

"You *do* have doubts about me," Holly said. "Don't you?" She sighed. "Linda told you about the will, didn't she?"

Conor looked at Holly. *She's incredible.* Any piece of incriminating evidence he could find and she's first out of the gate with it. Conor replayed that thought in his mind. *First out of the gate? A horse-racing analogy? Jesus! I'm becoming Ralph.*

"Yes, she did," Holly said, her pout still intact. "I can tell by your eyes."

"According to Linda Lawton, you stand to inherit—"

"Two hundred million dollars," she cut in.

"Is that true?"

Holly crossed her legs, smiled. "Yes."

Lirim appeared with the cosmopolitan. He placed it in front of Holly without a word then quickly withdrew.

Conor got right to the point. "Your sister-in-law thinks that isn't what your husband wanted to happen in the event of his death. She says your husband never got around to changing his will."

Holly lifted her glass. "Cheers."

Conor followed suit. "Cheers."

They clinked glasses, took sips.

"Walter was divorcing me. So what do *you* think? You think he really wanted to leave me two hundred million dollars?"

"No. I don't."

"Neither do I," Holly said, her tone matter-of-fact. "He was probably planning to cut me out completely."

Conor almost smiled. There she went again, right out front with anything that might make her look guilty or give her a motive.

"So the theory is what? I knew Walter hadn't rewritten his will so I killed him before he could make any changes?"

It was obvious to Conor that Holly was toying with him. Pirouetting around the edges of the case, dancing just out of reach. *Catch me if you can*, she seemed to be saying.

"That's what everybody's thinking," Holly said. "Isn't it?" She placed a finger against her lips. "Is that what *you* think, Conor? That Walter and I were out to dinner and on the way home I pulled a gun from my purse, forced him to stop the car, walked him into that empty lot, and then shot him six times?"

This woman is good, Conor thought.

"Did you kill your husband?" he asked.

Holly's pout returned. She made a face.

"I had to ask," Conor said.

Holly adjusted the hem of her dress, which had crept upward, pulling it toward her knee as if to signal that Conor's chance of getting under it was diminishing with each question.

His eyes moved from the hem down to her high heels. "By the way, what size shoes do you wear?"

Conor knew that Holly knew why he wanted to know.

"Why?" she asked. She slowly pushed a stray strand of hair from her forehead. "Are you thinking about buying me a present?"

Conor frowned. "I don't think I could afford to on my salary."

"Well, just in case you get a raise, they're size seven medium. Try Christian Louboutin. You can't go wrong."

"I'll keep that in mind."

Holly leaned over and probed Conor's eyes. "Seriously, Conor." She raised her leg high, pointing her toes at the bar. "Can you picture me stomping through a field in shoes like these?"

But Conor's eyes weren't on the shoe. There was another view that caught his attention.

"Conor!" She lowered her leg and put her hands on her hips.

"No, actually I can't," he said.

She took his hand again. "So when are we having dinner?"

"Soon," Conor said, playing along. "But in the meantime, can we clear up a few things?"

Holly sighed, rolled her eyes. "If you must."

"Your sister-in-law said she intends to challenge the will in court."

"Wouldn't you?"

"Yes. I guess I would."

"So there's no surprise, right?" Holly took a sip of her cosmopolitan. "What am I going to do about the will? Is that your question?"

Behind Holly, a woman walked toward them. She had brown shoulder-length hair, intense dark eyes, her presumably perfect body hidden under a white cashmere coat.

"Holly," she said as she stopped next to them.

"Susie." She motioned to Conor. "This is Conor. He's a detective. He's investigating Walter's murder."

Conor stood, faced Susie.

"Nice to meet you," he managed.

"Nice to meet you, too," Susie said. She extended an exquisite offering of five slender fingers which glided slowly into Conor's palm. Her touch was so delicate that he felt a tingling sensation dancing up his arm. She slowly withdrew her hand and slipped out of her cashmere coat, tossing it off her shoulders, revealing a little black dress almost identical to the one Holly was wearing. Of course they couldn't be identical, not on these two. Different designers for sure.

"Where can I check my coat?" Susie asked.

"By the front door," Holly answered.

Susie gave Conor a come-hither look, then turned and walked away.

"Susie is beautiful," Holly said. "Don't you think?"

"Yes, she is," Conor said, staring at Susie while she checked her coat. He couldn't help himself. Autopilot had kicked in again.

"Conor," Holly said, saying his name like she was aching to have him.

Conor turned back toward the bar.

Holly's pout made an appearance again. "What are you going to do, Conor? Suspect me of murder for the rest of my life?" She reached over and stroked his hair. "I hope not. Because I think we could have a really good time together."

Holly stood, stepped in front of Conor, wrapped her arms around his waist.

"I've had wealthy men," she said. "And I was always so unhappy. Even though you probably look at me as some rich bitch, I'm just a simple girl who has paid her dues. I'm finally ready to be with someone because I *want* to, not because I have to or because they have money."

Or because they're trying to lock you up for murder, Conor thought.

"We could be so good for each other," Holly continued. "We could balance each other. We could—"

In one swift motion, she pressed herself into him, kissed him like she really meant it. It happened so fast, Conor didn't have time to resist. As Holly's lips devoured his, he thought of how insane this was. A murder suspect coming on to a detective in her late husband's favorite haunt. Yet Conor found himself totally immersed in her kiss, his senses heightened, his eyes closed. Had he completely lost his mind?

Conor's grasp on reality returned with a jolt, his bizarre lapse in judgment finally over. He opened his eyes.

Monica was standing there.

First Heather. Now Holly. What the hell was he supposed to tell Monica *this* time?

Chapter Forty-one

Conor eased Holly off his chest and looked at Monica. She appeared to have taken a great deal of care in getting ready for their last encounter before she returned to Albania. Her hair was freshly coiffed. Her makeup applied with precision. She wore a purple V-neck top with a diaphanous scarf around her neck. Black slacks. Medium heels on her shoes. Everything about her was in sharp contrast to the way Holly and her friend were presenting themselves. Monica was elegantly demure. Holly and Susie were all about strutting and posturing. *How can this be happening?* Conor thought. Any possibility that had existed with this classy woman standing in front of him may have just been kissed away by a first-class bitch.

"Monica," he said, trying not to sound caught.

"Hello, Conor," Monica replied, understandably confused.

Holly moved an appropriate distance away from Conor. "Hello, Monica. I'm Holly."

"Hello, Holly," Monica said.

Susie suddenly appeared next to them.

"Monica," Holly said, "this is my friend Susie."

"Hello, Monica," Susie said.

"Hello, Susie," Monica said.

Monica looked at Conor. Susie looked at the floor. Holly looked at the ceiling. Lirim watched it all with bemused curiosity.

Seconds passed. They seemed like hours to Conor.

"Nice to meet you, Monica," Holly finally said, tossing her hair in full territorial display. She hooked her arm into the crook of Susie's elbow. "Susie, why don't we go to our table?"

"I think we should," Susie said, fighting a grin.

Holly and Susie, arm in arm, started out of the bar. They were quite a sight. Sleek blonde, svelte brunette. Holly looked over her shoulder at Conor. "Maybe you and Monica can join us for a drink after dinner."

Holly and Susie both flashed their cosmetically enhanced pearly whites, then disappeared around the corner.

Before Conor could offer any sort of explanation, Lirim leaned over the bar and looked at Monica.

"*Si jeni,*" he said, smiling broadly.

"*Mirë, faleminderit,*" Monica replied.

"*Nga të kemi?*"

"*Jam nga Shkodra, por jetoj ne Tiranë.*"

"*Une jam nga Tropoja,*" Lirim responded. He looked at Conor. "We are both from the north."

Lirim was doing everything he could to provide a buffer between the awkward encounter at the bar and the equally awkward conversation that would inevitably take place at the table. Conor gave Lirim a nod of appreciation.

Monica and Lirim spoke in Albanian for a couple minutes, which provided a welcome respite for Conor, precious time to figure out what to say about the scene Monica had just witnessed. But how do you explain a lip-lock on a bar stool?

"When is your reservation?" Lirim asked Conor.

"Eight."

Lirim checked the clock behind the bar. "You better go inside. They don't hold a table for too long."

"*Gëzohem që të njoha,*" Monica said.

"*Gjithashtu,*" Lirim replied.

Conor and Monica walked in silence to the front of the restaurant. A maître d' was standing sentry in a tuxedo.

"Good evening," he said, his accent mild but unmistakably Albanian.

"We have a reservation," Conor said. "The name's Bard."

"Detective Bard," the maître d' said, placing emphasis on the word *detective*. "Lirim told me you'd be dining with us tonight. And he told me you would be sharing the table with a beautiful Albanian woman." He looked at Monica. "*Domethënë ti je Shqiptare.*"

"*Po.*"

"That means 'yes,'" Conor interjected. "Lirim told me that's the only word I need to know."

The maître d' smiled. "Lirim is a wise man."

Conor and Monica followed the maître d' into a large area crammed with tables, all occupied. Just as they entered, the maître d' motioned to the right. There was a booth tucked away from the clamor.

"I reserved our most intimate table for you," he pointed out.

"Faleminderit," Monica said.

She edged into the booth first, then Conor sat next to her.

"The waiter will be with you in a minute," the maître d' said. "Enjoy your dinner."

He walked away. The moment Conor dreaded had arrived. To make matters worse, as wonderful as the seating was, it happened to be facing the table where Holly and Susie were having dinner directly across the room. Monica smiled sweetly and looked at Conor.

"Who is Holly?" she asked.

Conor cleared his throat. "She's the wife of the lawyer who was killed."

"Isn't she a suspect?"

"She's a person of interest. Yes."

"Well, you *did* seem very interested. Do you usually kiss your suspects?"

"Not usually."

"Sometimes?"

"Never before."

"What happened this time?"

"She grabbed me."

"Just like that?"

"Just like that."

Monica smiled sweetly. "Seems like every time I see you, there's some woman hanging on to you."

"I must be irresistible," Conor said, joking.

Monica didn't laugh.

A waiter arrived, his timing impeccable. Conor ordered a martini and a bottle of red wine from Sicily. Southern Italian wines, especially when made entirely from the Nero d'Avola grape as this one was, stood up well to sirloin. Besides, the price was southern too. South of a hundred dollars.

When the waiter walked away, Monica took Conor's hand.

"Look, Conor. It's not like we're in a relationship. You can do whatever you like."

"Monica . . ."

"Please. I don't want to talk about it, okay?"

"Okay."

Monica withdrew her hand and surveyed the dining room.

"Our waiter?" she said. "He's Albanian."

"According to Lirim, Albanians are taking over the restaurant business."

"Sometimes waiting tables is the only job an Albanian can get in America. Take my brother-in-law, Fatmir. Even though he had a professional certification as an engineer in Albania, the documents meant nothing here. So now he's a doorman." Monica shrugged. "But it doesn't matter. We still all dream of coming to America."

The waiter appeared with a bottle of wine and held the label so Conor could see it. It wasn't the bottle he had ordered.

"Mrs. Lawton would like to offer this to you," the waiter said before Conor could protest.

Conor looked over and saw Holly waving at him. *She won't quit, will she?*

"It's a Super Tuscan," the waiter explained. "Eighty percent Cabernet, twenty percent Sangiovese. It's among the best wines in the world."

"I'm sure it is," Conor replied. "I'm sorry, but no."

"Mrs. Lawton doesn't usually take no for an answer."

"I'm well aware of that," Conor said. "Would you please bring the bottle I chose?"

The waiter nodded and walked away. Holly motioned with her hands. *What happened?*

Conor scanned the wine list for the bottle Holly had offered. "Unbelievable."

"What?" Monica asked.

"A three-hundred-and-seventy-five-dollar bottle of wine."

Monica stared across the room at Holly. "Either she's definitely guilty or she desperately wants you." She turned and looked at Conor. "Maybe both," she said.

Chapter Forty-two

The waiter arrived with the martini and the bottle of Nero d'Avola. He uncorked the wine and poured a little for Conor to taste. Conor swirled it around in the glass, doing his best to appear knowledgeable about the sampling of fine wine, which, to some degree, he was. But his usual purchase was under ten dollars, and no amount of aeration would revive *those* grapes.

"Very nice," Conor said, doing his best to sound like a connoisseur.

The waiter filled their glasses. "Are you ready to order?"

Conor didn't need a menu. Although he had never eaten at Coals, he often dined at Frankie and Johnnie's on West Forty-fifth Street, an old-style New York steakhouse on the second floor of a low-rise building. All steakhouses offered virtually the same fare. He ordered two sirloins and several standard sides.

Conor raised his martini. Monica lifted her glass of wine.

"*Gezuar*," Conor said.

Monica smiled. "You speak Albanian?"

"*Po*," Conor replied.

Monica laughed. The melody filled Conor's head.

"*Gezuar*," Monica said as they touched glasses.

"You looking forward to going home?" Conor asked.

"I am." Monica flashed a sardonic smile. "But I hate to leave you here with all these aggressive American women. I feel like I should stay in New York to protect you."

Conor smiled. "Maybe the safest thing for me to do is fly to Albania."

Monica brightened. "You would come to see me?"

"Sure. Why not?"

"I'd like that."

"Speaking of flying to Albania, how are you getting to the airport on Tuesday?"

"I changed my flight. I'm leaving Monday."

"Why?"

"My mother called. My father is not doing well."

"I'm sorry."

"He's been sick for a long time. His heart. The family is already gathering at the house. I thought I better get back before . . ." Monica's voice trailed off. "I'm moving up to my brother-in-law's apartment in the Bronx tomorrow. Spending my last night with my niece, Olta."

Conor's cell phone rang. He slipped it out of his

pocket, checked the caller ID. "The precinct. Sorry. I need to take it."

Monica nodded.

Conor flipped open his phone. "Bard."

"Hey, Bard." It was Amanda. "I got an answer for you on that cell phone."

"That was fast."

"Don't ask."

"So you have a name for me, an address?"

"Got both."

"Great."

"The name," Amanda said, "is Radio Shack. Which is located at the following address: 2194 White Plains Road in the Bronx."

"What?"

"It's a prepaid phone," Amanda said.

Conor sighed. "I need a list of calls made from that phone."

"This time of night, that's tough. But I know a judge who I can probably get to sign a warrant right away. I'll call him at home."

"Thanks, Sarge."

Conor snapped the phone shut. His face broadcast disappointment.

Monica looked at him. "What's wrong?"

"Fitim Bregu's phone. It's a prepaid."

"Of course it is," Monica said. "A lot of Albanians either have bad credit or no credit. I see it at the bank every day."

"So now our best bet is to try triangulation. As

long as he's using the phone, we can pin the location down to a couple blocks."

Monica seemed puzzled. "How did you get the number?"

"A confidential informant in the Bronx," Conor lied.

"Well, at least you have the number. That's good, right?"

"Better than nothing."

"You said the other night that Fitim Bregu was a suspect?"

"Maybe. We know he figures into this somehow."

"How?" Monica wondered.

Conor hesitated, then: "We know he was in possession of the murder weapon at some point."

Monica looked across the room at Holly.

"You see the problem," Conor said, following Monica's eyes. "Nothing seems to connect. Holly had the motive. Fitim had the gun. How they found each other, if that's what happened, is the two-hundred-million-dollar question."

"Two hundred million?"

"That's what she stands to inherit."

"That's a lot of motive," Monica said softly.

"Tell me about it."

"You know what you need?"

"What?" Conor asked.

"A shocking discovery. Like on Dominick Dunne's *Power, Privilege and Justice*."

"Yeah, you're right. That's exactly what I need."

During dinner, Conor and Monica talked about

when Conor might have time to travel to Albania. It was a rush for him, to actually be planning a trip.

"I'm excited about you coming to Tirana," Monica said.

"So am I," Conor replied.

A busboy appeared. "Are you finished?"

"Yes," Conor said.

As the busboy reached for a plate, he frowned and looked at Monica.

"Monica?"

Monica stared at the busboy. She put her hand over her mouth. "Oh, my God! Krenar?"

"Yes. It is Krenar."

Monica laughed. "I can't believe this."

She got up from the table. Krenar put the plate down. They embraced.

"Krenar. When did you come to America?"

"Last year."

Monica turned toward Conor. "Conor, this is Krenar. We were neighbors when I was growing up in Shkodra."

Conor stood. "Nice to meet you."

"I haven't seen Krenar for, what?"

"A long time," Krenar said.

"Let me see." Monica calculated in her head. "Twelve years."

They spoke in Albanian for a moment. Conor made out the word *besa*. Either they were talking about Monica's sister or the *besa* beliefs. Conor guessed they were talking about the sister. He was correct.

"I'm sorry about what happened to Besa," the busboy said, dropping back into English. "Did they ever catch the guy?"

Conor frowned. Did he hear that right? *Catch the guy? What guy?*

"*Jo,*" Monica said. "*Ato nuk e kapen.*"

Jo *means no*, Conor thought. His knowledge of Albanian was minuscule. But at the moment, it was proving useful.

Krenar glanced over his shoulder nervously. "I have to work now. We get together?"

"I'm sorry, Krenar," Monica replied. "I'm leaving on Monday."

"Maybe next time." Krenar began clearing the table. "I give you my number." He looked at Conor. "Nice to meet you."

"Same here."

Krenar scooped up the plates, stacked them quickly, then hurried away.

Conor and Monica sat back down.

"What happened to Besa?" Conor asked cautiously.

Monica's eyes misted. "She was raped and killed."

Conor didn't know what to say so he put his arm around Monica's shoulder. She buried her head in his neck and cried.

Chapter Forty-three

Monica picked up her napkin and dabbed the tears from her eyes. "I'm sorry."

"It's all right," Conor said, rubbing her back. "It's all right." He looked at her, the makeup that she had meticulously applied now streaked, her eyes red, her hands trembling slightly. All she had been through, the struggle just to survive, and then something like this? A tide of feelings swirled around in him and he no longer could distinguish between any of them. Sympathy, compassion, anger, sadness. "How long ago was this?"

"Six years, two months, five days."

The jaded cop attitude Conor had long ago adopted was no help to him now. *Counting days*. That's what some animal had done to Monica. Caused her to count days instead of living them. "Where?"

"In the Bronx." Monica squeezed Conor's hand. "Will you excuse me for a moment?"

She stood and walked to the restroom. Conor

processed what he had just heard. Some low-life son of a bitch was still out there walking around a free man. He swore right there and then he would find whoever was responsible. Whatever it took.

"Would you like to join us for a nightcap?"

Conor looked up. Holly was standing there.

"This is not a good time for a nightcap," Conor said with an edge. "Trust me on that one, Holly."

"I saw your friend crying. Is everything all right?"

"Yes." Conor just wanted Holly away from him.

Holly struck a sexy pose. "You sure you won't—"

"No."

"Okay. You know where to reach me."

"I do."

"Good night, Conor."

"Good night, Holly."

Conor watched her stroll over to join Susie. They walked together toward the bar. Susie waved. Holly blew Conor a kiss.

Monica returned from the restroom, having done a good job of putting herself back together.

"I'm really sorry," she said as she sat down.

"There's nothing to be sorry about."

"It's very painful to think about."

"I know. It must be."

Conor wanted to know more, *needed* to know more. Who was this scumbag? He wanted to assure Monica that he would find him, make him pay for what he did.

"Do you know who did this?" Conor asked.

Monica didn't respond for a long time.

"His name is John Hicks," she finally said, her voice barely a whisper. "His DNA was at the scene, but they never found him."

DNA? So the miserable bastard was a repeat offender. Conor gritted his teeth. John Hicks was going down. "I'll find him."

"I know why you're saying that, Conor. But it's not your responsibility."

"I *am* going to find him," he insisted.

Monica reached over and brushed Conor's cheek. "I'm sorry it came up. I'm sorry it made you feel bad."

She's sorry it made *him* feel bad? She was worried about *him*? Conor found it incredible that she could be concerned about the way *he* felt while she was clearly being consumed by the fire of an unimaginable private hell.

"Can we stop talking about it?" Monica asked softly. "Please."

They ordered cheesecake, the standard finish to a steakhouse dinner. Then they walked out onto Fifty-third Street and ambled toward Second Avenue, arm in arm.

"You should have seen your face when I walked in the bar," Monica said.

"Let's put it this way. That wasn't my finest hour."

They stopped at the corner.

"Where are we going?" Conor asked.

"Seventy-third between Second and Third."

Conor hailed a cab. They climbed inside.

"I'm warning you," Monica said. "I've been packing, so my apartment is a mess."

"You should see *my* place. And I'm not even packing."

Monica laughed. By now, Conor knew the melody by heart. And he had a feeling it would fill his head long after she was gone.

Monica's building was a typical Upper East Side high rise. Conor and Monica entered the lobby. A doorman, dressed in a drab green uniform, regarded Conor suspiciously.

"Good evening, Miss Kodra," the doorman said, keeping an eye on Conor.

"Good evening, Michael," Monica replied.

They went into the elevator and Monica pressed floor seven. The doors lumbered shut.

"Your doorman didn't look too happy to see me," Conor observed.

"I haven't had a man up to the apartment since I got here," Monica explained. "I think he was a little shocked."

Conor was pleasantly surprised.

They got off on the seventh floor and walked to one of the indistinguishable doors. Monica inserted a key and they entered her small one-bedroom. It was functionally furnished, much like he imagined a corporate pied-à-terre might be. And, as Monica said, it was a mess. Three open suitcases dominated the middle of the living room.

Monica gave Conor the tour, which didn't take very long. Bedroom. Bathroom. That was about it. They wound up in the kitchen.

"All I have to drink is a bottle of red wine," Monica said. "It was on the counter when I got here."

"And you never opened it?" Conor smiled. "You *aren't* much of a drinker, are you?"

"No."

"Do you even have a corkscrew?"

"I think there's one in the drawer."

Conor opened the drawer and found a small plastic corkscrew. While he popped the cork, Monica retrieved two wineglasses from the cabinet. They headed into the living room. Monica snapped on a CD player. Soft jazz flowed from a set of speakers. Finally, they settled in on the couch.

Conor held up his glass of wine. *"Gezuar."*

"Gezuar," Monica replied.

They touched glasses, took sips, and then in tandem placed the glasses on the coffee table. When they leaned back, they found themselves in each other's arms. Conor kissed her. He felt a charge pulse through him. *This* was a kiss, loving and sensual at the same time. He kissed her again. But then Monica leaned away from him.

"Conor . . ."

"Yes."

"I'm sorry."

"For what?"

Monica looked into his eyes. "I want to be with you. I do. But not right before I leave America. It doesn't feel right." She squeezed his hand. "I'm sorry. The way I was brought up—"

"You don't have to explain."

From the moment he met her, it was apparent to Conor that Monica was operating under a different set of rules than the women he had known in the past. How could he argue with that? The truth was, he had always picked the *wrong* women. Maybe now, for the first time, he had chosen well. He wasn't about to ruin it with some sophomoric attempt at seduction.

"You'll come see me in Tirana?" Monica asked as if she wasn't sure.

"Are you kidding? This is *one* case I definitely want to close." He brushed her hair with his hand. "But there's a problem."

Monica frowned, concerned. "What?"

"I don't know how to reach you in Albania."

"I was wondering when you were going to ask." She reached over and picked up her purse from the coffee table, dug out a business card, and handed it to him. "My office number, home, cell, and e-mail."

Conor glanced at the card and burst into song. "*Conor, don't lose that number, you don't wanna call nobody else.*"

"Steely Dan," he explained. "'Rikki, Don't Lose That Number.'"

Monica laughed. Conor savored the melody of

her laughter as it played for the last time in America. He held her for a long time before he left.

The evening had come to a close the only way it could have. Monica was returning to Albania on Monday, which had to be stressful after spending six months in New York. And then there was the unfortunate encounter with Krenar at Coals, forcing Monica to relive the horror of her sister's rape and murder. *Yes*, Conor told himself, *it ended well tonight, with a promise of the future*.

It was almost one in the morning, but no way Conor was going home, facing that empty apartment. So he went to the precinct. It was quiet. As he walked past the bulletin board of mug shots, he was hit with a sudden fury. He strode to his desk and sat in front of the computer, logged into the criminal database, and typed the name John Hicks. After a few seconds, Hicks's file appeared. What Conor saw on the screen disgusted him. Staring from the monitor was the face of evil itself. Hicks was in his mid-forties. He had deep-set, beady eyes. Rat's eyes. His skin was pasty white, which made his scruffy reddish-brown beard stand out. Conor shuddered. *This face was the last thing Besa saw?*

Hicks had a long rap sheet but the most recent activity in the file was the arrest warrant for Besa's murder six years ago. Conor read the details of the crime and immediately regretted it. Results from the autopsy indicated that Besa had been tortured, raped repeatedly, then disfigured, and finally, brutally beaten to death.

Conor felt nauseated. He had never been involved in a homicide investigation where he was even remotely connected to the victim. It was hard enough to remain detached when a body turned up, but he had always found a way to focus. *Solve the crime. Find the killer.* That was his job. But now, reading about Besa, it wasn't just a job anymore.

Let those liberals who oppose the death penalty read this, Conor thought. *Let this happen to somebody they love and see how they feel.*

He tapped the keyboard. The printer whirred to life. He reached over, pulled several sheets of paper from the tray, then spread them out on his desk. He stared at the cold white pages, wishing he could change what they said. And then one overriding thought filled his head like thunder: *John Hicks is a dead man walking.*

Chapter Forty-four

Conor had more than the usual trouble sleeping. His last night with Monica, the revelation about Besa, Holly's bizarre behavior, all these things kept him thrashing around. So when his cell phone rang at seven, he was half awake. He rolled out of bed and staggered to the living room. The phone was where he always left it, on the coffee table. *Why don't I just put the phone by the side of the bed?* he thought.

The caller ID said "private." Conor flipped open the phone. "Hello?"

"Hey, Bard. It's Ross Marks. Sorry to call you this early on a Sunday morning."

FBI Agent Ross Marks was the Bureau's liaison officer with the NYPD. After 9/11, a new age of cooperation between federal and local law enforcement had been ushered in. Despite the inherent suspicion the NYPD had for the feds, Marks was effective in his job. All the cops liked Marks and often spent nights hanging out with him in neighborhood bars. He was a straight shooter, sharing what he could on an official basis, sometimes slipping them what they needed to know on a very unofficial basis.

"I have some information that you might find interesting," Marks said. But he didn't want to discuss it on the phone. "Why don't you stop by and have breakfast."

Conor called Ralph.

"You're up early," Ralph said.

"How fast can you get to Manhattan?"

"I'm already here. Sitting at my desk."

"At seven o'clock?"

"Me and this desk have been through a lot over the years," Ralph said, nostalgia reverberating in his voice. "I want to spend as much time with her as possible before I retire."

"Stop," Conor said. "You're going to make me cry."

Conor showered quickly and headed out of the apartment. When he walked into the precinct, he laughed.

"What are you doing at *my* desk, Ralph? Cheating on *your* desk?"

Ralph held up a piece of paper. It was a page from Besa's autopsy report. "We don't have enough to do? You've got to pull cold cases out of the freezer?"

"That's Monica's sister," Conor said quietly.

"The girl's sister?" Ralph tossed the page on the desk like it was burning his fingers. "Jesus!"

Ralph stood, headed for his desk.

"Marks over at FBI called," Conor said. "I think he's got something for us."

Conor and Ralph walked outside and climbed into the car. By the time they got to the FBI field office on Tenth Avenue, Conor had told Ralph about Holly's antics the previous night at Coals.

"So wait a minute," Ralph said. "You telling me the wife had you pinned against the bar?"

"That's what I'm telling you."

Ralph shook his head. "There's no accounting for taste."

"Thanks a lot."

"That's not good." Ralph's tone turned serious. "She's playing a game and you're letting her get away with it."

"*Letting* her? Ralph, I'm not letting her do anything. It all happened so fast and—"

"Somebody pulls a gun. That can happen fast too. You're trained to respond without hesitation."

"What was I supposed to do, punch her?"

"You shouldn't have put yourself in that position."

Conor was getting annoyed. "I appreciate the lecture, Ralph. But you weren't there."

"I was at her house. I saw the way you looked at her."

Conor wished he hadn't brought it up.

"Look, Conor, I'm older than you are. You have to listen to me."

"Should I call you Dad?"

"If you like." Ralph's voice took on an edge. "You need to stay away from her or hand off the case. Those are your two options."

"How am I supposed to investigate Lawton's murder without any contact with his wife?"

"Exactly."

"Which means?"

"Figure it out."

Conor turned and stared out the window. He knew Ralph was right. He couldn't keep indulging in whatever charade Holly had dragged him into while the investigation was still open. Maybe that was Holly's intention all along. To force him off the case.

Ralph punched Conor's shoulder. "Take it easy, kid. We're just going through a little separation anxiety, that's all."

Marks was sitting at his desk eating a sausage biscuit when Conor and Ralph walked in.

"Hey, guys," Marks said. "Have a seat."

Conor and Ralph sat across the desk from Marks. Ralph looked longingly at the food in Marks's hand.

Marks motioned to a cardboard box full of paper-wrapped sandwiches. "You want one?"

"Sure," Ralph said without missing a beat. He grabbed a biscuit, peeled back the paper, and stuffed it in his mouth like he hadn't seen food for a year.

Marks looked at Conor. "You?"

Conor frowned at the greasy concoction. "No, thanks."

"Coffee?" Marks asked as he chewed.

"That would be great," Ralph mumbled, his mouth full.

Conor nodded. "Thanks."

Marks reached over and picked up two cardboard cups of coffee. He placed them in front of Conor and Ralph.

"So what's up?" Conor wanted to know.

It didn't take long for Marks to drop a bombshell.

"Two weeks ago," Marks said, "we offered Salvatore Zeffri a deal."

Conor frowned. "What kind of deal?"

"The Bureau dug up some new evidence on Zeffri that we thought was a slam-dunk racketeering case. The U.S. attorney disagreed."

Conor and Ralph both knew full well what that was like. How many times, when they thought they had a perp in the bag, had the DA refused to indict?

Marks took a sip of coffee. "But the U.S. attorney *did* think the evidence was strong enough to take a shot and float a plea bargain. So he contacted Zeffri's lawyer."

"Walter Lawton?" Conor asked, already knowing the answer.

"You got it."

Marks stood, walked across the room, and shut the door. "What I'm about to tell you stays in this office."

"Of course," Conor replied without hesitation.

"Goes for me, too," Ralph said as he gobbled down the last of the sausage biscuit.

Marks returned to his desk, eased into his chair.

"Lawton was indignant," he continued. "Said his client Zeffri was innocent and would never entertain accepting *any* deal. Since the evidence implicated Zeffri in a few cold-case contract killings, we turned everything over to the Queens DA. He decided he would use what we gave him to retry Zeffri on one of the homicides, which had resulted in a hung jury a few years ago. The decision by the Queens DA was a very bad thing for Zeffri. And I'm not talking about legal issues."

"So what are you saying?" Conor asked. "That Zeffri was whacked because a federal plea bargain was on the table and an indictment in Queens was hanging over his head?"

"It certainly looks like a mob hit," Marks allowed. "But offing a guy like Zeffri, considering his position in La Cosa Nostra, would have taken a high-level sitdown. And as far as we know, there hasn't been one lately."

Conor started to tell Marks about the dinner Holly had at Coals with a rogues' gallery of mafiosi but then thought better of it.

Marks got up again, walked to the window, and stared out at the city.

"Anyway, after we tendered our offer to Zeffri through Lawton, later that night we picked up some interesting chatter on one of our wiretaps at a location I'm not at liberty to disclose. The exchange took place between a man named Pietro Delprete, a capo in the Gambino crime family, and an underboss named Vincent Marchetti. At one point Marchetti tells Delprete he got a call from Lawton and then goes into detail about the deal we offered Zeffri."

"I guess consigliere pays more than lawyer," Ralph said.

"I don't know if I'd elevate Lawton to consigliere status," Marks countered, "but it certainly appears that his relationship with the Gambino family was unusual and complicit."

Marks walked to his desk, sat down, and popped the last bite of his sausage biscuit in his mouth. He reached over and opened a cardboard box. "Want a doughnut?"

"Yeah," Ralph said, "I'll take one of those."

"I'm fine," Conor replied. He glanced at Ralph and grimaced. *How can you eat so much?*

Marks removed a doughnut, then shoved the box at Ralph, who wasted no time fishing one out himself.

Marks continued. "So Marchetti is telling Delprete what a good soldier Lawton is. And pretty soon we realize that Zeffri wasn't the only client Lawton sold down the river. He was setting up any client who looked to be a canary."

"Bastard," Ralph said.

"From what we've been able to determine, very few people in the family knew about Lawton's coziness with Delprete. Only a handful of trusted associates had any idea. Which is the way Delprete wanted to keep it." Marks chomped on his doughnut. "Why? Because when some low-level mobster was charged with a crime, where did Delprete send him?"

"Lawton," Conor answered.

"Right," Marks said. "And who better to know whether these guys were looking to cut a deal?"

"Lawton," Conor said again.

"And what did Lawton do when someone was offering to squeal on the mob?"

"He didn't approach the DA," Ralph said, his voice muffled by glazed dough.

Marks smiled. "No, he didn't. Lawton went straight to Delprete, which is a little violation of the attorney-client privilege, wouldn't you say?" Marks leaned over the desk. "So Marchetti's going on and on about the rats who would've copped a plea if Lawton hadn't tipped them off. And Marchetti's spouting off names, dates, even who carried out the hit."

Ralph shook his head. "Don't these guys ever learn? That's what brought Gotti down. He couldn't shut up."

"Which is good for us," Marks said. "Now, most of the guys Lawton handed over to Delprete were career thugs. But one was a nineteen-year-old kid busted for driving a truckload of cigarettes up from North Carolina."

Conor frowned. "Are you telling me Lawton set up a teenager?"

"Marchetti was cursing this kid like a dog," Marks

continued. "He even mentioned where the body was buried. An empty lot over by Kennedy Airport. We sent a team over there and guess what we found?"

"A nineteen-year-old," Ralph said, disgusted.

"Right where Marchetti said he would be. The worst part is, that kid probably had nothing worthwhile to give up anyway."

"So what are you doing about it?" Conor wanted to know.

"We're moving on Delprete's crew in the next week or so," Marks replied. "My guess is somebody's going to flip. I'll keep you posted."

Ralph eyed the box of doughnuts then looked at Marks. "Can I have another one of those?"

"Sure. Go ahead."

Ralph dug into the box. Conor stared at him in disbelief.

"Anyway," Marks continued, "the whole time Marchetti is talking, Delprete isn't saying anything, he's just letting Marchetti ramble on about Lawton. So Marchetti finally finishes and there's a long silence. And then this."

Marks reached over and pressed PLAY on a tape recorder that was sitting on his desk. After a few seconds of silence, Delprete's voice vibrated out of the small speaker.

You know what I think? I think that fucking lawyer knows too much about our fucking business.

Conor and Ralph looked at each other. They both knew what a statement like that meant, especially coming from a capo. Even though Lawton may have been considered a friend of the family, perhaps even a consigliere, he was still an outsider in Mafia terms. And an outsider with insider secrets but no real sense of *omertà*, the Mafia code of silence, could be problematic.

"You see where I'm going with this?" Marks asked.

Ralph rubbed his forehead. "You're saying Delprete had Lawton whacked."

"A strong possibility," Marks said.

Conor almost laughed. "No good deed goes unpunished."

"At this point it's just a theory." Marks sipped his coffee. "I know the agency and NYPD have not had the best relationship over the years. But this is the new FBI. We're all about cooperation. Lawton? Zeffri? Seems to be just mob business as usual. So, if you want, we'll take it from here."

Conor and Ralph exited the FBI building and walked up Tenth Avenue.

"What did I tell you about lawyers?" Ralph said, shaking his head.

"We're not talking some ambulance chaser," Conor pointed out. "It goes way beyond that. If this is true, Lawton was lining people up to be executed."

"And you're *surprised*? What makes you think Lawton had a soul? He used it to pay for law school."

They stopped at the car.

"A nineteen-year-old kid?" Ralph sighed. "And now we're supposed to give a damn who killed Lawton?"

"Like Marks said, we could let the feds deal with it."

"We could do that, but murder isn't a federal crime. This is still our case. And if Delprete *did* whack Lawton, then Delprete's *our* collar." Ralph opened the car door. "Besides, if you really wanted to hand this off to the feds, you would have told Marks about Holly Lawton's dinner at Coals."

But withholding that piece of information from Marks had nothing to do with jurisdiction. Although Conor wasn't entirely sure why, he knew he didn't want the FBI swarming all over Holly Lawton. At least not for the moment.

Chapter Forty-five

Ralph started the engine and pulled away from the curb.

"Let the feds do what they do," Ralph said, "and we'll do what we do."

"Yeah, but the thing is, if the feds haul Delprete in on a RICO, we'll have to stand in line to get our shot at him."

"Sometimes, kid, you've just got to play the hand you're dealt."

"What is that supposed to mean?"

"It means we're not going to fold just yet," Ralph said. "We've got to keep poking around. Playing our cards."

"There's something I've been wanting to tell you for a long time," Conor said. "The way you always use gambling or sports to make your point drives me crazy."

"You know why I do that? Because life's a game. And if you don't take risks, how you going to win?"

"What if you bet and lose?"

"Just double the stakes next time."

"That's what all compulsive gamblers say."

"Oh yeah? You think Henry David Thoreau was a compulsive gambler?"

"Thoreau? You dragging him into this now?"

"Thoreau said . . ." Ralph stared off, reciting. "'The mass of men lead lives of quiet desperation.'" He glanced at Conor. "In other words, people who don't take chances."

"I don't think he was talking about gambling."

"How do you know?" Ralph thought for a moment. "You know what else he said?"

"I'm sure you're going to tell me."

"'There are a thousand hacking at the branches of evil,'" Ralph offered in his best baritone, "'to one who is striking at the root.'" He took a deep breath. "That's what we're doing right now. Hacking at branches. We've got to get to the root of all this."

"Quoting Thoreau. I'm impressed. I didn't know you were so well-read."

Ralph shrugged. "Like I told you. Had a lot of long nights the past couple of years."

They drove a few blocks without speaking, then Ralph turned and looked at Conor. "I'm guessing you didn't get laid last night. Especially after the thing about the sister."

"Nice, Ralph. Really nice."

"Well, *did* you?" Ralph pressed.

"No," Conor said. "But I had a great time."

"You didn't get laid and you're *still* saying you had a great time? You better hang on to this girl." Ralph took a right and headed across town. "When's she leaving?"

"Her flight's tomorrow."

"You seeing her again before she leaves?"

"No. She's moving to the Bronx for the night. To spend some time with her niece."

"How's she getting to the Bronx?"

"I don't know."

"You don't *know*?" Ralph frowned at Conor. "Do I have to tell you *everything*?"

The car swerved.

"Watch where you're going," Conor said.

"She's got suitcases, right? What? She taking a train? With suitcases?"

"Her brother-in-law will probably come get her. Or she'll take a cab."

"You going to let her drag suitcases around looking for a taxi?"

Conor had wanted to take Monica to the Bronx, to have an opportunity to see her one more time. But the previous evening had ended on such a tender note, he figured it was better left the way it was.

Ralph looked at Conor. "You like this girl, right?"

The car swerved again.

Conor grabbed the edge of his seat. "Can't you look through the windshield when you talk?"

Ralph whipped the steering wheel to the left. "You call this girl. Offer to take her to the Bronx. No.

Don't offer. *Insist*. Pick up some flowers on the way over. Give her a proper bon voyage. That's how you do it."

"You really *are* starting to sound like my father."

"You do what I told you," Ralph said. He seemed suddenly sad. "I'm going to visit Laura."

The car swerved again. Conor braced himself against the dashboard with one hand.

"If you don't watch where you're going, you'll be *joining* her," Conor said.

Conor looked at Ralph and could see the deep crevices of loss etched on his face. Laura had been his whole world for so long. Conor recalled how different Ralph became when she died. The way his shoulders stooped like they never had before, the change in his gait, slower, more deliberate, the light in his eyes suddenly dark. It reinforced Conor's notion that loving someone wasn't worth the inevitable pain.

"You don't get second chances," Ralph said. "Listen to me. I'm older than you."

"You already pointed that out."

"It's worth repeating."

Conor turned and stared out the window.

"You don't want to have regrets, kid," Ralph said. "I couldn't live with regrets."

Ralph dropped Conor off at the precinct. Conor took out his cell phone and dialed.

"Hello?"

"Good morning."

"Conor." Monica was pleasantly surprised.

"What are you doing?"

"Just closing up my suitcases."

"When are you planning to head to your brother-in-law's?"

"I was just about ready to call the car service."

"Don't call them."

Monica laughed. "I can't *walk* to the Bronx, Conor. It's too far."

"I'm picking you up and taking you."

"Oh, no, Conor. That's—"

"That's what I'm doing."

"Conor . . ."

Conor remembered what Ralph had said. *Insist.*

"I'll see you in fifteen minutes. I hope you're still there when I get there."

"Conor . . ."

Conor snapped the phone shut. He walked into the precinct, grabbed the keys to one of the unmarked cars, and then started out the door. He stopped, suddenly realizing he had never taken a photo of Monica. He hurried to his desk and pulled a compact digital camera from a drawer.

Monica was on the phone when she let Conor into the apartment. She was nervous, full of anxiety. He'd never seen her like that.

She tilted the phone away from her mouth, mimed

the words *have a seat*, then turned her attention back to her conversation.

"How about if I go through Rome instead of Milan?"

As Conor sat on the couch he glanced down at a piece of paper on the coffee table. Several phone numbers were written on it. Lufthansa. Alitalia. American. United. Delta. British Airways.

"So *everything* is booked?" Monica sighed. "Okay. Thank you." She snapped the phone shut, walked over, and dropped on the couch next to Conor.

"I can't believe you did this."

"Did what?"

"I was going to call the car service and—"

"And I wanted to see you one more time before you left. So just pretend I'm a car service and we'll both be happy."

Monica hugged him. "Thank you."

Conor's eyes wandered to the scrawled list of airlines.

She noticed. "I spoke with my mother this morning. My father is getting worse."

"I'm sorry."

"So I was trying to get on a flight tonight. There are plenty of seats tomorrow, but tonight . . ."

For the savior in Conor, this was the perfect time to pull off a miracle. He'd be happy to use his NYPD position, get some airline manager on the phone, explain the situation regarding Monica's father.

"You want me to make a call?"

"It's all right. Even if I got a flight to Milan or Rome or Zurich or wherever, I'd still be on standby getting to Tirana."

"I could contact one of the airlines and—"

"No," Monica said. "Maybe it's better this way. When I told Olta I might be leaving tonight, she started crying. I'd rather spend time with my niece instead of being stuck in some airport. I just hope my father doesn't . . ." Her eyes misted. She stood and walked to a bulging suitcase that was in the middle of the floor. "Okay. Let me finish with the bags." She sat on top of the suitcase and struggled with the zipper. It wouldn't budge.

Conor laughed. "You're not heavy enough."

"Thank God."

"Get up. Let me do it."

Monica got up. Conor walked over and started to close the suitcase. Something caught his eye: a huge, Costco-size jar of peanut butter. He looked up at Monica.

"You think you have enough peanut butter?"

"Okay," she explained, "here's what happened. When I was a teenager, the United States sent eighty-three million dollars of aid to Albania. So we all got these big boxes of food. There was a lot of peanut butter in the box." She shrugged. "I guess I got hooked. But then, like everything in Albania, the government screwed it up. Instead of handing out the food, they hoarded it and started selling it. We couldn't afford peanut butter and eventually the government sold it all. After that, there was no more peanut butter in Albania. Once in a while you can find it somewhere but it's very expensive. So the first thing I bought when I came to America was peanut butter. And now I'm taking as much as I can back with me."

Monica smiled. Conor felt a twinge inside him, an overwhelming compassion. How many peanut-butter-and-jelly sandwiches had he wolfed down as a kid? It had never crossed his mind that he'd have to worry about where his next Skippy fix was coming from.

Conor looked at her. She had so many reasons to be bitter. The abject poverty, the heavy hand of communism that stole her childhood, the loss of her sister. And yet she exuded happiness. She had found the joy in life when most of the privileged people he knew seized upon every opportunity to be miserable. He wanted to grab her and hold her, tell her everything was going to be all right. But he was too afraid to make such promises.

Conor pressed down on the top of the suitcase with one hand, zipped it up with the other.

"It's nice to have a man around the house," Monica said.

"Don't forget that when you get back to Albania."

Conor hoisted the suitcase onto its wheels. "Where do you want this?"

Monica pointed to two other small suitcases. "Over there. By the door."

Conor moved the large suitcase next to the two smaller ones. Ralph was right. What if he hadn't come? He couldn't picture Monica dragging three suitcases down to the curb by herself.

Monica looked around the room. "I'm going to miss my New York apartment."

Conor walked over and put his arms around her.

"Thank you for being here," Monica said as she held him tightly.

Ralph's words echoed in his head: *You don't want to have regrets, kid.* Conor knew, holding Monica in his arms like he was, that someday, somehow, he would have regretted it if he hadn't shown up to take her to the Bronx. *Thank you, Ralph,* Conor said silently. But then, in the midst of comforting Monica, he felt a need for comforting himself. Monica was leaving. Ralph was leaving. Before long, two people who were important to him in different ways would be gone from his life.

Chapter Forty-six

Conor and Monica walked through the lobby, Conor carrying two suitcases, Monica pulling a small one behind her.

Conor stopped. Monica frowned at him. "What?"

Conor reached into his jacket pocket and produced the camera. He held it up. "Photo op."

Monica made a face. "*Now?*"

"I don't have a picture of you, so now's as good a time as any." Conor pointed to a wall. "Stand over there. By the plant."

"Conor—"

"Come on."

Monica sighed, walked to the wall, and posed next to a large plant. Conor aimed the camera and took a snapshot. Monica started walking toward him.

"One more," Conor said.

Monica dutifully stepped back over to the plant and posed again.

"Are we done?" she asked as Conor lowered the camera.

"Not yet." Conor turned, held the camera out to the doorman. "Would you take one of us together?"

"Sure," the doorman said.

"Conor . . . ," Monica protested.

The doorman took the camera. Conor walked over, placed his arm around Monica's shoulder.

"How do you say 'cheese' in Albanian?" he asked.

"*Djathe*," she replied.

"Dee oth," Conor repeated, fumbling the pronunciation.

Monica laughed. Conor laughed. And the flash of the camera caught the moment forever.

Conor eased the car into the smattering of Sunday-afternoon traffic heading north on the West Side Highway. He reached over and took Monica's hand.

"Remember what I told you," she said. "No touching in front of my brother-in-law."

"I'll do my best."

Monica pulled her hand away from his. "I'm serious, Conor. You have no idea how bad that would be."

"Relax. I get it."

"I don't think you do." She turned sideways in the seat, faced him. "For an Albanian to see a female member of his family having any physical contact at all with a man who is not her husband would bring dishonor to the whole family."

"And then?"

"And then I would be considered a *përdalë*. A whore."

"Just for touching?"

"In public, yes."

"Wow."

"Don't forget, Fatmir is from the north. That's the way they think. Which is why I moved to Tirana as soon as I had a good excuse."

"So what does Fatmir do for a living?"

"He's a doorman."

"In the Bronx?"

"No. West End Avenue. A Hundred and Sixth Street. One of those old buildings."

"Yeah. I know. Prewar. They're beautiful."

Conor reached across the seat.

"Can I touch you now?"

Monica smiled. "All you want."

Conor parked the car on the corner of 205th Street and Grand Concourse. He and Monica, carrying suitcases, walked down the block to a six-story building. As Conor eyed the assortment of young men hanging out on the corner, who were clearly up to no good, he wished Monica wasn't staying there even for one night.

Monica pressed a button on a panel near the entrance. A buzzer sounded. They pushed through the door and spilled into a small, dingy lobby.

"Remember," she whispered.

"No touching," Conor whispered back at her.

They climbed a flight of stairs. When they reached the second floor, a door opened. Fatmir greeted them. He was short and skinny, with black, unkempt hair, around forty years old.

"Hello, Monica."

"Fatmir, this is my friend Conor Bard. Conor, my brother-in-law, Fatmir Lisi."

"Nice to meet you," Conor said.

Fatmir didn't reply. He just nodded, a dour look on his face. *Friendly guy*, Conor thought.

"Teze!"

The voice belonged to Olta, who ran from inside the apartment and wrapped herself around Monica's legs. *"Teze!"*

"That means 'aunt,'" Monica explained to Conor. She rubbed Olta's head. "Olta, this is my friend Mr. Bard."

Olta stared up at Conor.

"Hi, Mr. Bard."

Wrinkling her nose and squinting up at him was an eight-year-old miniature version of Monica. Same dark hair, same dark eyes. Only half the size. Conor felt a paternal twinge. He wanted to pick her up and hug her.

"Hello, Olta," he said.

Olta ran back into the apartment. Monica and Conor followed. Fatmir shut the door.

"Put the suitcases in there," he said, pointing down the hall.

Monica led Conor to a small bedroom. Conor dropped the suitcases, checked to make sure Fatmir couldn't see him, then grabbed Monica around the waist. She pulled away and pointed a finger at him, frowned, then walked out. Conor followed her back into the living room, where they found Fatmir perched rigidly on a wooden side chair.

"Have a seat," Fatmir said.

Conor sat on the couch. Monica walked to a love seat on the other side of the room.

"Monica tells me you're a detective," Fatmir said.

"Yes."

Fatmir stared at him in a way that made Conor vaguely uncomfortable.

"A lot of crime in New York," Fatmir observed.

A Latina walked out of the kitchen. She appeared to be in her mid-twenties. Pretty, not gorgeous, but sexy in a way seemingly patented by Latin females. You could almost feel the heat emanating from her body.

"Monica!"

Monica stood and embraced her.

"I am going to miss you *so* much," the woman said in a heavy accent.

"Oh, Consuela," Monica said. "I'm going to miss you, too."

They hugged tightly for a long moment. Monica motioned toward Conor. "Consuela. This is my friend Conor Bard."

Conor stood. "Nice to meet you."

"Monica has told us so much about you," Consuela said.

Conor was pleased. He had no idea that Monica had even mentioned him to anyone. Fatmir stood quickly and disappeared into the kitchen. Apparently *he* wasn't so pleased.

"Would you like some coffee?" Consuela asked.

Conor, wondering if he should accept or just leave, looked at Monica. She nodded.

"That would be great," Conor said.

Consuela walked into the kitchen.

"I'm sorry," Monica whispered. "It's just that Fatmir—"

"It's okay," Conor said. "I'll have a little coffee then head back."

Olta came running out of a doorway. "*Teze.* Will you come look at my new painting?"

"Sure, Olta. Can Mr. Bard come too?"

"Okay," Olta said.

Conor and Monica followed Olta into her room. It was full of little-girl things: dolls, stuffed animals, frilly pillows. But what really caught Conor's attention were the photographs. Of Besa. They had been conspicuously absent from the living room, yet in Olta's tiny corner of the world they were everywhere. And there was no mistaking the fact that Besa was Monica's sister. The same eyes, the same mouth, the same hopeful expression on her face. As his gaze moved from photo to photo, Conor could feel himself being caught up in opposing whirlpools of mourning and fury, each fast-flowing current as strong as the other.

"That's my mommy," Olta said, pulling Conor back into the moment. "Isn't she pretty?"

"Very pretty," Conor replied.

He found it odd that Fatmir wouldn't have pictures of his wife on display where guests could see them. Maybe it would be too painful a reminder for him. Or maybe Consuela, and perhaps many others like her, had replaced Besa. Either way, it was strange: images of the lovely Besa, who bore Fatmir such a precious child, relegated to the back of a Bronx apartment.

Olta held up a large piece of stiff paper. "This is a painting of where we live."

It was a watercolor of the neighborhood around Grand Concourse. *Rather detailed for an eight-year-old*, Conor thought. Olta had even depicted the dangerous group of men who were obviously a fixture on the corner. In her innocent view, they were just people, not drug dealers or pimps or rapists or killers. If only Olta's innocence could last. But not here. Innocence dies hard in neighborhoods like these.

"That's beautiful, Olta," Monica said.

"The best painting I ever saw," Conor agreed.

Olta beamed. "Really?"

"Really," Conor said.

Olta seemed a little embarrassed, becoming all knees and elbows. "I like to paint."

"And you paint very well," Monica assured her.

Conor was suddenly mesmerized by one of the

photos of Besa, an eight-by-ten color print in a silver, easel-type frame placed on a dresser between a candle and a plastic flower. The picture captured an instant in the life of a youthful woman standing in a meadow full of spring blooms, a mountain rising behind her. As he looked into Besa's eyes, she became truly present to him. *I'm going to find the man who took your life*, Conor almost whispered aloud. *I will not rest until I do.*

"Conor?" Monica touched his arm.

He snapped back to the confines of the Bronx apartment.

"Are you okay?" Monica asked.

Conor looked around. Olta wasn't there. He glanced down at Monica's hand on his arm.

"No touching," Conor said with a smile.

"Coffee's ready."

They were both startled. Fatmir was standing in the doorway. Monica quickly withdrew her hand. Fatmir walked away.

"That was *your* fault," Conor whispered.

Monica bit her lip, then quickly left the room.

Chapter Forty-seven

The time Conor spent drinking his coffee was as awkward a five minutes as he could remember. Monica, who had once again strategically positioned herself on the love seat across the room from where he was sitting, seemed painfully ill at ease. Fatmir was about as talkative as a statue. Consuela was overly affectionate, even sitting on Fatmir's lap at one point, accentuating the fact that Fatmir appeared to have left his dead wife's memory far behind. Olta sat on the floor in the corner, combing the hair of a doll that Conor imagined looked a lot like Besa.

As Conor downed the last of his coffee, there was a lull in the conversation so deafening it was unbearable. He could hear a clock ticking, the swish of Consuela's panty hose as she crossed her legs, Fatmir's uneven breathing. *Time to get the hell out of here*, he thought. Although Conor was glad he had brought Monica to the Bronx, it might have been better to have had only the night before to remember.

"Thank you for the coffee," Conor said as he stood. "I better get back to work."

"On a Sunday?" Consuela asked.

"Unfortunately, criminals don't take days off," he replied.

Fatmir stood. "Thank you for bringing Monica up here."

His tone was dismissive. The way Fatmir said it, Conor felt as if he were being thanked for dropping off a bag of groceries.

Monica got up from the love seat but stayed planted in front of it, not daring to take even a step toward Conor.

"Olta," Monica said. "Say goodbye to Mr. Bard."

Olta obediently scrambled to her feet. "Bye, Mr. Bard."

Everybody stood rooted in his or her own spot. Conor wondered what to do. Monica walked slowly into the foyer and Conor followed her. They stopped in front of the door. Monica opened it.

"Thank you for everything," she said. "It was nice meeting you in America."

"It was nice meeting you, too."

Conor carefully caressed Monica's eyes for the last time before turning and trudging down the stairs.

The traffic had begun to build in the southbound lanes of the West Side Highway, people returning early in the day from their weekend retreats, so Conor took the exit at 125th Street onto Riverside Drive. He crisscrossed the Upper West Side, choosing whatever street was clear, and found himself on Broadway and Ninety-sixth.

Conor stared blankly at the red light. *So that was it? Standing at the door, close to her but far away?* His defenses kicked in. *There's a cultural divide between us. It could never work. I'll never go to Albania. What was I thinking?*

Conor didn't wait for the light to change. He turned on the flashers, stepped on the gas, and blasted through the intersection. Now he was speeding down Broadway, siren blaring. But where was he going? Not home. Definitely not home.

Conor turned off the flashers and sirens, then drove slowly south. The car seemed to float, a branch drifting down a lazy river. When he reached the lower tip of Manhattan, he had no recollection of having driven there. He turned toward the Hudson and then pointed the car north, back on the West Side Highway.

On the way uptown, he realized he needed to buy guitar strings. He stopped by Sam Ash on Forty-eighth Street and picked through the various brands. Sometimes he opted for steel, sometimes nickel-plated. Round-wound or flat-wound, depending on his mood and what his song list would be for that night. He bought several sets of each type.

As he left the store he wondered when he would be able to schedule another gig. That, of course, would depend on where they were with the Lawton homicide. It occurred to him that he had never put his music career first. Ever. *I should just quit the job*, Conor told himself. But he couldn't, not in the middle of a case. And there was another consideration: money. Could he *afford* to quit?

Conor ran through the reality of his financial situation. Not that much cash socked away. A few stocks, some mutual funds. He calculated what his pension would be if he took early retirement. In a couple months he would complete twenty years of service, which meant he would receive half of his eighty-eight-thousand-a-year salary. Forty-four thousand. And there would be additional payments of twelve thousand a year from the Variable Supplement Fund. That added up to fifty-six thousand a year, probably thirty-five or forty thousand after taxes. Pretty good if you lived anywhere but New York City.

What if he stayed on the job a little longer? He was a detective second grade. Why not go for a promotion to detective first grade? A raise in pay would mean more pension when he retired. But that was the trap almost every cop he knew had fallen into, chasing a higher pension until they were too old to enjoy it.

Yet if he retired now, the pressure to succeed on the music front would really come to bear. Was he up to the challenge? *I've got to wrap up this Lawton thing one way or another*, Conor thought. *And then I can think clearly about what to do next.*

Conor decided to head back to the precinct and

pore over what scant evidence existed. *Maybe I missed something*, he thought. *Maybe there's something right in front of my eyes that I didn't see.* But he knew what he really needed was a "shocking discovery," as Monica had put it. Without something unexpected dropping in his lap, he was going nowhere. It didn't matter how good a detective he was, he was at the point where he had to get lucky.

Amanda, a piece of paper in her hand, ambushed Conor the minute he walked up to his desk. "DeBellis just faxed this," Amanda said. "He located that guy you were looking for."

"What guy?"

"That Albanian," Amanda replied. "Fitim Bregu."

Chapter Forty-eight

Conor couldn't believe it. "DeBellis found Bregu? That's great. So where is he?"

"Right now he's probably about fifty thousand feet over the Atlantic," Amanda said.

"What?"

"DeBellis just received a communication from Homeland Security," Amanda explained. She perused the fax in her hand. "Fitim Bregu boarded Alitalia flight six-zero-five to Milan, booked through to Tirana, Albania. It left at five fifty-five this afternoon." She checked her watch. "Half an hour ago."

"Why weren't we notified *before* Bregu got on the plane?" Conor was annoyed. "He must've checked in around four o'clock."

"What can I tell you?" Amanda said, arms open. "Somebody dropped the ball."

"When did he book his ticket?"

Amanda checked the sheet of paper. "Friday night.

Ten forty-seven. First class, no less. Seems the plane was full and that's all he could get."

Conor sighed in frustration. "*That's* when someone should have called us. Isn't there supposed to a be a watch list? What if Bregu was a terrorist?"

"Look, Bard. I totally agree with you. There are too many cracks in the system. Too many slimeballs slipping through the crevices. Something's definitely got to be done. But, for now, it is what it is."

"Can we detain Bregu in Milan?"

"Sure," Amanda said. "First you've got to get the DA to file charges. Then contact the Italian government and *then* get the Italians to move on it. He arrives in Milan at seven fifty-five a.m. local time. So you've got seven hours. On a Sunday night. Good luck."

She handed the fax to Conor. He stared at it in disbelief.

"Laura says hello," Ralph said as he walked up to them. "I was going to go home but then I thought I'd stop by and . . ."

He looked at Conor and Amanda. The expression on their faces signaled something was wrong.

"What's up?" he asked.

"Bregu flew the coop," Conor replied. "Literally."

Conor and Ralph reconvened in Amanda's office.

"Okay," Ralph began. "Let's walk through this. We're going to have to get the DA to file charges if we want to intercept Bregu in Milan, right?"

"Charge him with what?" Amanda asked. "You guys can't link Bregu to Lawton's death, so murder one's out of the question. What's left?"

Ralph scratched his forehead. "Criminal weapons possession?"

"Yeah," Conor agreed. "But we'll need Fat Albert's testimony to pull that off, and he's in L.A."

"You don't have proof Bregu threatened anyone, do you?" Amanda asked. "And he wasn't seen with a gun at a school. So none of the requirements for felony gun possession exist."

"Which leaves fourth-degree criminal weapons possession," Conor offered.

"A class-A misdemeanor," Amanda noted. "I don't think misdemeanor gun possession is going to get the Italian police all worked up."

Conor looked at Ralph. "So we get more on Bregu, hang him with something that'll stick, then seek extradition."

"*If* we can find him in Albania," Ralph said.

Amanda tapped the keys on her computer keyboard, peered at the screen. "The extradition treaty between the United States and Albania was signed in 1935. It says the two countries agreed that, quote, 'upon requisition duly made as herein provided, deliver up to justice any person who may be charged with, or may have been convicted of, any of the crimes or offenses specified in Article Two of the present treaty.' End quote."

"What does Article Two say?" Conor asked.

Amanda tapped the keys, scrolled down. "Article Two: 'Persons charged with or convicted of murder are explicitly subject to extradition.'" She looked up at Conor. "The operative words are *charged* and *convicted*. Bregu is neither."

"How about as a material witness?" Ralph asked. "Can we bring him back to the U.S.?"

"Let's see," Amanda said as she typed. She scanned the computer screen for a long moment. "Here's a case where an Albanian man is attempting to block extradition to the United States by claiming the extradition treaty between the United States and Albania is no longer valid because the Kingdom of Albania no longer exists."

Conor frowned. "Kingdom?"

Amanda continued. "The defense lawyers are asking the court to rule that Albania is not a signatory to the original extradition treaty because whatever agreements the *Kingdom* of Albania made with other countries were rendered invalid when the *Republic* of Albania was formed in 1946."

"In other words—" Ralph began.

"In other words," Amanda interrupted, "if you think slogging through the criminal justice system in New York is a pain in the ass, try making your way through the swamp of international law." She tapped the keys again. "Or even worse, politicians. It says here that any treaty between the United States and another country after a governmental change in that country is a *political* question, not a question for the courts."

"All right," Conor said. "Whatever hoops we have to jump through to get him back here, that's what we do. We track Bregu's contacts in New York. Find out who he was calling in Albania." He turned toward Amanda. "You get Bregu's phone records?"

"No," Amanda said. "I did not get Fitim Bregu's phone records." She sighed. "I couldn't get a warrant."

Conor slumped. "What about that judge? You said—"

"I know what I said," Amanda interrupted. "But the bastard told me he didn't see any convincing evidence that Bregu was involved in Lawton's murder." She shook her head. "That guy's never going to see *my* bare ass again."

Conor and Ralph were momentarily stunned by Amanda's comment.

"Hey," Amanda retorted. "You try being a woman with my hours. You take what you can get."

She stood and walked around her desk to Conor and Ralph. "You guys bring me something more, I'll go back to the well. I know other judges."

Conor didn't want to ask.

Amanda looked at Ralph. "By the way, I thought you retired on Friday."

"I did."

"So why are you here?"

"Why are *you* always here?"

"Good point." Amanda slapped the side of Ralph's shoulder. "See you tomorrow night."

* * *

Conor and Ralph walked through the squad room.

"What are you doing for dinner?" Conor asked.

"Got a gorgeous redhead with big tits stopping by to grill me a steak."

"So you're free. That what you're saying?"

"I'm cheap, but I'm not free."

"Let's grab something to eat," Conor said. "Have a little farewell party. It's on me."

Ralph stopped. Conor stopped.

"Did I hear you right?" Ralph was incredulous. "You're buying me dinner?"

They started walking again.

"Where you taking me?" Ralph asked.

"McDonald's."

"Can I supersize?"

Chapter Forty-nine

Maria Pia was packed. Conor and Ralph sat at Conor's usual table, two martinis in front of them.

"I shouldn't be drinking this," Ralph said, taking a sip.

"It can't be worse for you than a Fat Albert sandwich."

"Yeah, I guess you're right. One's bad for your heart, the other one's bad for your liver." Ralph took a healthy swig of his martini. "What the hell? Something's gonna kill me someday. Might as well taste good."

"That's a pleasant thought," Conor said.

"So how'd it go in the Bronx?" Ralph asked.

Conor shrugged. "It was okay. The brother-in-law's strange, but the niece is a cute little girl. Looks like Monica. Made me want to have kids."

"So you're glad you went?"

"Yeah."

"Can you say 'Thanks, Ralph'?"

"Thanks, Ralph," Conor said. "It was the right thing to do."

Ralph sipped his martini. "I hate to leave you with this Lawton mess."

"Yeah. But according to NYPD, you're too old to be much good anyway."

"They're probably right."

"Besides, you don't really care that a lawyer was murdered, do you?"

"No, I don't," Ralph said. "You want to know why?"

"I think you already told me, didn't you? Over and over and over."

"I never told you *this*." Ralph looked down at the table. "I usually don't talk about it."

Conor waited for Ralph to continue but he just kept staring at the table.

"Ralph? You okay?"

Ralph looked up at Conor. "When Laura got sick, the doctors told me she needed an operation. But the insurance company said it wasn't necessary. The *insurance* company?" He drained the last of his martini. "So I called, wrote letters, made a real pest of myself. I finally got the woman assigned to Laura's case to sign off on the surgery."

Conor twisted the stem of his martini glass, unable to look at Ralph.

Ralph smiled, remembering. "Laura and I celebrated that night. I bought a really good bottle of champagne. The next day, I get a call from the woman at the insurance company. The CEO had overruled her recommendation that Laura undergo the procedure. So I called the CEO. He wouldn't take my calls. I went over there, walked right in his office. He had security throw me out. And then I found out that the CEO was a corporate lawyer who was paid big bucks to take over the insurance company. And you know what his specialty was when he was practicing law?"

Conor finally looked at Ralph. "What?"

"His specialty was defending major corporations against wrongful-death suits." Ralph's eyes watered. "That's why the insurance company brought in that son of a bitch. So when they let people die they had a hired gun sitting in the executive suite who knew how to squash the lawsuits." He swallowed hard. "After that, I tried everything, called every hospital, every doctor in the country, begged them to perform the surgery. I even called places in Europe. China. Russia. Mexico. Wherever. And then it was too late. Laura was gone."

"I'm sorry, Ralph."

Ralph cleared his throat to keep from choking up.

"Why didn't you tell me this before?" Conor asked.

"Why didn't you tell me you were color-blind?"

"That's a little different," Conor replied.

"No. It's the same thing. I don't know what colors you see. You can't possibly know what it's like to lose the most precious thing in your life for no reason other than corporate greed." Ralph held up his empty martini glass. "I think I need another one of these."

Conor looked toward the bar, motioned to Ralph's glass, held up two fingers. The bartender set about making another round of martinis.

"Where were we?" Ralph asked, rubbing his eyes.

"Talking about the Lawton case."

"Oh, yeah." Ralph leaned toward Conor. "I was thinking. Maybe you ought to forget it. Not because of what I just said but because it's what you should do under the circumstances."

"Yeah, you're right," Conor agreed. "Bregu's in Albania. Fat Albert's in L.A. The wife is untouchable at this point. Anatoli Sidorov is already serving life in prison, so even if Sidorov was somehow involved, what do we gain? Zeffri's dead. Who else we got? And what leads we going to follow? The shoe prints? The only suspect to come out of that was you."

Ralph laughed, then shook his head. "Maybe it *is* all mob business. Like Marks said. Simple as that. A bunch of scumbags killing each other. Which is hard to get too worked up about."

"Then what about Bregu? How does he fit in to this?"

"Probably nothing more than a guy who buys and sells guns. A little extra cash on the side."

"So I should just let the feds do the heavy lifting?"

"That's what I'm thinking." Ralph patted Conor's shoulder. "Besides, without me here to help you, you'll never solve the case anyway."

A waiter delivered two fresh martinis. Conor stared at the glass. Besa's smiling face formed on the surface of the shimmering vodka. And then slowly disappeared.

Conor was filled with a sudden resolve. He was done with the Lawton case. There was only one killer he wanted to track down. The monster who ended the life of Monica's sister and robbed Olta of a mother's love.

Chapter Fifty

Since it was a send-off of sorts for Ralph, Conor didn't spare his wallet or his palate when it came to the wine. He selected a very good bottle of Italian red, a Feudi di San Gregorio Serpico. It seemed a fitting libation for the occasion, not just because of its viticultural genealogy but also because it bore the name Serpico, the moniker of a cop who, in 1970, exposed widespread corruption within the NYPD.

"Frank Serpico," Ralph said as he examined the label. The connection between the wine and the cop hadn't escaped him. "Shot in the face with a twenty-two-caliber handgun."

This was something else that made the wine appropriate, although Conor hadn't thought of it. A .22-caliber weapon was used to wound Serpico and kill Lawton. Conor hoped that once they finished the bottle, it would be the last he would hear of the number 22 for a very long time.

As they waited for the food to arrive, Conor and

Ralph segued into stories from their long partner-ship.

"I remember the first time we went on a raid," Ralph recalled. "You were scared to death."

"No, I wasn't."

"You *weren't*? Then how come when the thing was all over, I looked at your gun and you still had the safety on?"

"Because you were running around in front of me and I didn't want to shoot you."

"Okay. But what about the time you lost the evidence?"

Conor frowned. "What evidence?"

"The robbery at that bodega." Ralph roared with laughter. "You picked up that glove with the end of a pencil. I mean, you were *so* careful. Next thing I know, the Crime Scene Unit gets there and the glove is nowhere to be found."

"I told you," Conor said, "somebody stole it."

"Stole it? Who would steal one glove?"

"All I know is I put it in an evidence bag and left it on the counter."

"You should've kept your eye on it."

"Me? *You* were the senior partner. Why didn't *you* secure it?"

"If the glove's been taken, it's *you* who's mistaken."

Conor had to laugh. "What? You're Johnnie Cochran now?"

"At least *I* never did anything dumb," Ralph said.

"No, Ralph. You were a perfect partner."

"Thank you."

Ralph took a sip of wine. "This stuff is pretty good."

"Nothing but the best for my perfect partner."

"Actually, I wasn't perfect."

Conor raised an eyebrow. "Really?"

"No. There was one time when I thought I had made a mistake, but I was wrong."

"Very funny, Ralph."

"Seriously, though, I know I wasn't perfect. But compared to you . . ." Ralph smiled, held up his glass. "Here's looking at *you*, kid. It's been a helluva ride."

Conor picked up his glass. "I'd like to say the same thing." He paused. "I'd *like* to say the same thing, but . . ."

They both laughed, clinked glasses.

Conor studied Ralph for a moment. Ralph appeared to be drained. He always looked that way after visiting Laura's grave.

"Why don't you take the day off tomorrow?" Conor said. "You know, relax before your big night."

"I already took half a day off today," Ralph protested. "Why do I want to take tomorrow off?"

"Because I'm tired of looking at you."

"You know what? I'm tired of looking at you, too. So I *am* going to stay home tomorrow. Sleep till noon. Eat bacon and eggs in my boxer shorts. Head to the track and get a few dollars down on the ponies."

"Do me a favor. Whatever horse you pick . . ."

"Yeah?"

"Place a bet for me on every other horse in the race."

"Sure. How much? Ten? Twenty each?" But Ralph didn't expect an answer. His mood turned serious. "What are you going to do at the hearing tomorrow morning?"

Given the events of the past couple of days, Conor hadn't thought much about the fact that he was due in front of a tribunal at ten thirty, standing opposite his accuser, Captain Frank Reynolds.

"I don't know," he said. "I'll play it by ear."

Ralph sighed. "That's the problem with you. You don't listen. I already *told* you what to do. Hit them with the ex-girlfriend thing right away. Reynolds is humping Heather. That's why he wrote you up. Who's going to give a damn that you pulled a gun in a bar after hearing that?"

A waiter appeared with dinner. Conor and Ralph dug in immediately. After a couple minutes of cutting and chewing without speaking, Conor glanced at Ralph. "How's your pasta?"

"You hear me saying anything?" Ralph stuffed a forkful of linguine in his mouth. "So we agree?"

"That the food here is good?"

"No," Ralph replied. "That you're dropping the Lawton case."

"Don't worry. It's history."

"Good. No way you could be objective anyway."

"What are you talking about?"

"What do you think I'm talking about?" Ralph scooped up more pasta. "The wife."

"What is that supposed to mean?"

"It means what it means. I don't care what any-body says, she could be right in the middle of this thing, *especially* if it's mob business."

"You're right, Ralph. She *could* be in the thick of it. Which is why I *really* want to get off the case. So it won't be a conflict of interest to *get off* with Holly Lawton."

"*Right*," Ralph said, his voice dripping with sarcasm.

"What? You think that couldn't happen?"

"That woman is so scary it probably *could* happen. But I'm hoping you've got more sense than that. You know why? Because at your age, you can't afford to keep wasting your energy on fucked-up women. And didn't you just meet someone you care about?" Ralph pointed a finger at Conor. "You want my advice?"

"Not really."

"Well, I'm going to give it to you anyway. Explore the situation with that Albanian girl before you chip off another piece of your soul for some bitch. And then you do what we talked about this morning. You go after this guy who killed the girl's sister. You put that bastard's mug shot in your wallet and you look at it every day until you find him."

"Mug shots in my wallet? I'll be just like you."

"You could do worse."

"Okay, Ralph. So now I've got a mug shot in my wallet. What good's it going to do? This guy's been on the lam for six years. What? I'm going to bump into him on the street?"

"You never know," Ralph insisted. "There was a detective, name was Carney. He was positive this doctor killed his wife. There was no body, she was listed as a missing person. No evidence. Just his gut told him the doctor killed her. Six months Carney works the case, finally gives up. Then one day Carney hears about an auction of rental cars. Hertz, Avis, I don't remember. Now, these cars take a lot of abuse, but the thing is, they're almost new, a year old, and they're cheap. And that's what Carney needed. A cheap car."

Ralph poured more wine for both of them.

"So Carney buys this car," he continued. "Takes it home. He opens the trunk and what does he see?"

"Okay," Conor said, resigned, "I'll play along. The wife's body was in the trunk."

"No such luck. What he finds is a little piece of metal. He picks it up and realizes it's a slug. So Carney gets the rental history of the car. A name jumps out at him."

"The doctor."

"The doctor's mistress. Carney goes over to her house. Turns out she and the doctor had split up. Which is always a good thing, to have an ex you can lean on. You know that saying: Hell hath no fury like a woman scorned."

"Tell me about it."

"Carney confronts the mistress about the bullet. She breaks down. Admits to helping the doctor move the body. The bullet must've fallen out when they put the dead wife in the trunk. Turns out the barrel marks on the slug match a gun owned by the doctor. End of story." Ralph leaned across the table. "What I'm trying to tell you is, these things happen all the time. *You* should know, of all people. Last weekend when you collared Willis at the Rhythm Bar? What do you call that?"

"I call it a hell of a coincidence."

"Einstein's a pretty smart guy, right? E equals MC squared? Well, that's nothing compared to what he said about Robert Willis walking into the bar that night."

"I didn't realize Einstein was on the job."

Ralph leaned over the table, his expression intense.

"'Coincidence is God's way of remaining anonymous.' That's what Einstein said. And if ever God needed to intervene, it's on behalf of that poor girl whose autopsy report is sitting on your desk."

Coincidence? Divine intervention? Conor wasn't planning to wait around for either one.

Chapter Fifty-one

Conor and Ralph stood in front of Maria Pia. "You hanging out?" Ralph asked.

"Yeah," Conor replied. "I really don't feel like going home."

"Just do everything I told you, kid, and you'll be okay."

"Yes, *sir*."

"See you tomorrow night."

"Tomorrow night?" Conor pretended he had no idea what Ralph was talking about. "What's tomorrow night?"

"Jesus," Ralph replied, slapping his forehead. "I forgot. You weren't invited."

"That's all right. I'll just crash the party." Conor grew serious. "You okay to drive? I never saw you drink so much."

"Yeah, I guess I did pound down a few tonight. But I'm fine. Really."

Ralph headed down the street. Conor watched

him until he turned the corner and disappeared. Their long partnership was over, which filled him with a profound sense of loss. He headed back into the restaurant and sat at the table. *Change sucks*, he thought. *Why can't everything just stay the same?*

Conor thought about having a *scropino*, which was a cross between a cocktail and a dessert. It was made with vodka, fruit-flavored liqueur, and lemon Italian ice. It was rather sweet, so you had to be in the mood to drink one. Conor wasn't. He ordered another martini then stared through the front window, mindlessly watching people drift by—mostly couples, hand in hand. He imagined that everyone in the world was happy except him.

Conor's cell phone rang. He pulled it out of his pocket and checked the caller ID.

It was Holly.

He sighed. Now what? He thought about not answering but his hand seemed to have a mind of its own. It flipped open the phone.

"Hello, Holly."

"Conor. Am I disturbing you?"

"Actually . . ."

"I saw a play and I was about to head home but then I thought: Why not call Conor?"

Conor almost laughed. *When did we become best friends?*

"Where are you?" Holly asked.

"I just finished dinner and I was about to—"

"Have a drink with me."

"Holly."

"Just one drink. I can't face that house right now."

Conor sighed, looked out the front window. Another blissful couple floated past. *Maybe not everyone is so happy*, he thought. *There's me. And there's Holly.*

"Okay," he said.

As it turned out, Holly was only a few blocks away, reclining in the back of her limo at Eighth Avenue and Forty-fourth Street. Conor gave her Maria Pia's address and then hung up. *This should be interesting*, Conor thought.

Holly arrived five minutes later. When she walked into the restaurant, every waiter, every busboy, every male patron drew in a sharp breath. As usual, she looked absolutely stunning. She had shed her coat in the limo and made her grand entrance in a pair of tight-fitting jeans capped by a crisp white blouse unbuttoned to the top of her unfettered breasts. Her high-heeled boots clicked on the floor.

Conor stood. Holly swept toward him so fast that she had her arms around his waist before he could even greet her.

"Conor," she said as she hugged him.

"Hello, Holly."

Conor eased her arms away and pulled out a chair. The minute they sat down, Holly scooted her chair closer to him.

"What would you like to drink?" Conor asked.

"I don't know," Holly replied, crossing her legs. "Surprise me."

"You ever had a *scropino*?"

"I love *scropino*," Holly said.

Of course, Conor thought. *Is there anything she hasn't had?*

Conor flagged down a waiter, ordered a *scropino*.

"I saw this very interesting play tonight," Holly said.

"What was it?"

"It wasn't on Broadway or anything. It was in one of those little theaters on Forty-second and Tenth. The woman who does my nails?" Holly paused to admire her perfectly manicured fingers. "Her daughter is an actress. And she was pretty good. You should see it."

"What's the play called?"

"I don't remember," she said, still examining her nails. "*Passion* something."

Conor studied Holly. She had a way of making you wonder if what she said was the truth even if you knew it was. *Did she even see a play?* he wondered.

"I wanted to talk to you about Walter's murder," Holly said. "I don't think—"

"I'm not on the case anymore."

"Really?"

But Holly didn't seem all that surprised he was removing himself from the case, which reinforced Conor's notion that this had somehow been her plan all along.

A waiter placed a *scropino* in front of Holly. She picked it up, took a sip.

"Very nice," she said. Then: "What I was going to say was, I don't think Sal killed Walter."

Conor picked up his martini. He had to have a healthy shot of vodka after hearing *that*. Wasn't she the one who was so convinced that Zeffri *was* the shooter?

"What makes you say that?" he said as he placed the glass back on the table.

"Oh, come on, Conor. You know very well who my husband's clients were."

"I do."

"Well, I heard through the grapevine that Sal didn't do it. No matter what else Sal was, he was a good soldier. He wouldn't have killed Walter without approval. And no way it was sanctioned by . . ." Her voice trailed off.

"Delprete?"

"I think we both know who we're talking about," Holly replied coyly.

Chapter Fifty-two

The FBI had all but confirmed that Lawton was indeed whacked by Delprete. Conor wanted to explain to Holly that these people she referred to as "my husband's clients" were ruthless scumbags capable of anything. Of course Delprete didn't want Holly to know he was the one who had made her a widow. That could cause complications. So Delprete floated some disinformation and Holly bought it.

Or did she? As Conor studied the lovely feminine form perched on the chair next to him, it suddenly struck him that maybe *he* was the one being fed misinformation. After all, could he trust anything Holly said? She had wanted Zeffri arrested. Now Zeffri was dead. So what if Delprete had sent Zeffri to kill Lawton then had Zeffri taken care of as well? Had Holly been dispatched by Delprete to tie up loose ends, deflect the investigation away from the mob?

Conor felt a creeping paranoia overtaking his sense of reason. He tried to shake it off. *Holly can't be part of a Mafia conspiracy*, he told himself. *She just can't be.* But hadn't she just described Zeffri as a "good soldier"? Which meant she'd screwed a guy she *knew* was a mobster. If drama was Heather's drug, then danger was obviously Holly's choice of stimulant.

"I want Walter's killer brought to justice," Holly said, taking another sip of her *scropino*. "Whoever it is."

"So do I," Conor said. "I'll let you know who takes over the case."

Holly tilted her head, smiled. "No one can take your place, Conor." She seemed suddenly sad. "You know what I feel guilty about when I think of Walter?"

"What?" Conor asked. He expected her to say, *Fucking Sal Zeffri.*

Instead, she said, "That night I embarrassed Walter at Elaine's."

Elaine's. On Eighty-eighth and Second. Conor had been there a couple of times with a retired detective who frequented the place. It was known as a celebrity joint but few people knew it also was a favorite spot for cops.

"What did you do?"

"Well, Walter was a regular at Elaine's before we met. We had our first date at Elaine's, but he didn't like to take me there after that. He told me he used the place for business and he didn't like to mix business with pleasure. After a while, I figured out that he would take his girlfriends up there. That's really why he didn't want to take me."

Conor wondered if this was the incident Linda

Lawton had referred to, a night when Holly had made a scene at a restaurant.

"Anyway," Holly continued, "Walter told me he had a business dinner at Elaine's. I knew that wasn't true. So I sat home, got a little drunk, and went up there." She sighed. "I acted so badly. It was terrible. All his friends were there watching. That was the only time I ever saw Walter cringe."

Holly stared off for a moment. "I met with Linda this afternoon," she said abruptly as she turned toward Conor. "Walter's sister."

Conor braced himself for some horrific account of that meeting.

"You asked me last night if I was planning to fight Linda over the will," Holly continued.

"Are you?"

"No," she replied. "Linda and I made a deal."

Conor shook his head slightly. Holly certainly was full of surprises.

"I thought about it all last night," Holly went on. "And I realized that I would be fighting Walter's entire law firm. I *could* win, I realized that. But I could lose, too. Plus, even though Linda never liked me, I didn't want to put her through a long court battle. She worshiped her brother, you know." She smiled sweetly. "So I made her an offer she couldn't refuse."

Coming from anyone else, that would have sounded like a joke. But from Holly, considering her connections, it rang ominously.

"Which was?" Conor asked.

"I keep the townhouse," Holly explained. "I really do love that place."

"You keep the townhouse."

"Right. And besides the ten million in the prenup, I get another twenty million. She would have spent that anyway on legal fees."

Conor frowned. "You stood to get over two *hundred* million. Thirty million doesn't sound like much of a compromise."

"I'm not done."

Conor smiled. *Of course she's not done.*

"So I'm happy with the thirty million I'm getting. Who needs more than thirty million? But that means Linda is getting a hundred and eighty million of the money Walter left to me in the will—before he was planning to divorce me, I mean—*and* her own inheritance, which is half a billion . . ."

Conor's head was swimming. Numbers like those were unfathomable to a cop on a salary.

"So . . ." Holly crossed her arms. "I told her she had to donate fifty million dollars to breast cancer research."

Conor was stunned. Not only did Holly walk away from a fortune, not that thirty million wasn't fortune enough, but she managed to create a windfall for charity.

Holly uncrossed her arms and crossed her legs. She leaned back in the chair. "What do you think, Conor?"

He smiled. "All I can say is, well done."

Holly soaked up Conor's approval for a moment. "You see," she said, flicking her hair with her hand. "I'm not so bad, am I?"

"No," Conor said, a smile creeping across his face. "Not so bad."

Holly yawned. She quickly covered her mouth. "Oh, I am *so* sorry. But I didn't sleep a wink last night."

"It's all right. That's a natural impulse."

"I love natural impulses." Holly took Conor's hand. "Now that you're not on the case anymore, can we have dinner one night?"

Conor wasn't sure what to say. After all, she still wasn't cleared of involvement in her husband's murder and might never be entirely free of suspicion— not to mention what Ralph had said about chipping off a piece of his soul.

"Let's talk about that later," Conor replied, being polite.

Holly pouted. "Okay." She rubbed her eyes. "I really *am* tired. I should go."

"Yeah," he agreed. "I should head home too. I've got an early day tomorrow."

"You want a ride?"

"No," he replied. "I only live three blocks away. I could use the fresh air."

"Walk me to the car?"

"Sure."

They stood and made their way outside to the waiting limousine. Conor opened the back door.

"Thanks for listening to me," Holly said. She

leaned forward and kissed Conor on the lips. It was a soft kiss, a breeze caressing a willow branch. Then she eased into the backseat.

"Good night, Conor."

"Good night, Holly."

Conor shut the door. He watched the limo glide down the street, then went back into Maria Pia. Luca walked up to him.

"Who was *that*?" Luca asked.

"I don't know," Conor said. "I really don't know."

Chapter Fifty-three

Conor entered his apartment and stood just inside the door, a blank stare on his face. He was a zombie, moving at the will of voodoo princess Holly Lawton. *Why does seeing her always do this to me?* Conor asked himself. He recalled the first time he'd met her and relived the dream that had troubled him so much that Sunday night.

Heather smiling at him, then disappearing. He was alone somewhere. Feeling empty, afraid. A kiss on his cheek. A hand taking his. His nostrils filling with perfume. Turning and pulling her against his chest.

But it wasn't Heather in his arms in the dream. It was Holly Lawton. Conor shuddered at the recollection. He remembered thinking then that Holly had found her way deep into the primal level of his consciousness. He had shaken off the bizarre notion at the time, but now he realized with horror that it was true. He had no idea what inside his psyche allowed her to affect him the way she did. Sure, she was gorgeous, sexy, excitingly crazy, but how many women had he met like that? Maybe not as stunning as Holly, but damned close. And these women were definitely as insanely sensual as Holly was. But they had never gotten to him the way Holly had managed to do. Why?

And there was another why.

Why was Holly seemingly so attracted to him? He was a cop, a blue-collar kind of guy. He didn't have male-model looks, far from it. He didn't have money. So what did she find so irresistible about him? The best answer Conor could come up with was the fact that he was investigating the death of her husband. That's what made him unique to Holly. And if that was the sole reason she was all over him, it only served to reinforce the possibility that she had been somehow involved in the murder. But that wasn't even the worst of it. *She could be up to her pretty ass in mob business*, Conor thought. *What the hell is wrong with me?*

Conor decided he would never see Holly again. *Never.* By this time tomorrow, the Lawton homicide would be somebody else's headache and there would be no reason to get anywhere near Holly's intense gravitational pull.

Thoughts of Monica enabled him to break free of Holly's orbit. The week with Monica seemed suddenly surreal, something that had never actually happened, and he was filled with melancholy. Albania loomed in his mind like an alien planet that he could see in the sky but would never visit. He tried to tell himself he would, in fact, plan a trip there. But when? How soon? A month? Two months? Would there still be a spark between them when and if he made his way to Tirana? Would it be the same? *Could* it be the same?

Conor wondered if he should just drop everything, take the couple weeks of vacation he had coming, accompany Monica back to Albania, keep the immediacy of their relationship from shattering into pieces of yesterday's imagined intimacy. He could surprise her at the airport, passport in hand. But how would she react? Would she be happy? Would she be freaked out? It didn't matter, because showing up at the gate unannounced was simply too daring a thing to expect his pragmatic mind to permit him to do. So, at least for now, he'd have to trust fate, or whatever or whoever it was that writes the future upon the wall.

Conor walked into the kitchen and pulled a bottle of vodka out of the freezer. He poured a small amount into a water glass, just enough for a quick nightcap, and headed into the living room. He passed his guitar, which was leaning against the wall, and was drawn to it. He picked it up, settled on the couch, and began mindlessly strumming. At some point, the melody of "For What It's Worth," a Buffalo Springfield song, became recognizable. Conor started singing. *"There's a man with a gun over there. Telling me I got to beware."*

Conor stopped. Of all the songs that could have spontaneously sprung from his lips, it had to be one with a gun reference. Obviously, his subconscious was working overtime. And what was his subconscious trying to tell him? Stop thinking about your love life and get ready for the disciplinary hearing. But he *was* ready, wasn't he? He would hit the brass with Reynolds's Heather connection and that would be that. He laughed out loud. It occurred to him that the source of all his angst had to do with one woman or another. Heather. Holly. Monica. *I should have been a priest*, he mused. *They drink all they want and never have to worry about women.* He took a sip of vodka. *Maybe it's not too late.*

Conor awoke exhausted, as if he hadn't slept at all. His eye sockets felt like metal rings inside his head and his neck hurt every time he twisted it to the right or left. A hot shower did little to ease the pain. He splashed ice-cold water on his face in an effort to reduce the puffiness around his eyes but that didn't work either. At least he would dress well. He pulled his suit for special occasions from the closet.

Conor wasn't sure if Amanda would be on duty but when he walked into her office, there she was. Just like always. He wondered why Amanda even bothered to have a home.

"Got a minute, Sarge?" Conor asked her.

"A minute," Amanda replied. "That's all I've got." She waved her hand at a pile of folders. "Has to be processed today."

"I wanted to talk to you about—"

"Hold that thought." Amanda looked past Conor. "Come on in."

Conor turned. A man was standing in the doorway. Young, probably no more than twenty-five. Medium height. Light brown hair. An athletic build.

"Thank you, Sergeant," the man said. He entered the office.

"Bard," Amanda said, "this is Steven Clyde. Just transferred in from the Three Four. I'm partnering you two."

Conor was caught off guard, a little annoyed, in fact. Amanda could partner him with whoever she wanted but Conor felt he deserved to be consulted. As it was, this adolescent—that's what he looked like—was being thrust upon him. But what could he do at this point? Conor extended his hand. "Conor Bard. Nice to meet you."

"Steven Clyde."

Steven grabbed Conor's hand in a firm handshake. Conor felt sharp pains in his knuckles. *Jesus, this kid is strong,* he thought.

"Why don't you guys go somewhere and get acquainted," Amanda said.

Conor looked at Amanda, his eyes saying he still had something to talk to her about.

"Come back in twenty minutes," Amanda said.

Conor and Steven left the office and walked toward their desks.

"When did you get your shield?" Conor wondered aloud.

"Two months ago."

It occurred to Conor that Steven had to be at least thirty years old to make detective, but he sure as hell appeared to be a lot younger.

"You mind if I ask your age?"

"I'm thirty-one," Steven replied.

Conor frowned. *I'm forty-two and look older, he's thirty-one and looks younger.* That *sucks.*

They reached their respective desks.

That's Ralph's *desk,* Conor thought as he watched Steven take a seat.

"What would you like me to do?" Steven asked.

"Whatever I tell you," Conor said, dropping into his chair.

"Of course. You're the senior partner."

Two things struck Conor about Steven's response. First of all, Steven didn't appear to have a sense of humor. Conor was joking when he said "Whatever I tell you." Steven was probably nervous and wanted to make sure he got off on the right foot, so Conor would reserve judgment. The content of what Steven said, however, had more of an impact than the humorless manner in which it was delivered. Steven had referred to him as the senior partner, which was true, but Conor had been junior partner for so long, actually since he'd made detective and teamed up with Ralph, that it sounded strange to be referred to as senior.

"Should I go over the Walter Lawton file?" Steven asked. "You're working that case, right?"

"*Was*," Conor replied. "I'm asking to be taken off the Lawton homicide."

"Whatever you say," Steven said reverentially.

Conor smiled. He hoped Steven would get over his awe soon. Conor needed a partner, not a dependent.

He checked his watch. It was quarter to ten. "I've got a meeting at ten thirty."

"The disciplinary hearing," Steven said.

Conor was surprised. "You know about that?"

"Everybody knows about that," Steven said, then added, "I just want to tell you that I would have done the same thing. That perp Robert Willis needed to be off the street. So I'm sure they won't take any action against you."

"Thanks for the vote of confidence. I'll let you know how it goes."

"Actually, I've got to go to the Three Four and complete the rest of my transfer papers. But I should be back by—"

"You know what, Steven?" Conor interrupted. "I've had a rough couple of days, so why don't we just start in the morning."

Steven stood. "Whatever you say."

"I'll see you tonight at Ralph Kurtz's retirement party?"

"Am I invited?"

"You just were," Conor said. "I want you to know what a tough act you have to follow in Ralph Kurtz."

"I'll do my best not to let you down," Steven said.

No quick comeback, no stinging counterpunch. *God, I hope he develops a sense of humor,* Conor thought.

"So I guess I'll see you tonight," Steven said.

"That you will."

Steven walked away. Conor recalled what Ralph had told him a couple of days ago. "*You're going to miss me,*" he'd said. Why was Ralph always right?

Conor looked down at his desk and found himself staring at John Hicks's rap sheet. *That bastard,* Conor thought. He opened a drawer, found a pair of scissors, picked up the rap sheet, and cut out Hicks's photo. Then he dug his wallet from his pocket and slid Hicks's mug shot inside.

Conor leaned back in his chair. Senior partner? Mug shot in his wallet? Had he *already* become Ralph?

Chapter Fifty-four

Amanda was on the phone when Conor walked in. "I'll have to get back to you," Amanda said into the phone, then hung up. She looked at Conor. "What's up, Bard?"

"The Lawton homicide."

"Yeah. How's that coming?"

"It's not."

"I didn't think it was."

"I'd like to be taken off the case." Conor readied himself for an argument.

"Okay. As of now, you're off the case."

Conor was surprised. "You're not going to give me a hard time?"

"You want me to?"

"No."

"The way I see it," Amanda said, "is that you and Kurtz gave it your best shot and you didn't get anywhere."

Conor was stung by the way she put it. Unfortunately, she was correct. He started to tell her about the meeting with Marks at the FBI field office, how the Bureau was convinced it was a mob hit, but then he remembered Marks had asked that what he told them stay in the room. *Let the new guys on the case figure it out*, he thought. *Not my problem anymore.*

"And since you're starting with a new partner," Amanda continued, "you're better off with a clean slate."

"Thanks, Sarge."

"Don't mention it. Just pull all your Lawton material together and get it to me as soon as you can." Amanda glanced at a clock on the wall. It was almost ten. "You better get going. The hearing's at ten thirty, right?"

Conor nodded.

"Good luck," Amanda said.

Conor headed downtown on the West Side Highway. He was berating himself for not getting an earlier start but since there wasn't much traffic, he felt confident he wasn't going to be late. *That* would be a disaster.

His cell phone rang. He checked the caller ID. It was Monica.

"Monica."

"Conor."

They let a wave of silence wash over them.

"I'm sorry about yesterday," Monica finally said.

"It's okay," Conor replied. "I understand."

"You do?"

"Yes."

"Thank you for saying that."

Conor was happy to hear that she felt as non-plussed as he did about their painfully uncomfortable goodbye.

"What time is your flight?" he wanted to know.

"Five fifty-five."

"Alitalia flight six-zero-five," Conor remarked.

"How did you know?" Monica asked.

"Fitim Bregu was on the same flight yesterday."

"So you caught him?"

"No. He had already taken off before we found out."

"I'm sorry."

"How are you getting to the airport?"

"Fatmir is driving me."

Another wave of unspoken communication, then: "I'll call you as soon as I get to Tirana."

"You'd better."

"Mirupafshim herën tjetër," Monica said.

"Does that mean goodbye in Albanian?"

"No," she replied. "I don't want to say goodbye. It means I hope to see you well next time."

"Meeropashin hear in teeter," Conor said, mangling the language so badly it made Monica laugh.

Conor snapped the phone shut with Monica's laughter still echoing in his head. The melody erased all doubt. He would plan a trip to Tirana as soon as he could arrange it.

*   *   *

Conor parked in front of One Police Plaza. It was 10:27, assuming his watch wasn't running slow. He hurried inside and took the elevator to the ninth floor. A uniformed officer was waiting for him.

"Detective Bard?"

"Yes."

The officer had the expression and demeanor of an executioner. He led Conor down a long hallway and stopped in front of an unmarked door. "In there, sir," he said flatly.

Conor opened the door and entered a conference room. At the head of the conference table were a deputy chief, a lieutenant, and a captain. Frank Reynolds, carefully avoiding eye contact, sat on the side.

"Good morning, Detective," the deputy chief said, his voice devoid of cheer.

"Good morning, Chief," Conor replied. He looked at the other two members of the three-man jury who would judge his actions that night in the Rhythm Bar. "Lieutenant. Captain."

"Have a seat, Detective," the deputy chief said.

Conor sat across from Reynolds.

"If no one has any objections," the deputy chief said, "I think we should begin." He stared at Conor. "You know why you're here, Detective. According to eyewitnesses, you drew a weapon in a room full of civilians when it was unnecessary to use lethal force, thereby creating a potentially dangerous situation."

Conor felt a sudden surge of anger. He bolted to his feet.

"No, Chief," Conor said. "That's not why I'm here."

The deputy chief frowned. "Why do you *think* you are here, Detective?"

"I'm here because Captain Frank Reynolds is fucking my ex-girlfriend."

Reynolds paled.

The lieutenant and the captain looked at each other in confusion.

"Excuse me?" The deputy chief said.

"Her name is Heather Calvert. Last week she came to me and told me that Captain Reynolds was extremely jealous of me and was unable to get over the fact that she and I had a relationship prior to the time Captain Reynolds met her."

Reynolds stood. "Chief, I don't see what any of this has to do with—"

"Captain Reynolds," the deputy chief said, his voice rising in admonishment. "Please let Detective Bard finish his statement."

Reynolds sighed heavily, eased back into his chair.

"You may continue," the deputy chief said.

"Thank you, Chief," Conor said. "Miss Calvert also related to me that Captain Reynolds had vowed to retaliate against me in some way and had told her about this scheduled hearing in a manner consistent with someone offering confirmation that he was actually carrying out that threat. I can provide you with Miss Calvert's contact information so she can be called in to testify."

Reynolds looked cornered. The deputy chief cleared his throat. "Would you please wait outside, Detective Bard?"

Chapter Fifty-five

Conor left the room and paced down the long hall-way. He felt a sense of relief. One way or the other the incident at the Rhythm Bar would be resolved. And no matter the outcome, he could live with it. A suspension? So what? He'd just use the time to concentrate on his music.

After nearly half an hour, the lieutenant emerged.

"Detective Bard?"

"Yes."

"We have decided not to pursue any disciplinary action against you at this time. You are free to go."

"Thank you, Lieutenant."

The lieutenant turned and went back into the room. Conor stared at the closed door. He wouldn't want to be Reynolds right now.

Conor entered the precinct, a spring in his step. Amanda spotted him from her office. She got up and walked over to him.

"How'd it go?"

"They dropped all disciplinary action."

"Congratulations. How'd you pull *that* off?"

"I just told them the truth."

"Which was?"

"Which was that Reynolds was sleeping with my ex-girlfriend."

"*What?*" Amanda stared at Conor in disbelief.

"I've been meaning to tell you."

"That's all right," she said, her voice steeped in sarcasm. "I can see why a minor detail like that would be something I didn't need to know."

"Well, now you know."

Amanda grimaced. "Reynolds screwing your ex-girlfriend? What a creep. What a bitch."

"You got that right."

When Conor sat behind his desk, he half-expected to hear Ralph make some pithy comment. But Ralph wasn't sitting across from him, and Conor would just have to get used to it.

Conor spent almost an hour gathering his Lawton notes and files, creating a stack on the left side of his desk. He smiled. It felt good to unload the case. He looked down at his suddenly clear desk. All that remained were a few sheets of paper. Besa's autopsy report and John Hicks's rap sheet, missing a section where he had cut out the mug shot.

Conor leaned back in his chair and began formulating a plan. He would do as Ralph had suggested, comb through every database, even the consumer search engines like Google, and learn as much about John Hicks as he could. He would build an extensive dossier. What were Hicks's past addresses? Who were his neighbors? Did he have any known acquaintances in the area? Where were his family members? In which prisons was he incarcerated? Who were his cellmates? Any scrap of information was not too insignificant to be thoroughly vetted.

Conor leaned forward and hunched over the keyboard. He would start with the criminal database, catalog all Hicks's previous offenses, going backward in time arrest by arrest, conviction by conviction.

Conor pulled up Hicks's most recent arrest before he murdered Besa. Hicks had been charged with rape, kidnapping, and various other counts relating to the crime. According to the police report, Hicks had abducted a twenty-three-year-old woman and repeatedly attacked her in an abandoned warehouse over the course of several hours. The outcome of the case was labeled: Acquittal. How was that possible?

Conor switched to the legal database and found the indictment and several documents pertaining to that case. He opened the file containing the trial transcript and scrolled past all the heading material to where the particulars began. The date. The charges. The name of the judge. He scrolled farther down. Conor's face grew ashen. *It can't be*, Conor thought. *It just can't be.*

But there it was, in undeniable pixels glowing from the computer screen. John Hicks was free to roam the city streets and kill Besa after his prior arrest because of the brilliant defense mounted by his attorney.

Walter Lawton.

Chapter Fifty-six

Conor stared at the screen. Walter Lawton had represented Besa's killer in a prior arrest. Conor was investigating Lawton's murder. His mind reeled. Fragments of encounters and conversations rose from his consciousness. An image of Fatmir formed in Conor's mind. Fatmir was from northern Albania. They practiced *Gjakmarrja* in the north—the taking of the blood.

Conor struggled to recall what Lirim, the bartender at Coals, had told him. He conjured up Lirim's voice.

When a member of your family kills someone, then a member of that family must take the blood from your family. So the family of the man my brother killed, by the law of the Kanun, must now kill my brother. They cannot find my brother. But they still want to take the blood.

Was that it? Did Fatmir want to take the blood but couldn't find John Hicks so he went after a surrogate? Walter Lawton. Did Fatmir kill Lawton? Did he pay Fitim Bregu to do it?

That seemed logical to Conor. An ancient Albanian law brought to bear in America. Fatmir took the blood. It was a clean theory, perfectly linear.

But there was something wrong here. How did Monica fit into that scenario? Conor had met Monica, Besa's sister, on a street corner. It was a chance encounter, wasn't it?

Coincidence is God's way of remaining anonymous, Ralph had told him, quoting Albert Einstein. Conor now found himself wanting to believe that, *needing* to believe it. *Monica had nothing to do with Lawton's murder,* Conor convinced himself. They happened to meet on the street corner. By accident. That's all there was to it.

He stood and headed out the door with no idea where he was going. He knew only that he had to start breaking everything down into manageable investigative chunks. By the time he climbed behind the wheel of his car he had decided that step one would be to determine Fatmir's whereabouts at the time Lawton was killed. If Fatmir had an unimpeachable alibi, then he wasn't the shooter, although he could have still hired Bregu.

Where did Fatmir work? Conor replayed the drive to the Bronx with Monica.

So what does Fatmir do for a living?

He's a doorman.

In the Bronx?

No. West End Avenue. A Hundred and Sixth Street. One of those old buildings.

West End Avenue and 106th Street was Conor's destination now. He turned on the flashers and the siren and sped up the West Side Highway. A few minutes later he was bounding from the car and walking into a building. Fatmir wasn't employed there so Conor crossed the street and entered another prewar structure. A doorman greeted him.

"May I help you?" the doorman asked.

"Does Fatmir Lisi work here?"

The doorman looked at Conor with suspicion. Conor badged him.

"Does Fatmir Lisi work here?" he asked again, holding the gold shield in the doorman's face.

"Yes."

The doorman had an accent that Conor was now able to easily identify as Albanian.

"What are his hours?" Conor asked.

"Four to twelve."

Lawton was killed during those hours. *Maybe,* Conor thought, *Fatmir does have an alibi.*

"Is he working today?"

"No. he's off Mondays and Tuesdays."

"So he works Sundays?" Conor pressed.

"Yes."

"How about last Sunday?"

"You mean yesterday? He took the day off."

"No. The Sunday before that."

"I'll have to check the log." The doorman walked

over to the desk. He opened a drawer and pulled out a black logbook. He flipped through the pages, stopped.

"Yes," the doorman said, looking up at Conor. "He was working."

Conor rubbed the back of his head. *Okay, but he had to take breaks. Dinner break, bathroom break, whatever.*

"What happens when you want to go to dinner?"

"The handyman fills in."

"Who was here that Sunday?"

"The handyman."

Conor was losing his patience. He took a step closer to the doorman. "Who was the handyman working Sunday before last?"

"José."

"Is he here now?"

"He's off Mondays."

"You know how I can find him?"

Conor located José at his home, which was a small apartment on East 119th Street in the center of Spanish Harlem. José was a diminutive man with a full head of jet black hair that Conor found himself envying.

"Fatmir went to dinner at eight," José said, "like he always does."

"When did he come back?"

"At nine."

There was always the possibility that José was lying to protect Fatmir, but Conor's instincts told him that José was being truthful.

"Did he take any other breaks?" Conor asked.

"Sure."

"When?"

"A couple of times," José said. "To go to the bathroom."

"Was he gone long?"

"Five minutes."

Conor wasn't sure if he was happy with this information or not. On the one hand, it seemed to eliminate Fatmir as the shooter. On the other hand, just because Fatmir was at his post didn't completely exonerate him. In fact, having Fitim Bregu kill Lawton during the hours that he was working could be construed as convenient timing for Fatmir.

As Conor walked to his car, a question popped into his head, one that he asked himself over and over. How did Lawton wind up standing in the middle of an empty lot by the Hudson River? Someone lured him there? Forced him to drive there? But who? *Lawton had a rendezvous with a woman that night*, Conor remembered. Where did he take her?

Holly, Conor thought. *She all but told me*. Conor pictured Holly sitting next to him at Maria Pia. He could hear her voice.

We had our first date at Elaine's. But he didn't like to

take me there after that. He told me he used the place for business and he didn't like to mix business with pleasure. After a while, I figured out that he would take his girl-friends up there.

Conor climbed into the car. Elaine's. It was worth a shot.

Chapter Fifty-seven

Conor parked in front of the restaurant, near the corner of Eighty-eighth Street and Second Avenue. A large window with *Elaine's* written across it in golden script dominated the storefront while a bright yellow awning covered the entrance. The place had been immortalized in countless books and had made an appearance in a great number of films, most notably Woody Allen's *Manhattan*—the opening montage ends with a shot of the window, and the first scene of the movie takes place inside.

It was with some reverence that Conor approached such a famous establishment during daylight hours and on police business.

The door was locked. Conor pressed the buzzer. After a moment, a woman appeared.

"We're closed," the woman said dryly.

"I'm not here for a drink." Conor took out his shield.

The woman pulled the door open. Conor entered.

Elaine was sitting at the bar. She had run the place since 1963 and over the years had engendered a fierce devotion from her regular customers.

"Hey, Detective," Elaine said. "Nice to see you."

Conor wasn't sure if she actually remembered him or had seen his gold shield when he came in.

"You were here with Selzer," Elaine said. "April."

The good news was that Elaine never forgot a face. The bad news was that the Sunday Lawton was killed happened to be one of the extremely rare nights when she wasn't at the restaurant until late. She had gone to an event at the Museum of Natural History and didn't get back until after Lawton had left.

"Diane told me Walter was here that night," Elaine said, then smiled. "At least he had a good meal."

Diane, the longtime manager, was the woman who had let him in. She recounted that Lawton had arrived at eight and left early, around ten fifteen, ten thirty.

"He was upset," Diane said. "I couldn't give him his regular table because we had a party of forty back there."

Conor felt he was finally on to something. The witness who had heard shots when she walked her dog said it was ten forty-five. If Lawton left Elaine's at ten fifteen or thereabouts, that would put him in the lot right on time.

"The woman who was with Walter Lawton," Conor asked Diane. "What did she look like?"

Diane sighed. "It was so busy I didn't have time to notice anybody."

"Can you give me a general description?"

Diane thought for a moment. "I don't know, dark hair. She had an accent. I think she was Spanish. Anyway, she looked Spanish."

Conor jolted. Of course. Consuela. A woman as sexy as Consuela could lead a man anywhere. So that was it. Fatmir places himself in the lobby of a building on West End Avenue, creating an alibi. He hires Bregu to kill Lawton, then gets Consuela to make sure Lawton winds up in the lot, where Bregu could pop him.

"Sorry," Diane apologized. "That's all I can tell you. Like I said, we had a party in the back. David Black's birthday party. The place was a zoo."

Conor needed to confirm that Consuela was Lawton's date. But how? Then it occurred to him that people take pictures at a birthday party. Lots of pictures.

"David Black?"

"He's a writer," Elaine explained.

Diane retrieved Black's phone number and address from a stuffed Rolodex. When Elaine asked Conor why he wanted to know who was with Lawton, Conor simply replied that the woman might be of some help in retracing Lawton's final hours. Elaine didn't press for details. Conor turned to leave.

"Come in for dinner sometime," Elaine said.

"I will," Conor replied.

When Conor arrived at David Black's apartment in Greenwich Village, David, in his early sixties, with snow white hair, was doing what writers do. He was writing.

David frowned. "You want to see my *what*?"

Conor felt a little foolish. From the look of the awards, book covers, movie posters, and television stills on the wall, he was interrupting a very busy man just to look at photos.

"The pictures from your birthday party," Conor repeated. "If you don't mind."

David was confused. "Why do you want to see the pictures of my birthday party?"

Conor offered David the same bare-bones explanation he'd given Elaine. David shrugged, led Conor to his desk, and motioned to a chair.

"You know how to use iPhoto?" David asked.

"Yeah."

David leaned over, grabbed the mouse, navigated to the iPhoto interface, and pulled up the collection of photos from the party.

"Let me know if you'd like to order prints," he said. "I'll be right back."

Conor sat down, placed his hand on the mouse. He was filled with anticipation. Who would he see dining with Lawton at Elaine's? Consuela? He focused his attention on the photos. There were about a hundred of them, but none seemed to have captured Lawton. He scrolled down and noticed one wide shot with tables in the background. He opened the photo and zoomed in. There was Lawton and his lovely date.

Monica.

Chapter Fifty-eight

Conor didn't want to believe it. Blood rushed to his head. His mouth became dry.

"You find what you were looking for?" David asked as he walked back into the room.

"No," Conor replied.

He thanked David for his time, then, almost staggering, made his way to the elevator. Images came at him in flashes. The ceiling. The floor. Overhead lights. He steadied himself against a wall.

The elevator arrived. Conor stepped inside next to two women. He grabbed a brass handrail.

"Are you all right?" one of the women asked.

Her voice echoed in Conor's ears. *Are you all right, right, right . . .*

"Yes," he managed.

The sudden downward motion of the elevator added to his disorientation. Finally, he was in the lobby and then out the door onto Seventh Avenue. Everything around him seemed hyperreal. Colors bled into each other. Buildings appeared to sway around him. Every step he took was in slow motion. He strained to remember where he had parked the car. Ninth Street between Sixth and Seventh Avenues. *Yes*, Conor recalled. *That's where it is.*

He rushed to the car and climbed inside. He stared through the windshield. What now? He checked his watch. It was almost four. Monica's flight was scheduled to leave at 5:55. *She's at the airport by now, checking in.* He started the engine and pointed the car east toward the Midtown Tunnel. He took out his cell phone, thumbed through the phonebook, and hit SEND.

"Miller," a voice said.

"Hey, Ben," Conor said, "it's Conor Bard."

"Detective Bard. What's up?"

Lieutenant Ben Miller was Conor's contact at the Port Authority Police, the law-enforcement entity charged with protecting bridges, tunnels, airports, and seaports in and around New York City and northern New Jersey. Conor and Miller had come in contact a couple of times, when Conor was traveling and had to pass through airport security with his gun.

"I need to intercept someone at Alitalia," Conor said.

"Who?" Miller asked.

Conor thought for a moment before responding. That was a good question. Who was Monica, really?

"A possible witness," he finally said.

* * *

It took half an hour to get through the tunnel to the Long Island Expressway, which wasn't necessarily a bad thing. In those thirty minutes, Conor was able to focus on the undeniable fact that Monica was involved in the murder of Walter Lawton in some way. There was no magic-bullet theory that could offer an alternate explanation.

Conor remembered the first night he took Monica to dinner. She had denied knowing anything about Lawton.

Maybe you read about it, Conor had said. *Big-time lawyer shot and killed. Name was Walter Lawton.*

But Monica had shaken her head no.

Yet, fifteen minutes before the murder, Monica had been with Lawton.

Conor recalled a brief exchange he'd had with Monica the next time he saw her.

"How's your case going?"

"Like wading through seaweed."

"Seaweed? Is there seaweed in the Hudson River?"

But Conor had never mentioned anything to Monica about Lawton being killed by the river. She could have read it in a paper, of course, developed an interest in the case after he had talked about Lawton that first night. But Conor now knew that wasn't why she'd said what she did. *Is there seaweed in the Hudson River?* Why hadn't he picked up on that?

Conor recalled the night he and Monica were at Pongsri. It was Friday. *One of our possible suspects is a man named Fitim Bregu*, he had said. And then, dinner over, Monica had asked: *What time is it?* He had checked his watch and told her it was ten fifteen. Conor remembered she took his hand. *I don't want to go but I think I should,* she had said.

So Monica had left at ten fifteen, which was significant, because when Conor learned that Bregu had fled the country on Alitalia flight 605, he had asked Amanda when Bregu had booked his ticket. *Friday night,* Amanda had replied. *Ten forty-seven*—half an hour after Monica went home, armed with the information that Bregu was a suspect. Had she tipped off Bregu? There seemed to be little doubt.

No wonder Monica was desperate to book a flight Sunday night. She knew he was getting close, too close, and wanted to bolt to the relative safety of Albania. If she had in fact warned Bregu, that warning was about to cost her. Bregu had booked the last seat on Alitalia flight 605, leaving her to scramble for a reservation on other airlines.

Conor pounded his fist on the steering wheel. *How could I have been such an idiot?* He wanted to feel sorry for himself, to bemoan the betrayal. Monica had played him. And, oh, the way she had played him. Absolutely brilliant. Their "chance" meeting on the street corner, which obviously wasn't serendipity, was choreographed with the precision of a ballet. Hell, *she* didn't even approach *him. He* was the one who ran after *her*. How could she have known he would be so pathetically susceptible to such a setup?

And how about the tender kiss in her apartment

and everything that led up to it? All a lie. Every moment he had spent with her was a scene from a carefully crafted script. She was good. Very good. And she had made a complete fool out of him.

But did Monica actually kill Lawton? Did she really gun down a man in cold blood? *No way*, Conor thought. *Not Monica*. She may have been able to pull off a masterful charade but he couldn't see her holding the gun. That had to be Bregu. Bregu was the shooter. But if that was the case, what was Monica's role? Did she lead Lawton into an ambush on the banks of the Hudson River? And what about motive? Was it retribution for Lawton's role in putting John Hicks back on the street so he could kill Besa? Was it the taking of the blood? Had to be. Monica must have been a willing and active partner in crime and therefore could be charged with felony murder even if she hadn't pulled the trigger. At the very least, she was guilty of a laundry list of offenses: conspiracy to commit murder, hindering an investigation, obstruction of justice.

The traffic slowed to a crawl near the Van Wyck Expressway, which led to JFK Airport. Conor checked his watch. It was a couple minutes past five. He hit the flashers and the siren, drove down the shoulder at times, and finally pulled up in front of the terminal at 5:20.

Conor tossed his NYPD placard on the dashboard, locked the car, and hurried toward the entrance.

"You can't park there," a Port Authority cop shouted.

Conor flashed his shield. "NYPD."

"I don't care," the cop countered.

"Tow me," Conor said as he headed toward the terminal, almost jogging now.

"Detective Bard?"

A thirty-something man in a dark blue suit swept up to Conor.

"Yes." Conor held up his shield.

"Detective Mark Owens. Port Authority Police. Lieutenant Miller asked me to meet you."

They headed into the terminal.

"Alitalia six-zero-five, right?" Owens asked.

"Yes."

"Gate twenty-one," Owens said, leading the way. "You sure you don't want backup?"

"No," Conor replied. "It's a low-risk operation."

They stopped at the security checkpoint. Owens held up his Port Authority badge. "Owens. Port Authority. We're going through."

A TSA security officer nodded. "You're clear, Owens, but—"

Conor held up his shield. "Bard. NYPD."

"You have a ticket?" the TSA officer asked.

"He doesn't need a ticket," Owens said. "I'm his escort."

Two more TSA officers wandered over, ready to forcefully exert the power bestowed upon them within the confines of their little fiefdom.

"What's the problem?" one of the officers growled.

"I'm taking Detective Bard to gate twenty-one," Owens said.

Conor withdrew his gun. The three TSA officers leaned away.

"You want to hold my gun? Here it is."

Owens stepped in. "Detective Bard is going through security on my authority. *With* his weapon."

Conor holstered his gun.

"Take off your belt and shoes," one of the TSA officers said.

Owens ushered Conor around the metal detector.

"Go ahead," Owens told Conor. "I'll deal with this."

"Thanks," Conor said as he jogged toward the gates. "I owe you dinner."

"Wait!" a TSA guard shouted at Conor. "Your shoes have to go through X-ray!"

"*Shoes?*" Owens bellowed. "The man has a loaded weapon! What the hell do you mean, *shoes?*"

Conor could still hear Owens's booming voice as he rounded the corner for gate 21. The loudspeaker crackled to life. *Alitalia flight 605 to Milan, Italy, is now ready for boarding.*

Conor's jog quickened to almost a sprint. When he reached the gate, he saw a line of people queueing up to enter the Jetway. Where was Monica? Would he have to pull her off the plane? That was something he wanted to avoid. And then he spotted her, standing off to the side, waiting to merge into the flow of passengers. She was wearing jeans and a red cotton blouse. A large pocketbook was slung over her shoulder, a blue blazer draped in the crook of her arm, a magazine in her hand. A young woman on vacation. Not a killer on the run.

Conor stopped, out of breath. He stared at her. She turned slowly and saw Conor standing there. Her face flushed in surprise.

"Conor?"

They locked eyes. Conor took his time closing the distance between them. Monica smiled sadly.

"You're not here to see me off, are you?"

Conor pointed to an area by the window. "Let's go over there."

They walked away from the line of passengers and stood staring out at the runway.

"I'm sorry," Monica whispered without looking at Conor.

Conor felt an urge to grab her, shake her, slap her, ask her how the hell she could have done something so terrible. But before the questions, there was something he had to do.

"You have the right to remain silent," Conor said evenly. "Anything you say can and will be held against you in a court of law."

Fear filled Monica's eyes. "Conor. That's not necessary."

Conor's resolve weakened. He fought to separate the reality of Monica the suspect from Monica the woman standing next to him. "You have the right to have an attorney present during questioning," he continued, his voice now cold. "If you cannot afford an attorney, one will be appointed for you."

"Conor . . . please . . ."

"Do you understand your rights?"

"Conor . . ."

"Do you understand your rights?" he repeated, this time with barely contained rage.

Monica swallowed. "Yes."

Conor took a deep breath. "Was it Bregu?"

Monica didn't answer for a long time.

"He got me the gun," she finally said.

Chapter Fifty-nine

How unreal it all seemed. Conor placed his hand on the back of a nearby chair. It was not so much to steady himself as it was to grab something tangible, something that could anchor him in the physical world.

"What happened, Monica?"

Conor willed himself to adopt a sympathetic tone. *This is an interrogation*, he told himself. *Get a detailed confession. That's your job.* His objective now was to draw her out, keep her talking.

Monica stared off, her eyes gazing across the Atlantic. "The night before I came to New York, my father pulled me close to him. And he said, 'Find the man who killed Besa, my daughter, your mother's daughter, your sister, and take the blood.'"

"Take the *blood*?" Conor's voice rose to a crescendo. "This isn't ancient Albania, Monica. This is twenty-first-century America. You don't take the blood."

Monica looked down at the floor. Conor stifled his welling anger, which was directed not only at Monica but also at himself. *Don't let your feelings get in the way. Keep building the case against her.*

"So your father asked you to commit murder? Is that what you're telling me?"

"Yes."

"And what did you say?"

"I said, 'But, Papa, I am a woman.'"

Conor gritted his teeth. "Your father didn't have a son who could do it. So the job fell on his lovely daughter."

Conor needed to be on top of his game now, not only to elicit the confession from Monica but also to determine the involvement of anyone else who may have played a role.

"What about Fatmir?" Conor wondered aloud. "He's a man. Why didn't he take the blood?"

Monica shook her head. "He doesn't care about tradition anymore. He lives his life in the American style. Gambling, drinking, hanging out in clubs. After Besa died, he started going after Spanish girls." She paused. "I used to hate him for that. But now I see that's his way of getting through it, that's how he—"

Conor cut her off in midsentence. "And so you just decided to fly to New York and kill somebody?"

"No! How could you say that?"

"How could I *say* that?" Conor was agitated now. "I was the one standing over Walter Lawton's body, remember?"

Monica's pretty features grew tortured. "As soon as I got here, I went to the police in the Bronx and asked them about John Hicks. The detective I spoke to didn't seem to care." She clenched her fist. "He took a phone call from his girlfriend while I was standing there." Tears formed in her eyes. "I cried all night."

Conor understood the reaction. Besa's murder was a cold case. A lot of homicides had gone down in New York since Besa had been killed. It was hard enough just keeping up with the fresh bodies.

Monica pulled a tissue from her purse, wiped the tears that were now flowing down her cheeks.

"Go on," Conor said.

"Conor . . . Don't make me . . ."

"I want to know what happened." Conor's tone was no longer sympathetic.

Monica folded her arms around her stomach. "We have access to legal databases. At the bank. So I looked up John Hicks and saw he was represented in a previous case by—"

"Walter Lawton."

"Yes. I called Lawton's office, to ask him if he had any idea where John Hicks might be, but he never called me back. So I went to the law firm. Insisted on seeing him. While I was talking to the receptionist, he walked by."

Monica looked away, recalling that day. "We went into his office. I sat on the couch. He sat next to me. I explained why I was there and he said he was sorry, he had no idea how to find John Hicks. And he said if I happened to find John Hicks to let him know because Hicks still hadn't paid his legal fees. And then he laughed." Her chest heaved. "He made a joke, Conor! A *joke*!"

Conor winced. *What a fucking jerk!*

"After that, he put his hand on my knee and invited me out to dinner." Monica moaned. "*Dinner?* The man who got John Hicks off so he could rape and kill my sister? I got up and ran out of the office."

Monica rubbed her forehead, collected her thoughts. "So I decided to research Hicks. Find him myself. I pulled up the transcript of Hicks's trial."

"You mean the rape trial . . ."

"The year before Besa was . . ." Monica couldn't bring herself to say it anymore. She was really crying now, breathing heavily to keep from sobbing. "Did you read it?" she asked, her lips trembling. "Did you read the transcript of that poor girl's trial?"

Conor shook his head no.

"Lawton ripped the victim apart. *Destroyed* her. Dredged up every sexual partner he could find. Made her sound like a total whore. By the time Lawton was finished, she was a mess. Raped all over again in a courtroom. And a year later, you know what she did?"

Conor didn't respond. He had a good idea what Monica was about to say.

"She killed herself," Monica said.

Conor bent over slightly, his stomach in a knot.

"I tried to find John Hicks," Monica said. "I really did."

"And what were you going to do if you found him? *Kill* him?"

"Yes," she said softly. "At that point, yes. He deserved it."

Monica walked unsteadily to a chair, crumpled into it.

"Right after that, my father called. He asked me, 'Have you taken the blood?' He sounded so weak, so dead inside." Monica grabbed her knees, rocked slightly. "I told him that no one knew where John Hicks was, that he had disappeared after he killed Besa. My father said, 'Then take the blood of someone in his family. You must take the blood. Someone must pay for what happened to Besa.' I didn't know what to do. I couldn't find John Hicks. I couldn't find someone in his family." Her tears were gone now, her face suddenly filled with hatred. "But I knew where to find the man who helped John Hicks walk free, to rape and to kill my sister."

Conor stared out at the runway, unable to look at her. It was too painful. "So you called Lawton again?"

"Yes. I didn't know what I was going to say, what I was going to do. My hands dialed, my voice spoke, but it wasn't me."

Conor whipped around. "It *was* you, Monica. It was *you*. *You* stood there in that empty lot. *You* murdered an unarmed man."

"I know this is hard for you to understand—"

"No, Monica," Conor fired back. "I understand perfectly well. And so does Walter Lawton." He walked over to her. "So you spoke with Lawton . . ."

"And I told him I was sorry about that day in his office, that I was under a lot of stress at the bank." Monica's chest heaved. "Conor! He asked me if I wanted to go to the Hamptons with him for the weekend!"

Conor already felt like driving his fist through a wall. Every word out of Monica's mouth stoked his rage even more.

Monica started to tremble. "I told him I couldn't go to the Hamptons but I was free Sunday night. We arranged to meet at Elaine's."

"Because you were planning to kill him?"

"Yes," Monica said with no remorse.

It occurred to Conor that Monica's account made her guilty not simply of murder, but of *premeditated* murder. He had read her the Miranda warning. So this was a legally obtained confession, one that would hold up in court. The next few minutes of freedom could be the last she would enjoy for the rest of her life. He wondered if she realized that.

Monica sniffled. "So I called Fitim from a pay phone." She laughed. Only this time there was no melody. "I told you, Conor, all I watched were forensic shows. I knew better than to use my cell at that point."

"Why Fitim?"

"We had grown up together and I knew he was in New York. I hadn't called him before because he was always in some kind of trouble in Tirana. He

was bad. But I knew if anyone could get a gun . . ."
Monica stared off. "At first he didn't want to be bothered. Even when I told him why I wanted the gun, to
avenge the death of my sister." She shook her head.
"Fitim is not a man. He couldn't care less about honor
or respect."

"Not the kind of guy who would be a member of
the Besa club," Conor said between clenched teeth,
almost losing it on the spot.

Monica shook her head no.

Beautiful, Conor thought. Because of her, I had
a dozen cops crawling all over the Besa club in the
Bronx looking for Bregu.

"You met Lawton at Elaine's." Conor was now
only seeking information. All his emotion had been
spent.

"He kept touching me." Monica's face contorted in
disgust. "It made my skin crawl." She grew strangely
calm. "After dinner, he insisted I have a nightcap with
him at a club in Chelsea. So we got into the car, drove
across town, and headed down the West Side Highway. I pretended to be carsick and asked him to pull
over. He didn't want to. I told him that if he didn't, I
was going to throw up all over his expensive leather
seats. So he stopped on the side of the highway. I
reached in my purse, I was about to do it right there,
in the car, but then I saw that we were parked by an
empty lot. So I got out. And I really did throw up."

Monica relived that moment in her head, then:
"When he came to check on me, I pulled the gun

out of my purse. He was terrified. And that made me happy. What terror must Besa have felt? So I aimed the gun at him and I said, '*Kjo është per Besen*,' which means 'This is for Besa.' And then I shot him."

"Fuck!" Conor blurted out.

"He won't be able to defend another killer now. He won't ever help someone else get away with horrible things so they can do it again to someone else." Monica's eyes narrowed. "He had no conscience. Just greed." She was suddenly defiant. "I'm glad I did it. I'm sorry to say that but I am. I have taken the blood. I have made my father proud. I don't care what happens to me now."

The loudspeaker crackled to life. *Final boarding call for Alitalia flight 605.*

Conor stood and paced for a moment, then stopped and stared at her hard. "So meeting me . . ."

"That was Fitim's idea."

Conor's entire body tensed. Why hadn't he seen it coming? Why hadn't alarms gone off in his head?

"Fitim saw the article in the *Post*," Monica continued. "He called me. He was very upset. I guess he didn't really believe I would do it. So now he wanted to make sure he wouldn't be arrested for getting me the gun. I told him I threw the gun in the river, but he was still panicked. He told me to get the *Post*, that your picture was there and—"

"And he told you to hang around outside the precinct, run into me by chance, stay close, keep tabs on the case."

Conor could feel the heat on his face, his cheeks like two burning coals.

"Well?" he said, the veins on his neck now bulging. "Wasn't that the plan?"

"That's the way it started out. But that's not how it ended up. You have to believe me."

"I don't have to believe anything."

He stared out the window and watched a plane lift slowly into the skies. He knew what he needed to do, what he *had* to do. His hand slid under his jacket and found the cuffs that were clipped to his belt. The coldness of the steel pressed against his palm.

Monica stood.

"Conor . . ."

Conor turned and faced her, steadied his nerves. He drew in a breath, prepared himself to put an end to it all with the words *You're under arrest for the murder of Walter Lawton*.

"You better go," Conor said. "You're going to miss your plane."

Chapter Sixty

Monica hesitated, giving Conor a moment to reconsider what he was about to do—let a killer walk away. He reached for the cuffs again, then slowly withdrew his hand.

"Get on the plane," he said, meaning it.

Monica searched Conor's eyes for a heartbeat, then walked to the gate. She handed the agent her boarding pass and headed into the Jetway, pausing an instant to glance over her shoulder. And then she was gone.

Conor stood at the window watching flight 605 push back from the gate, taxi onto the runway, and then take off. He felt numb. No, not numb. He felt nothing, which was worse. He had never been so hurt by anyone. His career as a cop was over, and yet he felt nothing.

The drive back to Manhattan was slow. Conor had to contend with an endless stream of cars occupied by

Long Island residents making their nightly pilgrimage to the theaters and fine restaurants of Manhattan. The delay gave him time to decompress, absorb the blow, attempt to rationalize what he had just done. Lawton was a scumbag, defending criminals, handing over clients to be slaughtered. And John Hicks? An animal walking the streets, polluting society. Monica was a victim in all this. That's what he kept telling himself. Soon she would be out of reach, safe behind the vagaries of Eastern European extradition laws. Justice had been served. Even if the laws in this case were centuries old.

But the truth was, as noble as his motive may have been, there was no excuse for allowing Monica to board that plane. His job was to "protect and serve," not to be judge and jury. Tomorrow he would walk into the precinct and hand over his shield and gun. That was the right thing to do, wasn't it? After what he had done, how could he stay on the job?

Conor finally arrived in front of the Playwright Tavern on Forty-ninth Street, parked the car, then walked up the stairs to the second floor. Ralph's retirement party had just gotten under way. Conor scanned the crowd and spotted his old partner standing at the end of the bar.

"How's it feel to be on the NYPD scrap heap?" Conor asked as he walked up to Ralph. "Like an old car, huh?"

"Yeah," Ralph replied. "But even old cars still have a few miles left in them."

They embraced. Ralph frowned, looked at Conor. They knew each other too well not to notice when something was wrong.

"What's the matter, kid?" Ralph asked, concerned. "You look like you just lost your best friend."

"I did." Conor smiled. "He's moving to the DA's office."

Ralph studied Conor. "You sure you don't want to tell me?"

"Maybe one of these days."

Ralph slapped Conor's shoulder. "Get yourself a drink. We'll talk later."

Ralph walked away. Conor ordered a martini then turned and saw Steven Clyde, his baby-faced new partner, entering the room. Steven looked around nervously.

"Hey, Steven," Conor called out.

Steven spotted Conor at the bar, then walked over to him.

"You get those transfer papers done?" Conor asked.

"All filled in. Ready to fight crime in Hell's Kitchen."

Was I ever like that? Conor wondered.

The bartender placed a martini in front of Conor.

"What are you drinking, Steven?" Conor asked.

"I'll have a Diet Coke."

Diet Coke? What? The kid doesn't drink? Conor

turned toward the bartender. "Diet Coke, please."

The bartender walked away. Conor dug in his pocket, pulled out some cash, and placed two singles on the bar. When he stuffed the rest of the cash in his pocket, his hand brushed his wallet.

"I want you to look at something, Steve. Can I call you Steve?"

"Sure."

Conor pulled his wallet from his pocket and it flipped open. John Hicks's mug shot stared out from behind a plastic window.

"Who's that?" Steven asked.

"Name's John Hicks. Wanted for murder. Been a fugitive for six years."

The bartender placed a Diet Coke on the bar.

Steven picked up the glass, took a sip, then concentrated on the mug shot.

"Remember that face," Conor said. "You ever see him, take him down."

Steven nodded. "I'll keep my eyes open."

Amanda walked up to them. "Good. I see you guys are going through your male bonding ritual." She looked at the wallet in Conor's hand. "A mug shot? What? You're becoming Kurtz now?"

"He could do worse," Ralph said as he stepped up to the bar.

He looked at Steven. You could almost hear him thinking, *How* old *is this kid?*

"Ralph," Conor said. "This is my new partner, Steven Clyde."

Ralph and Steven shook hands.

"Ralph Kurtz. Nice to meet you."

"Same here."

Conor turned toward Amanda. "Now that I'm not saddled with the old guy, you're going to see me and Steven solve a lot more cases."

"Don't listen to that crap," Ralph said as he looked at Steven. "I've carried him all these years."

Steven seemed confused, not sure whether to laugh.

Ralph put his arm around Steven's shoulders. "Come on. Let's go meet some of the guys on the beat. And I'll tell you what a nightmare you're looking at, partnering up with that slacker over there."

Steven finally did laugh. A forced laugh. Ralph and Steven drifted into the crowd. Conor and Amanda watched them as they walked away.

"I'm going to miss that old fool," Conor said.

"Yeah," Amanda agreed. "Me too." Amanda's eyes continued to follow Ralph and Steven as they weaved through the crowded room.

"We're losing a lot of talent," Amanda said, concern in her voice. "A lot of guys retiring. The new kids coming in? Sure, they're eager, they're smart. But what they don't have is experience."

"Experience keeps you up at night," Conor countered.

Amanda checked her watch. "Better get back to work."

"Don't you ever take time off?"

Amanda thought for a moment. "Yeah. There *was* that day in 1998." She started walking away. "Better make my rounds. See you in the morning."

"Bright and early," Conor replied. *When I walk into your office and put my gold shield and my gun on your desk.*

He hunched over the bar and studied Hicks's mug shot. *Look at that son of a bitch. Where is that cockroach hiding?* He snapped the wallet shut, picked up his martini, and walked to one of the booths on the other side of the room. He stared out the window at the flashing neon sign of Colony Records on the corner of Broadway and Forty-ninth Street. How many times had he imagined seeing his CD on sale there? He drew a mental picture of a large free-standing display rack full of Conor Bard recordings. *I've got a music career to think about. I'm not getting any younger. It's now or never. I can't be a cop anymore.*

Conor opened the wallet again. Hicks was still there, peering up at him. *You low-life bastard.*

He looked across the room at Steven clutching his Diet Coke. *You going to find Hicks? I don't think so.* Conor turned his gaze back to the mug shot. And then, with Hicks's image scowling at him, suddenly realized he wasn't going to resign after all. Hicks needed to be caught, taken off the street, and tracking down Hicks would be much easier to do on the job.

Conor recalled the old adage: What doesn't kill you, makes you stronger. *Okay, you made a mistake. No, it was a choice. A human choice. And now it's your secret. Nothing like a good secret to make someone more interesting.*

Friday night. The Rhythm Bar. Conor was back in his element. It felt good to be onstage again. Especially tonight. The place was jammed. And not just with the usual suspects. During the past couple weeks, the run-down joint had been discovered by Hell's Kitchen's newest residents—young and successful professionals who now occupied the upscale condominiums built to attract them. In response to his demographically diverse audience, Conor had added a horn section consisting of a saxophone, a trumpet, and a trombone. He had also injected a little rock and roll into the repertoire in addition to his staple of R&B. At the moment, he was in the middle of a Rolling Stones song and the crowd was loving it.

Conor moved away from the microphone, allowing the sax player to step in and begin his solo. As the sax player wailed away, the bass player edged over to Conor.

"You sure can pick 'em," the bass player said, his eyes wandering to a table near the middle of the room.

Conor looked down at it. There she was. Exquisite, sexy, crazy, rich. Dressed down in torn jeans, T-shirt, and denim jacket, Holly was swaying to the beat. She smiled, blew Conor a kiss. He smiled back. It had been an incredible four days with her. Or rather, four nights. Danger, Conor had discovered, was a much more effective aphrodisiac than drama.

The sax solo ended. Conor stepped back to the microphone.

> *You can't always get what you want . . .*
> *But if you try sometimes you might find . . .*
> *You get what you need . . .*

Conor embraced Holly with his eyes, if not his heart. Whatever connection they shared wouldn't last forever. Then again, nothing does. For once he was living in the present.

And what a present it was.

Acknowledgments

My agent, David Vigliano, who encouraged me to write this book in the first place; Roz Lippel, my editor, who molded a manuscript into a novel; and Elaine Kaufman, a proprietor of Elaine's Restaurant, who is the best friend a writer can have.

Scribner Proudly Presents

CRYSTAL DEATH
Charles Kipps

Available in hardcover from Scribner

Turn the page for a preview of
Crystal Death. . . .

Chapter One

It had been two months since Conor Bard had taken to the stage at the Rhythm Bar, so he found it comforting that the joint was packed. It didn't matter whether people were there to see him perform after his long absence or just seeking refuge from the torrential rain that had transformed the streets of New York City into white-water rapids. He had a lively, appreciative audience and his adrenaline was flowing.

Even though the place was a dive, it was still a venue. And to Conor, each venue was a step on the way to achieving his dream: signing with a major record label. So why *hadn't* he been up there jamming for the past eight weeks?

It's my own fault. I should just quit the job.

The job was NYPD. Conor was a cop, a detective in the precinct that encompassed the most high-profile sectors of Manhattan. Times Square. Fashion Avenue. The Diamond District. All the Broadway theaters. Hell's Kitchen, which despite its recent gentrification still harbored remnants of its violent past. So there wasn't much time to pursue a dream when every day someone else's dream bled out on the pavement.

Conor strummed the nickel-plated strings of his electric guitar, a vintage Fender Stratocaster, then stepped up to the microphone and belted out the opening verse of the Temptations classic "I Wish It Would Rain."

"Sunshine, blue skies, please go away . . ."

Now *there* was a song that struck an emotional chord—about a man so miserable he wouldn't leave his house. *When was the last time I was really happy? Maybe never.*

Conor was forty-three. A hard forty-three. The crevices in his craggy face were growing deeper by the day, and his brown hair was in a constant battle with encroaching strands of gray. But he didn't dwell on these things. Instead, he spent most of his late nights in hollow hours of denial. Denial about getting older. Denial about his chances of actually making it as a singer. Denial about his aversion to romantic commitment. Denial about his drinking, which was becoming a real problem. Whenever someone asked him where he lived, he was always tempted to say, Where do I live? I live in denial.

"I wish it would rain . . ."

The crowd roared its approval at the irony inherent in his decision to sing that particular tune, considering the downpour that had lasted all day. As he soaked up the collective praise, he scanned the faces in the crowd. Many of them were familiar, particularly a pretty thirtysomething blond woman he had met the last time he played there. He struggled to recall her name. *Ingrid.* Yes, that was it. Ingrid. *She plays viola. Or is it violin? Something in the string section.* He had intended to get her number that night, but for some reason, he couldn't remember why, he never did. *Maybe I was drunk. Maybe it was because she was a musician. Musicians are fucked-up. What the hell? Maybe tonight I'll get her number.*

The door swung open, momentarily allowing the pelting rain to provide an appropriate, percussive accompaniment to the music. Conor was surprised to see Sergeant Amanda Pitts entering the bar. Amanda hadn't been to see him play for two years. But he didn't take it personally. She was always on the job, working twelve, fourteen hours a day, and when she wasn't at the precinct she was likely passed out from exhaustion. *Sarge looks different tonight*, Conor thought. Then again, he usually saw her under the harsh fluorescent bulbs in the office, which tended to accentuate the worst of her thirty-eight years. *That's what bar lighting will do.* Even though no one would ever call Amanda sexy, in the perpetual twilight of the Rhythm Bar, she was a contender.

Conor made eye contact with Amanda. She nodded an acknowledgment, then moved her hand across her throat in a slicing motion as if to say: *Cut!*

Amanda drifted to the back of the bar and disappeared into the darkness where he could no longer see her. He finished the song, but because he knew she was there and could feel her staring at him, his performance suffered. The paying customers didn't notice, however, and lavished applause as Conor hit the final chord, then swung the long neck of the guitar upward with a flourish.

Conor leaned into the mike. "We're going to take a short break. But we'll be right back."

That was the signal for Susie the bartender to trigger the iPod plugged into the sound system. She did this at the end of every set, to keep the energy level in the room from plummeting. But the band wasn't due to break for another twenty minutes, so she had been caught off guard. After a few seconds of confused hesitation, Susie lunged for the Play button. Johnnie Taylor's rendition of "Still Crazy" vibrated out of the speakers.

Starting all over . . . I've got to find what's left of my life . . .

Conor looked at the band. "Sorry, guys."

And he was. How many shows had he canceled because of the job? It wasn't fair to the other musicians, especially not to Richard Shorter, the piano player. Conor and Richard had gone to high school together. Richard had stuck with him ever since, never complaining about the uncertainty of their schedule. Peter, the drummer, who was a veteran known as the "Human Metronome," and Gordon, the bass player, a twenty-two-year-old African American who brought a youthful energy to the group, were recent additions to the quartet. But how long would they stick around without a steady or, more to the point, reliable flow of gigs?

Conor climbed from the stage and made his way to the back of the room, where he found Amanda propped against the bar.

"Hey, Sarge. Glad you could make it."

"You were in great form tonight."

"Thanks."

"We've got a homicide," she said abruptly. "And you're up."

He motioned to the stage. "I'm in the middle—"

"No problem. The house is full of detectives playing cards. I'll give it to one of them. I just thought you might want this one."

"Why?" Conor asked before he could stop himself.

"The victim's name is Zivah Gavish."

"Sorry. Doesn't ring a bell."

"She's Israeli. One of the biggest dealers in the world for something *you'll* never buy."

"And what's that?"

"Diamonds."

Conor grinned. "Maybe you're right about the diamonds."

"A Stanley Silberman called nine-one-one a half hour ago, at eight thirty. Owns one of those jewelry stores on Forty-seventh Street, in the Diamond District. According to Silberman, Zivah Gavish was supposed to meet him at the annual diamond dealers' dinner tonight. When she didn't show up at the hotel, I guess he was worried enough to phone it in."

Conor rubbed the back of his neck. No way he was going to let the job pull him from the stage. Not this time. *I've got a show to finish. Let her give this to someone else.*

"S-A-P-S is already at the scene," she continued, pronouncing each letter of the acronym.

"SAPS?"

"South African Police Service."

"What's their angle?"

"I don't know. The victim's a diamond dealer. South Africa produces diamonds."

Conor felt himself being reeled in, which he knew was precisely what Amanda intended and something he was definitely trying to avoid. If he was going to get back on the stage, now was the moment. But his legs were like stakes driven firmly into the ground.

Amanda shrugged. "A dead diamond dealer? South African cops? As far as cases go, it doesn't get any better than that." She motioned toward the stage. "Anyway, you should get back up there. Don't want to keep your fans waiting." She started walking away.

"Sarge," he called out.

She stopped, turned slowly.

"Meet you in front?" she asked, although she already knew the answer.